THE TIME O

A

Civilization annihilated . . . Earth transformed . . .
And Hawkwind rocks in the remains of ruined
London, avidly attended by the new Children of the
Sun. But deep in the heart of the planet is buried a
satanic Death Generator, at last triggered off by the
explosive sounds, whose rays bring the dawning of a
third Magical Age, an age manifested in the figure of
Colonel Memphis Mephis – the man who threatens
the survival of the Children unless Hawkwind and
their music intervene . . .

Watch out for the sequel to
The Time of The Hawklords,
to be published early 1977

QUEENS OF DELIRIA

THE TIME OF
THE HAWKLORDS

Michael Moorcock
and
Michael Butterworth

A STAR BOOK
published by
WYNDHAM PUBLICATIONS

A Star Book
Published in 1976
by Wyndham Publications Ltd.
A Howard & Wyndham Company
123 King Street, London W6 9JG

Copyright © Michael Moorcock 1976 and Michael Butterworth 1976

Printed in Great Britain by
Richard Clay (The Chaucer Press), Ltd., Bungay, Suffolk

ISBN 0 352 39894 9

For Dik Mik, Terry and Del

AUTHORS' NOTE

While the characters in this story are based on actual people we wish to make it clear that the descriptions of these characters are entirely fictitious and based on roles used by members of Hawkwind on stage and recorded performances.

Legend:

'And in the future of time, the prophecy must be fulfilled and the HAWKLORDS shall return to smite the land. And the Dark Forces shall be scourged, the cities razed and made into parks. Peace shall come to everyone. For is it not written that the Sword is the key to Heaven *and* Hell?'

HAWKCRAFT INVENTORY

At the time of the events presented in this book, the ever-changing crew of the HAWKWIND Spacecraft are:

Baron Brock – (David Brock, lead guitar, 12-string guitar, synthesizer, organ and vocals).

The Thunder Rider – (Nik Turner, sax, oboe, flute and vocals).

Count Motorhead – (Lemmy, bass and vocals).

Lord Rudolph the Black – (Paul Rudolph, bass and guitars).

The Hound Master – (Simon King, drums and percussion).

The Sonic Prince – (Simon House, keyboards, mellotron and violin).

Stacia . . . The Earth Mother – (Stacia, dance).

Astral Al – (Alan Powell, drums and percussion).

Liquid Len – (Jonathan Smeeton, lights).

Captain Calvert – (Bob Calvert, with Lucky Leif and The Longships).

Moorlock . . . The Acid Sorcerer – (Mike Moorcock, with Deep Fix).

Actonium Doug – (Doug Smith, Manager).

BOOK ONE

ROCKING ON THE EDGE OF TIME

THE LAST OUTPOST OF MAN

On the gleaming, scarlet surface of the stage, crouching like wide-mouthed monsters, sat the hulks of the speaker cabinets. Little whisperings and tiny shrieks occasionally issued forth, as if they complained of the silence enforced upon them. Soon they would roar as their power was released. Above, on a platform supported by candy-striped scaffolding, were the four drum kits. All the equipment, including the eight AU516 synthesizers and the newly invented Delatron Processor, was painted with swirling colours and designs: mind-blowing.

Through screwed-up eyes the cat girl watched the shiny, garish dais being completed. It had taken the designer, Barnie Bubbles, and Hawkwind's roadies the best part of a week so far, working slowly because of the unusually hot summer and the sheer size of the operation. Now it was ready. Now the final great rock concert – the longest running ever to be held on earth – could start.

The cat girl closed her eyes. She retreated back into her basking slumber where she lay upon the metal roof of the truck. It was real, then, she thought. She was roused, almost immediately, by a slight feeling of panic. Perhaps it was not panic but simply excitement which flushed through her bronzed body? The prospect of her appearing on stage again after the wasted, horrifying months between gigs suddenly made her feel tense.

All around her she could hear the subdued murmurings of the remaining population of Great Britain, about five thousand people. Like everyone else, they were still not sure if a civilized event were possible. Many of them had waited weeks for this moment. They had travelled half-starved from the northern-most wastes of Scotland, and camped out on the site in make-shift shelters and nearby derelict buildings. They had come cautiously, to hear the music, but also because of the promise of companionship with their fellows. She admired them, for the faith they had managed to find.

At last the roadies finished their task. And now they jumped down, bringing an expectant hush from the sprawling rim of Children below.

Reluctantly, cued to the subsidence of noise around the stage, and to the roar of the extra diesels starting somewhere in the distance, Stacia sat up, rubbing her eyes with black paws that might have been polished, they shone so brightly in the sun.

Simon House, the legendary Sonic Prince, was the first of the musicians to mount the stage, moving about his synthesizers in a flashing blue silk gown, checking the links, testing the master console.

At last the Sonic Prince paused by the shiny, ebony cube of the Delatron. The complex machine bristled with wires and jacks. With a simple, dignified movement, the Prince made his gesture of obeisance to the Delatron, then, amidst rising whistles and shouts, he arose and indicated the cube with his hand, drawing a swell of exultation from the Children.

Even as the shouting died, the Prince had vanished behind his keyboards and all that Stacia could see of him was a flash of blue silk, a lock or two of his thick black hair.

She was pulling her fish-net body stocking over her black leotard. She felt proud of the Prince. It had taken him years of research to perfect the Delatron, based on the cryptic and involved plans left behind by Detmar, a dwarf both benevolent and cunning, who had long-since left to further his studies in mystic lore.

Next came Lord Rudolph the Black, most recent champion sworn to the ranks of the Company of the Hawk. About his lips there played an eternal, mysterious smile as he adjusted the strap of his great bass called *Boneshiverer*, which all men feared and all women loved.

Then, following close on Lord Rudolph's heels, appeared Simon King, known as the Hound Master, famous for his keeping of fierce, untameable beasts who obeyed none but himself, and with him was the one who called himself Astral Al but was also known as Powell the Power. These two climbed long ladders to take their positions above the stage; the one with a stick-quiver bouncing on his tattooed back, the other with a white cotton suit, dark hat, and shades.

Soon, through the clear morning air, came the sharp explosions of practise rolls and riffs, ululations and shrieks from the synths.

The familiar sounds fired Stacia's blood. She rose gracefully to her feet, arching her back and cupping her slender arms above her head. She struck a defiant, regal pose with her black eye-mask and straight raven-black hair falling to her shoulders. The crowd applauded wildly.

From the side door of the Mercedes truck beneath her feet there came, suddenly, a jumbled, wailing blast of sax. And now Thunder Rider emerged, bearing with him a doom and a joy that was his alone, clad in a totally silver space skin to reflect the sun's heat, adorned with clattering silver medallions and chains, copper and brass and gold bracelets on his blazing arms, his red beard and hair glowing. Amidst the riotous applause, Thunder Rider leapt on stage and loped in slow, weightless motion towards the mike, blowing for all he was worth.

Simultaneously there stepped from behind the vast mixer unit the powerful figure of that brave and sagacious champion who, with Thunder Rider, had first conceived, with noble ideals, the Company of the Hawk, Baron Brock, Lord of the Westland. He held a jackplug in one hand, trailing yards of coiled black flex behind it. He walked, keeping his own counsel, in a faded T and brightly patched jeans, towards his stacks, the sleek and tawny guitar *Godblaster* held at his side. As he reached his stacks he swung *Godblaster* lazily over his powerful shoulders and the light flashed on his muscular, tattooed arms, his pale gold hair. He plugged in the jack and began, instinctively to play a short A minor progression.

Then came Lemmy, Count Motorhead, almost slipping down the front of the high stage, but regaining his jack-booted footing at the last moment and hauling himself up. He arose and looked around him, apparently dazed by the spectacle of the yelling, cheering biomass plastered against the skyline.

13

With a grin of self-mockery he drew his heels together sound-lessly and raised his arm in a salute, turning the shrieks to the friendly jeering he seemed to find more tolerable. But the enthusiastic roar returned as he bent down to retrieve his trusty Rickenbacker bass, *Gutsplitter*, from the blood-red panelling.

One by one the members of Hawkwind fell silent, and only the welcoming roar of the Children, now back to their usual enthusiastic selves, could be heard. Soon, that too ceased in a clatter of deafeningly sharp riffs sent up by Astral Al to command attention.

In the electric silence that followed, Thunder Rider's free-form sax burst out once more, almost inaudibly at first, but gradually mounting in volume, climbing up and down in the air. When the squealing noise reached an unbearable pitch, he allowed it to fade away. Before it could vanish altogether, the rest of the group let out a sudden, frightening crash of blurred notes and drum rolls from which snaked low, vibrant synth sounds prolonging the roll and the ethereal high pitch of the melatron. Just as suddenly, these sounds too faded away – this time into the echoing, clipped voice of Lemmy, who started to chant the old Calvert number, *Welcome To The Future*.

'Welcome to the future!' His voice boomed out, shattering against a million invisible canyons in the clear blue sky over-head.

> *'Welcome to the dehydrated land,*
> *Welcome to the south police parade,*
> *Welcome to the neo-golden age,*
> *Welcome to the days you've made you*
> *Welcome*
>> *You are welcome*
> *You are welcome*
> *Wel come*
> *Wel come*
>> *You are welcome*
> *Welcome to the future.'*

The introductory poem ended in a mighty, rising din of

drum, gongs and synth that strained the stacks and almost rent the five thousand shuddering rib cages. Then, after a full, tortuous minute the sound gradually subsided, and the group began playing their first, mind-blasting number, *Psychedelic Warlords*.

Unable to express herself adequately any longer on the small, slippery roof of the Mercedes, Stacia climbed down among the parked fleet in the compound, and headed for the stage.

From her new vantage point she was able to stretch out her limbs to their full extent, and interpret the music more freely. The Children spurred her on with their shouts. They had gone absolutely ecstatic, their shrieks and roars uncaringly trying to climb above the 50,000 watt wall of sound shoved out by the amps.

She felt pleased. The gig was going fine – fulfilling its purpose of unlocking pent-up feelings, and drowning the intense fear and excitement everyone felt in an orgy of sensual assault. After nightfall, it would be better still – when Liquid Len and the Lensmen would get the chance to set up their light machines.

The music made her feel extra good. It held an indefinable quality she couldn't put her finger on. She knew she had never heard music like it – anywhere. She knew how well her body usually responded to sound, able to express its most subtle meanings. This music melted into her very being – not just her ears – becoming a symbiotic part of her flesh. In its grip, she felt like a goddess, an all-powerful controller of Destiny.

Soon, the long, heavy organ notes of *Winds of Change* were sweeping through her body, forcing it to perform a series of slow, expressive pirouettes to match the changes in mood. The notes signalled an end for mankind, as well as a new beginning. Her flesh tingled with a feeling of dread mixed with a strange, unearthly bliss . . .

King Trash prickled to attention. One of his grubby hands was still automatically counting the pile of bank notes on the table in front of him.

He felt his skin crawl with dread as the temperature of the room unaccountably seemed to drop. The sound of the band playing was inaudible in here. The heavy, velvet curtains he had ordered blotted out all traces of the hideous outside world – but he *knew* the hippies had started something. He could feel it in his bones.

'Rastabule!' he shouted hoarsely for his servant, knocking over a pile of freshly counted bank notes before him, spilling them into the heap that were still to be counted. 'Here!'

Trying to shrug off the shakes, and prevent any further deterioration of order in the Counting Room, he reached for the elastic bands and secured the remaining piles. Then he put the piles into cardboard boxes and lifted them to the back of the room where he stored them, neatly. The work normally gave him a positive feeling of satisfaction. He knew that all those crisp, blue and orange notes were there, arranged in fat bundles of £5,000; furthermore that every single one of them had been lovingly counted by him. There was the personal sacrifice, too. He had stayed awake all night during the Seventh Recounting. This time, he felt sure, he would be well rewarded. Although only a few hundred thousand notes were left still to count, a job he could easily finish off tomorrow, he was confident that this month's count would agree with the previous month's figures. If it did, he would have obtained three consecutive count figures. This would mean that he could finish counting and concentrate on other important matters of royalty. One day, things would return to normal, he felt sure. Then he, King Trash, would be seen as the monarch who had preserved the great royal tradition.

'Rastabule!' he roared again. 'Where are you?'

'Here, Master,' came a high, timid voice. Out of breath,

Rastabule – a thin, scrawny servant with a warty face – appeared from behind the heavy oak-panelled door.

'Where've you been? I've been calling you for hours,' demanded King Trash, irritably.

'Sorry, Master. What can I do?'

'Peep behind that curtain will you? Tell me what you can see in the park.'

'Yes, Master.'

Rastabule curtsied like a girl servant, and did as he was told. Behind him, the great trembling bulk of the King cowered behind the door, hiding from the glare as the curtains were drawn slightly aside. The awful feeling inside him was getting worse – like a sodden crapping sensation down below, as though no longer able to retain proper control over his bowels. He waited a moment, then said impatiently:

'Well, come on. Come on. What do you see?'

'Only . . . the park, Master, and . . . you know, the . . .'

'Hippies?'

'Yes . . . Master.'

'Are there more of them today?'

'Many more, Master.'

'The buggers . . . what are they doing?'

Rastabule looked vainly through the King's powerful binoculars into the crowds populating Green Park. It was difficult to say, but it seemed as though there were some sort of a concert.

'A *concert*?' screamed the King. 'What sort of a concert? A *rock* concert?'

'It looks so, Master.'

'By God, Rastabule, the bloody nerve . . . the . . . that's what's giving me this terrible – oh my sweet Christ . . . quickly Rastabule . . . Help me!'

Rastabule ran across the soft carpeting to help relieve the collapsing monarch. He shouldered part of the weight of the twitching, leaden frame, and together they limped along the corridor and down several flights of stairs into the lower part of the Palace towards the Royal Chambers . . .

TOWER OF MINDS

At Control, in the heart of London, Press Reporter Seksass had one finger poised in readiness to flick over a file on his card index. The Twinny Triad Sex Affair – the most revolting in his entire press experience – was beginning to clear itself up. Only one final journey into Control's vast computer memory – where the minds of millions of Britain's former citizens, the Middle Classes, were on tape – was necessary to wind this horrible case up, and bring these three ghostly deviants inside to justice. It was his biggest assignment, and he expected promotion.

Before his finger had selected the Twinny card, he felt the terrible cold feeling grip hold of him. It began in his feet and spread up his body to the back of his head, icing over his brain and making his bowels heave and feel suddenly rotten.

'God in Heaven!' he muttered. 'What's happening to me?'

Lurching from his swivel seat, he flung himself across the room and threw open the window. He inhaled deeply from the warm, muggish air outside in the derelict City. The sickening drop to the heavily guarded forecourt below, at the foot of Control's massive tower block, made him feel even worse.

Leaving his office, he staggered next door into the gents, clutching at his already sodden trousers . . .

COLD PLANES OF CONTINUITY

The blinding sun tracked slowly, punishingly, across the steel blue sky above the park.

Through its dazzle, and the mistiness of exhaustion and sweat, Thunder Rider watched the rings of screaming Children surrounding him.

Together, they were speeding on a huge, never-ending trip

of orgasmic happiness into the future.

They had been playing for six hours almost without a break – longer than they had ever played before.

They had ignored all the rest intervals that had been carefully scheduled. They had deliberately followed one request with another as soon as it had been shouted out by the crowd.

Now, the music had turned into a shapeless, free-form jamming session based loosely around the last request, *Assault & Battery*. It went on and on, inexorably, as though no one had the energy to stop it.

No one wanted it to stop, because of the indescribable feelings of withdrawal they would have to bear, to recall the horror, the loneliness of the devastated Earth.

Drunkenly, Thunder Rider let the sax fall from his lips and threw back his head with mirth. He roared with laughter at the sheer lunacy of what was happening. No one had expected Hawkwind music to be quite *this* powerful. It gripped everyone equally, inexplicably in its power, like the most lustful and enslaving woman.

Then, unexpectedly, he started to stagger backward, caught off balance by the mood of paranoid hilarity. Weakly, his legs collapsed under him and he fell to the floor against one of the giant stacks, unable to move, pinned down by the numbing tiredness.

The others saw him go, and immediately their last reserves of energy ran out. Helpless, they were forced to stop playing. Dead fingers refused to move.

Unthinkably, the music stopped.

From all about came a howl of disappointment as the withdrawal symptoms started up. Terrifying visions of torment formed inside each head. But this was followed bravely by a tremendous outburst of appreciative clapping and whistling.

Sweat-soaked, Hawkwind reeled away from their positions and instruments, and started to climb down into the dizzying compound below.

Thunder Rider opened his eyes where he had fallen. The noise, like a million shrieking sea-gulls, rose higher. Then he forced himself to his feet and half-climbed, half-fell down the stage wall.

As he followed the others towards the yellow Mercedes bus, he managed to wave a leaden arm at the Children, hoping they would understand. But they didn't. They never did. They were shouting and screaming for more. But he couldn't give them any more. Not . . . yet . . . anyway. He was almost collapsing again when at last he reached the bus and flung himself through the passenger door on to the rugs on the seat.

'Had enough, then?' The mocking voice of Higgy, their burly tour manager from Glasgow, came from the driver's seat next to him. The bearded Scot had been resting up across the front seat during the performance, together with the cans of beer, magazines and sandwiches, now half-consumed, which he had prepared for the group's refreshment during the intervals.

'Just get us back, Higgie,' Thunder Rider's voice was muffled by the rug.

'Dunno what you English people a' made o'!' Higgie jibed, shaking his head. 'Yer poor weak, pansy minds need a good drop o' Scots blood in yer t' clear awi' the fog.'

Thunder Rider sat up sluggishly, trying to think of a retort, but he couldn't raise the energy. He noticed the beer instead, and opened a can. Gulping, he turned to watch the others as they climbed unsteadily through the door, dropping half-dead and motionless on to the heaps of rugs and clothing.

Stacia complaining of her feet; Lemmy, looking sightlessly around like an electrocuted Hell's Angel; Astral Al, still drumming mindlessly; Hound Master, shaking his head in glazed amazement; and the ever-complaining Baron: 'It's not the *playing*, it's the bloody *demand* that gets me. And it's not just the kids – you can't blame them – it's us, too. The moment we stop playing and we get down off that stage, blam! It hits you like a brick in the cobblers!'

Last in was the Sonic Prince in his crumpled gown, looking strangely alert, for all the hard slogging. There was no room on the floor, so he climbed dextrously into the front. Thunder Rider pressed a can into his lap, without commenting.

Higgie started the engine. He knew better than to delay. Already, some of the Children were leaving their grassy seats and beginning to converge on the compound exit. Not that there was any harm in this in itself – the kids were a great bunch, most of them; but as chief wet nurse to the group, he felt bound to put the interest of his charges first. Hawkwind had promised to play again after dark, to celebrate the mammoth outdoor New World Party that was being arranged, and they needed all the rest he could get for them.

THE YELLOW VAN COMMUNE

The journey to the Yellow Van Commune in Notting Hill Gate, where Hawkwind had their base, was long and straining. The Mercedes edged its way through a mass of seemingly disjointed limbs and faces that peered in and smiled and waved. The congestion grew worse as they travelled further out from the compound into the sprawling mini-city of tents and shelters.

Thunder Rider winced unpleasantly at the sights.

The apparent cheerfulness on the faces outside was a pretence. Behind each mask was a terrified, panic-stricken gaze that stabbed him to the core. They were desperate for Hawkwind to return. But there was no way he could help until after dark when they had rested.

No one knew what was causing the bad effects. No one guessed at the start that the concert would have become anything other than a good, mindless freakout to dispel bad vibrations. They noticed the strange but beautiful high effect, that the music had. But they had not discovered the full extent of its power until they had tried to stop playing and rested up for a short, ten-minute breather. The effects had been instant, like the withdrawal symptoms from a highly addictive drug.

At last, the grimy, lemon-coloured Mercedes broke free of the clinging crowds, and they were speeding along the avenues forged out of the wreckage of stilled cars and other vehicles that choked the Knightsbridge Road – and most other parts of London.

Here and there, some of the more adventurous Children had set up shop or home, trying to breathe back life into the great city. Most of the few remaining habitable buildings were now in fact occupied. In parts, the pavements were even starting to look familiarly crowded again, especially in the Gate itself and on the Portobello Road where the commune was situated.

There were other pockets of indigenous life also remaining in London, called, simply, the 'Others' by the Children. They belonged to the older orders, the breed of men who had brought the world to its present, sorry condition. Some of them were dressed in uniform and carried guns to protect themselves and their Property from Others less privileged. But they were few in numbers, and rarely seen.

Higgie brought the van to an abrupt halt outside number 271 Portobello Road – the Yellow Van Commune.

The commune was so named in honour of the group's first (yellow) van back in the late sixties – the decrepit vehicle which in those early days had served literally as home for most members. The group had moved in during the desperate period of fighting and dying which had taken place after the British Army had failed to bring back law and order . . . and after their own homes had been burnt to the ground to provide night illumination for the insane mobs that had roamed the streets, mindlessly murdering and looting.

It was situated adjacent to the burnt-out shell of the legendary Mountain Grill restaurant – the supplier of good, plentiful food to many a starving freak who roamed the inhuman streets of the period. For some unaccountable reason, 271 had always attracted people of a certain fighting kind, who pledged their lives to revolutionary causes. The previous occupants had been outlaw publishers of underground pamphlets, friends of Hawkwind who had been hideously killed by marauding gangs of puritan vigilantes.

The entrance door was painted in Barnie's typical, swirling colours and designs, as was every square centimetre of exterior brickwork up to the roof. It led into a long, dark hall cluttered with dusty relics of the past, and decorated with distorted pictures of cars and long-dead people painted on to the walls.

The interior of the house had remained more or less as they found it, most of its effects belonging to the luckless publishers. The walls were lined with old mirrors and hangings from different periods, collected years before from the junk stalls that once lined the street outside with thriving business life. The common room where the group usually slept and relaxed, contained a similar, odd mixture of second-hand items – a long, green, dusty couch, a scarred, wooden chest of drawers, a creaking wicker-basket chair, a harmonium, a bed, and on the floor, several giant cushions and striped mattresses, as well as innumerable smaller items of curiosity.

The tired band climbed out of the van and clomped upstairs, oblivious of the small group of Children who had gathered to watch their return. They threw themselves down on to the first soft surfaces that presented themselves. But sleep was hard coming. Almost immediately, the terrifying sickness started to gnaw its way up from under the tiredness. It screwed-up their stomachs and slid wracking pains into their heads, making them long for the hour when their bodies would be rested, and once more they could pick up their instruments and play.

Eventually, with the help of downers procured by Higgy, they managed to sink into a turbulent, delirious kind of release.

THE NEW WORLD PARTY

Thunder Rider was the first to wake, opening his eyes to the weird glow of firelight coming through the holes in the curtains. Though he had been worn out, he had had an uneasy sleep, due to the withdrawal depression. He had experienced frightening dreams and unnerving physical pains and shakes. Not wanting to wake and face them properly, he tried to let himself drift off again. But a sudden, sharp cracking sound came at the window pane. Then he heard the voices of the Children outside, and realized they had woken him up. They were reminding Hawkwind of their pledge.

Stiffly, he arose and went to the window. He pulled back the curtains and peered out at the night scene. A large crowd of Children had gathered. They had built a roaring, crackling fire in the centre of the street.

Behind the derelict shop fronts opposite him, the intense, primitive blackness of the night was waiting, pressing in on the garish assembly. He felt a mournful excitement build up inside him as he watched. Most of the Children were looking at the window, and he waved to let them know he had seen them.

He turned away to survey the silent, sleeping forms jumbled frozen on the floor in the room. The scene in here looked deceptively normal. It could still be 1976. Only the sounds and lights coming from outside suggested otherwise. He debated whether to wake them, then decided to let them sleep on a few moments longer. They looked so peaceful.

Hawkwind had undergone so many changes. They had come so far, lived through so many periods. They had all come through and survived the last few months intact, except for one member – Actonium Doug Smith.

The still shape of their ex-Manager was sprawled sadly on a mattress, just as it had been for days, too morose to care. He slept with Clarence, his shaggy-haired Old English Sheep Dog, surrounded by his litter of cans and bottles. Ever since the old world had ended, he had made no attempt to adapt, and only slipped further into depression. Thunder Rider guessed, sadly, that it was because there was no Management role left for him to play.

He wended his way into the bathroom, switching on the battery lighting as he went. He was still dressed in his silver PVC suit. At close quarters, it didn't look so good. He had ripped holes in it in several places for ventilation. Elsewhere the aluminium was starting to rub off. He decided to change into something more casual for the party.

When he emerged twenty minutes later, he was dressed in faded denims and sweat shirt, wearing soft, brown, low-heeled boots, and a wide, pewter-coloured belt. The belt was fastened impressively with twin interlocking bison-heads, a piece of unusual gear he had once picked up from an alternative leather-craft shop in Belsize Park. Round his neck, he wore a silver medallion he had sworn to wear for ever – the parting love gift of a Mexican girl he met on an old tour. On his fingers he wore an assortment of rings – like controls, that flashed as he moved.

He felt much better, apart from the sick feeling in his head and stomach, which wouldn't go away until the music started again.

He went to wake the others.

By midnight, they were back on stage preparing for the second part of the marathon rock concert in celebration of the forming of the Children of The Sun – the new society of mankind. Everyone had had enough of the old world, full of its rules and regulations and its petty suppressions of natural behaviour. Looking around, it was all too evident that the old way of doing things had failed. Now, people wanted to try out the new ways of life which were instinctively felt to be better.

The population of Children had gradually spread away from the stage, throughout the wooded park. They had been working hard during the afternoon, transforming the park into a permanent festival city of tents and makeshift shelters fashioned out of scrap metal, plastic and other materials left behind by the previous civilization.

Inumerable fires were dotted about, and the night air was full of laughter, and heavy with the smell of wood smoke and the sound of Hawkwind's music.

Inside the compound, among the gaudily painted Commers and Mercedes, stood the most important ingredient of the party next to the music – the huge, insect-like bulk of a 5,000 gallon Bass Charrington beer tanker. They had found the tanker during a food hunt, rammed into the side of a tailor's shop in Oxford Street. While Hawkwind were sleeping, Higgy had got out an old Bedford cargo truck, and towed it in.

It gleamed wetly under the mercury stadium lighting, causing the crowd who were gathering to watch the opening ceremony to slaver at the mere sight of it. Its load was still, miraculously, intact but unluckily the engines and the vital air pump needed to get the precious fluid out had seized up. Higgy was leading the team of helpers who were vainly trying to break their way in. The crowd were getting impatient, banging tin cans and salvaged cups in a slow protest beat against the sides of the vehicles:

'Give us a swiggy, Higgy!
Give us a swiggy, Higgy!'

The bearded Scot swore and shouted, partly in reply, but also at the tanker which he cursed with all his heart. He had slaved at it for several hours now, and he was beginning to work up a real, celtic aggression. He made several more fruitless attempts to smash off the pumping assembly with a crow bar. Then, exasperated, he hauled himself up on to the roof and started hammering at the welded casement of the safety valve instead. His mighty, flesh-shuddering blows drowned the chanting chorus, filling the night air with a resounding, metallic clanging. Finally, the stubborn cap cracked and smashed off, amidst a wild, enthusiastic burst of applause.

'That got the bitch!' Higgy shouted out, triumphantly.

With the aid of a rusty fire bucket and a piece of dirty electrical cable, the flat booze was ladled out. Higgy took the first bucketful, clasping it with both hairy arms and putting it to his lips. He took a long slug, slopping it down his greasy sweat shirt. 'Doesna taste so bad for all that!' he shouted, grinning broadly. He took a second, long draught. Then he lowered it, half-empty to the amazed clientele below.

Soon, the flat booze was splashing and gurgling on its intended journey down the parched and indifferent throats. It was the first taste of alcohol for most people since the last distillery had been looted, and they weren't grumbling. It acted very quickly.

The noisy, jostling crowd surrounding the tanker suddenly grew in size as the good news spread. The time of the evening's performance approached.

The party-throwers loosened up, milling about in laughing, singing groups; sitting around the roaring camp fires, talking of the future. They brought out their guitars and strummed along with the music. Some of them were content just to lie back on the trampled ground to face the stars, and allow the pleasant sounds to carry them lazily off to sleep. For others, the revelrous atmosphere was a chance to catch up on lost love-making.

The dome of dark above them, now once again the unknown terrifying veil that had once kept their ancestors huddled round the dancing flames for security, gradually expanded, pushed back by the myriad pin-points of light and by the natural, human activities.

In front of the stage – the vital nerve hub of what was now called Earth City – Jonathan Liquid Len Smeeton and the Lensmen were busy setting up the clusters of light machines that would further add to the sense of togetherness with their splendour.

The gaunt figure of the Light Lord was clearly visible in the powerful lighting, fussily dressed in his green corduroy flairs, low black boots and short black leather jacket. He moved on nervous energy, striding about among the banks of equipment and the groups of sprawling Children. He battled with immense lighting problems inside his head. A circular stage provided no backdrop for the images of his projectors to fall on to, so instead he had had to devise a complicated-looking sculpture of tall plastic shapes and mirrors, which was now mounted on the stage. It rotated like a giant gyroscopic assembly, rising above the heads of the players.

Hawkwind themselves were quietly composing and rehearsing new numbers, while waiting for their cue from Liquid Len. To keep the bad feelings at bay, they had to keep playing for as long and as often as they could . . . driven on by the unceasing demands for their music. Any sort of Hawkwind music seemed to do, even the rehearsals. This suited the group, because it would have been difficult to arrange a second, practice site.

27

A shout went up from off-stage near by one of the projector mountings. Liquid Len finished checking the wiring behind the Master Console. He held himself impressively erect like a symphony hall conductor. Elegantly, he raised an arm in the direction of the stage as a signal to begin.

Abruptly, the big amplifiers, which had been working at only a quarter volume to save power, were turned back up to full again, and a series of long, loud drum rolls crashed out. Those among the Children who were still inside their shelters, heard the mighty call of Hawkwind, and made their way to join the swaying, cheering throng ringing the stage.

Next, Liquid Len killed the central battery of lights with a curt nod of his head. Satisfied at the sudden inrush of darkness that began to invade the site, providing him with the strength he needed, he turned his attention to the controls on the shining panel in front of him.

Gradually, the other two main lights dimmed out, and in the sudden, ageless dark that had returned to London, the Light Lord's powerful machines were brought to life.

The stage began to cartwheel slowly, then more rapidly in a vivid, heady explosion of colours and shapes. A gasp of disbelief exhaled slowly from the blackness round about. The tall, plastic fins sticking up in the air appeared to turn like spokes, rippling and undulating with the colours which were continually changing by merging into each other. The colours slid off the ends into the black sky, like the exhausts of a giant space craft.

The enormity of the illusion was so large that it caught many off-balance, and they staggered around in the dark, falling drunkenly into each other.

Thudding drums and hissing cymbals leapt out like angry animals from the strange-looking craft – the Hawkwind Spacecraft, formed so long ago by Captain Bob Calvert, who, legend had it, would one day return to them.

Stacia, (who *had* come back, with Lemmy), appeared on its platform from somewhere inside the swirling hull, draped only in a fine, colour-bombarded negligee. Her body was completely energized by the incessant rhythms of the ship's engines, and the magical sounds of the melotron as the Hawkcraft began gear-changing into the music of *Silver Machine*. As the sound stabilized, she released the veil. Her wholesome, naked body, clad only in the magical light began moving wildly and sensuously around the perimeter of the flashing panels. She fed her all into the grasping, sucking blackness of the primeval night – a perfect gesture of triumphant human love, a symbol of Earth, of optimism, of life yet to come.

Then the outer part of the ship seemed to break away like an unearthly jewel that whorled and flashed and pulsated with synchronized colour and sound. As one, the Children roared and screamed along with the familiar words, their voices sliding up and down with the rushing, careering scales of sound.

The notes travelled out over their heads, slicing unafraid through the darkness, through the unseen semi-ruins of London . . . travelling far beyond the mile-wide jam of bodies, tents and belongings in Green Park . . . reaching out soundless, powerful fingers of musical substance which probed every last remaining biologic cell of life on Earth. They heralded a new dawning for Mankind . . . an irresistable message which could not be ignored by anyone . . .

BLASTS FROM THE SKIES

In China, Kwa Wang, leader of the People's Resistance Movement, leapt off his bicycle as the shock of inspiration hit him. The bike collided into the others. Soon the entire foraging party was brought to a jumbled, buckled halt on the overgrown loess plain.

Out in this vast sea of rubbish, dotted with gnarled, leafless trees and fragile reed huts, and edged with the ruins of Chinese industry, the puzzling words of their Grand Master spoken moments before his death, suddenly became clear.

The old man, killed in the rioting, had simply said: 'Go

West.'

Wang realized now that somewhere in the Imperialist West must lie the secret of the Master's teachings . . . another of life's Great Paradoxes. As the knowledge dawned, each man, woman and child present felt the 'windless wind, the soundless sound, the visionless vision' that blew across the ruined landscape, beckoning them on towards its mysterious source, where they felt compelled to go . . .

In Argentina, in the normally crowded Calle Florida in Buenos Aires, the last great game of bidou was being played in the Café Bolonga. The death dice rattled across the marble table tops, deciding which of the solemn-faced señors and señoritas in the cafe should be next to pick up the loaded Colt ·45 and blast out his brains.

Life wasn't worth living in the abandoned city now that all its glamour and lights had died. The rest of Argentina was equally deserted, and communications with the outside world had ceased altogether.

But, unbelievingly, the dice suddenly refused to play. Each player threw a double six . . . time after time. Not one person could ever be the loser. Their depressions lifted, and life no longer seemed to lack purpose. Laughter broke out, and the game ended. Someone pulled out a pair of maraccas and the group left the café singing and dancing up the echoing, deserted street, to where the great transcontinental coaches were still parked in the Calle Lavalle . . .

In India, deep beneath the devastated, corpse-choked Calcutta alleys in the British Section, Rojan's wasted human shape splashed distastefully through the sewage. He clutched at the disintegrating dhoti wrapped between his legs, in a vain effort to protect himself from the heavy chill air and the suffocating blackness.

'It's just as bloody bad up there as ever,' he called out, partly to reassure himself with his own voice as he inched forward, and partly to announce his return to the other survivors who were camped further up the pipe in the dry flow

30

chamber, awaiting his news. He had been gone for some time, and the dreadful thought that they had died in his absence filled him with acute panic.

'The rats are still eating their dinners in our precious streets while we starve in their stinking old homes!' he called out again, but there was still no sound apart from the trickling of fluid. 'The only consolation you will have now, my friends, is that the wealthy shit you see flowing in this so holy venerable of channels, will cease to flow. From now on, gentlemen, all *castes*, all *men* are equal.'

Then, his terrifying plight forgotten, he froze as the strange, blissful feeling from thousands of miles away washed over him like a dam breaking. Entranced, he saw the shimmering, colourful stage surrounded by happy, beautiful people light up like a magical island floating in the blackness. At this distance, he couldn't hear the music, but he could feel the fresh warmth pumped into him and he could sense what it did for the crowds of lucky people gathered around.

The vision was real. It spelled the end to his appalling suffering, it gave hope to him and his friends. If only there was a way to reach it. Somehow, they *had* to. They had to take their chance on the deadly, rat-infested streets above and find their way to the stage . . .

In Uganda, near the ruined campus at Kyambogo, on the shores of the great chemical swamp, mud huts were growing again. Inside them, Angel and other ex-workers and students of the college were resting up after the successful overthrow of the corrupt Regime. Now there was no government, because there were no people left to govern. The once fertile land, and most of the teeming lifeforms it contained were both poisoned. Change, as in the rest of the world, had been brought about too late.

Angel felt the music start to thread its powerful rhythm through his veins. It started as a memory, of the young white-haired boy he had spent his early student days with in the London of '67. He remembered the English rock music they had heard together at the clubs and concerts, music so long

31

banned in his own country by the tyrannical will of his ex-president.

The picture of the boy on the mud wall smiled back in recognition, and he felt a strong urge to be there with him once again, away from the horrifying, sterilized African continent.

He arose from his squatting position on the hard earth floor – the first movement he had made for several days – then, with the others he strode out for Entebbe airport, energized by the Hawkwind music beating powerfully in his strong black body . . .

The musical emanations reached the Arctic.
'Mush! Mush!'
Through the fur of his upturned collar, Klute looked back at the glinting convoy of sleds and dogs, waiting to evacuate the last remaining Eskimos from their treacherous homelands of cracking ice.

His brown, slit eyes glanced over the fields of slowly melting snow . . . a landscape once familiar as the place of his birth, now punctuated here and there by abandoned, black skeletal shacks riddled with gaps, and by large, emerging heaps of last year's Coca-Cola cans and empty gas cylinders. The gassy waste of endless, thoughtless industrial processes had caused all this, he thought bitterly, trapping heat in the atmosphere and melting the ice caps. In the ensuing disaster, his kind had all but died out, and the survivors had suffered great hardship. Then the inexplicable urge to move had come. He had felt it first, like a migratory instinct, but gradually the others had felt it too – a happy, tremulous energy that seemed to come from everywhere and nowhere, inviting them to an unknown future.

The dog packs rose like withered ghosts, shaking themselves free of their slushy beds. Without waiting for food, they braced themselves ready for the long, hard haul to the boats at the port . . . to the promise of a new life.

'Mush! Mush!'
The waves, emanations, reached round the planet, holding it in a strange, vital new embrace. They stirred hope. They

inspired action.

They attracted hatred.

Nowhere on Earth was free of their powerful transforming effects . . .

THE WEBS OF NIGHT

'Whatever they are, sir, they seem to be coming from the North West, sir,' Cowers, Regimental Sergeant Major to the highly secret SOB Garrison, informed the Colonel. SOB ('Saudi Oil for Britain'), had been guarding the giant oil refineries at Ra Tannurah on the east coast of Saudi Arabia ever since HM troops had forcibly taken the UK's 'share' of the Eastern power wells. 'Lance Corporal Burk picked them up on his radio, sir.'

'Picked them up on his *radio*, Sergeant?' asked Colonel Memphis Mephis, semi-incredulously. 'Waves? Emanations?' His ascetic, military face looked deliberately puzzled.

'Well, whatever they are, sir.'

'He just "tuned in", did he?'

'Well . . . ' said the RSM, gripping his pointing stick more tightly behind his back, '. . . by positioning his transmitter, sir, and broadcasting a certain sort of, ahem, music sir, through, ahem, uni-directional speakers, sir, he was able to deduce which direction the, ahem, waves were travelling, sir.'

'Uni-directional speakers? What sort of music is that?'

'Pop music, sir.'

'*Pop* music? Sounds a bit far-fetched to me, Cowers.'

'Yes, sir . . . I mean no, sir . . . you know, Tony Blackburn tapes, sir, and the records belonging to the lads, sir . . . Bay City Rollers, great stuff, sir, great stuff . . .'

'Yes, yes. Get to the point, Sergeant! How did Burk discover the direction using, hm, pop music?'

'Easy, sir,' the RSM's face cracked in a parody of a smile. 'The lads were having a bit of a party . . . off-duty of course, sir. Burk happened to notice, sir, that the terrible effects of these damn rays, whatever they are, were neutralised when his speakers were pointed North West, sir.'

'Observant fellow. Well, Sergeant, you know what to do. We'll put a stop to this nonsense once and for all, now.'

'Yes, *sir*! Right away, sir. It'll be a relief not to have to wear these awful sanitary pads, sir.'

'Off you go, Sergeant.'

The RSM left the room.

The Colonel allowed the re-assuring, concerned, paternal look to slide off his face.

He seated himself in smouldering silence, his true nature revealed, casting a hating alien gaze over the table map in front of him.

'So, it looks as if I'm going to be proved right . . .' he muttered, a wicked sneer beginning to bend down his lips. 'If so, it will fit in nicely with my plans.' His finger traced a course North West across the map, through Persia towards Great Britain. 'As I thought! The stupid fool Cowers! I know more about the source of these "rays" than the lot of them put to-together . . . now let me see.'

He shuddered uncontrollably as the visions of the detestable, long-haired yobbos in Green Park returned to him. *They* were the offensive. *They* were the Enemy. They were what was turning his men into a bunch of ineffectual, spineless pansies . . .

The idiot Burk's radio might help to ease the ghastly effects, but ultimately . . . *They* would have to be eradicated.

The world situation had changed. There was no longer any need to protect the oil. With him at the head – by degrees the Colonel had come to assume that he was the highest-ranking officer remaining in the world – SOB Garrison would triumph over everything and everyone. It would rout a bunch of dirty hippy upstarts desecrating the Royal Parks in London . . . and it would do more.

While he schemed and plotted, his slender, manicured finger traced the precise route his killer Army would take . . .

34

LOSING CONTROL

Over the concert site, another plane roared laboriously off-course for Heathrow Airport. This one had the red Chinese star on its battered fuselage. Like the others, it flew erratically, heavily laden, and piloted by a desperate crew of amateurs. One of its jets had evidently packed up, for it only just managed to keep its height.

Hawkwind stopped playing momentarily, as all attention was diverted up into the sky. They could see the small, round, Chinese faces crammed at the portals, looking down and waving. The Children waved back and cheered. Then, abruptly, the plane's other engines misfired one by one, and shut out. In deathly silence, the giant airliner veered sharply earthwards with its human cargo. The crowd below gasped as it disappeared behind the jagged horizon of ruins in Piccadilly.

Several tense minutes elapsed before it became evident that the plane must have found space to crashland in Hyde Park. Somewhere at the back of the crush of Children, a detachment broke away and ran to help.

A bitter, unnatural chill began to grow in the summer air. The Horrors, kept at bay by the music, were already returning. Desperately, Hawkwind began playing again, fearing that the hellish feelings would soon sap the will of the gallant rescue party.

The last concert was well into its eighth day. They had been playing for up to ten hours at a time, unable to leave the stage because of the music's horrific withdrawal symptoms. Whenever they could, they drove back to the Yellow Van, but the next day, or sometimes at night, they would be persuaded back again by the hungry Children, their rest only half obtained. The music was like a hard drug – the more they played, the worse the after-effects became.

They had played on relentlessly, ignoring their own safety for the welfare of Earth City. Now, they began to wind down, unable to stay on their feet – equally unable to get the sleep they so desperately needed.

They could go on no more. The music had got them hooked – and it started to eat them away.

KINGS OF SPEED

The feeling was like a constant adrenalin trip, only worse. It could only be effectively stopped by heavy doses of the Hawkwind music, though chemical agents, if available, helped to ease the symptoms of paranoia and delusion. The whole of Earth City, and the other like-minded people in the world, were in its satanic grip. Still no one knew why or, properly, what caused it.

'We can't go on endlessly playing,' Hound Master spoke into the gloomy silence of the room.

He was sitting next to the Baron on one of the cushions at Yellow Van, clutching his drawn knees to his wiry frame, rocking nervously backwards and forwards in an attempt to stave off the speeding. 'We're worn out from playing. The paranoia's so great now we can't even get the small amount of sleep we're used to. Higgy's managed to eke out the few remaining downers. But now they're running low and we're having to take twice the dose before they'll work. What will we do when they run out altogether? . . . Maybe we should give the next performance a miss and use the time instead trying to work out some other plan.'

'Maybe you're out of your head, Hound Master!' The Baron spoke angrily. 'What do you think we're made of? Even if we could take the effects that long, the kids would throw a collective fit. Just listen to them!' He had been attempting vainly to focus his mind on a set of sunny travel photographs in an old *Telegraph* colour supplement. But now he slammed the magazine down and rose to his feet.

The Children had stopped gathering outside the window, as they used to. They were too low spirited to muster the strength.

It took them all their time to walk about organizing food. When Hawkwind were off-stage they spent most of their time in their shelters and homes, fighting off the collective madness. They tended to leave actual work to the hours covered by the music, when they felt instantly happy and energetic. During music hours they also slept. Unlike Hawkwind, they at least got much-needed sleep. But they were still in a bad way.

A young red-haired man in a green suit was freaking-out in the centre of the street as the Baron looked from the window. 'Another luckless victim driven over the edge,' he commented, bitterly, yet with compassion. The man tore at his hair with clawed hands, pulling away huge handfuls, and screamed frantically trying to oust the demon inside him. The Baron turned away from the sight, feeling the same desperation start to well up inside him. 'The poor bastards! You've got to remember Hound Master, they've not had the downers we've had to help them through.'

Everyone was quiet. From outside in the street, came more agonized shouts and wails from the Children of Portobello – constant reminders of the invisible front of negative energy that was slowly destroying their minds and bodies.

'What do you think we could plan, then?' Thunder Rider asked Hound Master.

'We could try to find out why our music's become so potent. Of course our music's always been good,' he managed a wry smile, displaying two missing front teeth, 'judging by the number of followers we've got. But it's never been *this* good . . .'

'Or bad . . .,' Liquid Len added. He was pacing agitatedly up and down a clear strip of floor. His hands were clasped whitely behind his back. He was trying, as were the others in their various ways, to take his concentration off the nightmare thoughts and pictures that were always ready to form inside their heads.

The same imagery came to everyone – earth that cracked and made gaping crevices into which poured the crumbling, sliding buildings of Man; demented faces of tortured human mutants which crawled out of the fissures, seeking revenge; calm, alien gazes from robot-like creatures standing patiently on the horizon of the devastated land; their own bodies transforming into squirming, gleaming tentacles of green, squid-like flesh if they dared to look down at themselves; showers of molten metal and burning acid fall-out lancing down through the ceiling from the sky, stinging their flesh and riddling their bodies through with millions of scorching holes . . .

'We must be under attack . . . that's the only explanation that stands up . . .!' Stacia shouted, eyes wide with fear. 'It's never been this bad before . . .!' Her teeth chattered, and she hugged her chest tightly with both arms, trying to still her hammering heart.

Actonium Doug cried in the corner, shuddering convulsively. His beer supply had run out. Clarence lay by his side, whimpering. His once radiant coat was now dry, and balding.

'Maybe it's all these bloody foreigners coming over here,' the Baron joked grimly. 'Why are they coming?' He looked to silent, smiling Rudolph the Black who simply shook his head.

'It must be the music . . .' someone said.

'What? I know it's loud, but it's not *that* loud!' the Baron smiled, painfully. 'I can't stand this feeling – it's crawling about under my skin. It feels like I'm coming down from an alky's trip.' He shuddered, and motioned as though to scratch himself viciously.

'We've got to come through, somehow,' Thunder Rider kept intoning. 'There must be a way of fighting it . . . maybe . . . if we took turns manning the stage and kept the music going . . .?'

'The equipment wouldn't stand it,' the Sonic Prince interjected hastily. He seemed to be able to resist the effects better than the others. He was seated at the harmonium, and every so often played a few jazzy notes in an attempt to lighten the mood.

'Try putting on the records again,' the Baron suggested.

'We've tried them a dozen times already,' complained Thunder Rider, 'but I'll try them again. It's something to do, at least.'

He strode jerkily towards the Goldring, which was mounted

on the chest of drawers next to a box containing the records. He selected the *Doremi Fasol Latido* album and set the disc down on the turntable. Then he left the room and climbed down the stairs into the hallway. The old bikes left by the previous tenants had been cleared out now, given away to the Children, and a diesel generator installed instead. He kick-started the engine. When it was running properly he stuck the exhaust outlet through a hole in the door and climbed back up the stairs. He switched on the player, and then sat down and waited in one of the wicker chairs.

The room went quiet as *Brainstorm* came over the speakers. But even as the first urgent notes of Lemmy's bass guitar work commenced, it became evident that the Hawklord space chant was not going to make any difference to the paranoia. If anything, it helped to increase it. Alarmed, Thunder Rider rose to his feet and tried *Lord of Light* on the reverse side, with no greater success. Despondently, he turned the set off. A loud, amplified click sounded over the speakers.

'It's no use. Live music seems to be the only remedy. If only we knew why . . .'

No one answered. The point had been discussed a hundred times already. As the Sonic Prince pointed out, the signals received by the loudspeakers were the same whether they originated from live instruments or a plastic disc. Technically, there was no reason why a live performance should work when a recorded one didn't.

'I think Hound Master's gotta point though, Baron,' Astral Al lifted his head finally from where he was crouched over a plastic sink bowl. He was still dressed in his showy white suit which was now much the worse for wear and stained with recent vomit. 'I mean about getting time to think and skipping the next gig. Maybe we gotta be cruel to be kind, eh?' He smiled, a little roguishly, but no one objected – that was his way. 'We can use up the rest of the downers and crash out for a few hours. That way we'll be able to think better.'

'I like that idea best,' Lemmy said. He had been lying next to Stacia, trying to space himself out by relaxing and keeping perfectly still, hoping the Horrors would eventually go away.

'We could get drunk on the rest of that home-made pigswill, too. There's about twenty bottles left in the alcove over the stairs.'

'That's because it really *is* swill,' Stacia said, retching slightly at the thought.

No one said anything to counter Hound Master's idea. They knew, at the back of their minds, that sooner or later they would have to do something of the sort. The downers were running out, and the threatening image warfare, whatever it was, was increasing in power, and very soon they felt it would take over their minds entirely.

'Who's agreed on that, then?' asked Thunder Rider. He could scarcely concentrate on the proceedings, and had to use all his energy and will to speak at all through the nervous collapse that was starting up. 'I know you don't like the idea, Baron. But it's worth trying. We're not getting anywhere simply by playing. All we do is stave off the Horrors a little longer . . . and they're getting worse all the time. If we don't do something else fast, we'll join that guy in the street.'

They were all silent again for a few moments, shivering in the heat, and battling for control. Eventually, they consented unanimously to miss the performance for the momentary relief that would be granted.

Wordlessly, Higgy arose from his mattress to fetch the remaining downers from the kitchen. When he came back, he handed them round, two to each person present including himself.

'Let's hope,' he said, as he tossed the empty bottle over his shoulder, 'ye can all come up wi' something when ye wake, or it's curtains for th' Human Race.'

Solemnly, they swallowed their tablets and lay down to await sleep – all except for the Sonic Prince. An idea of his own had occurred to him, and he wanted to check it out.

FILMING THE UNKNOWN

Outside Yellow Van, the air was even more close and humid, and full of the smells of rotting wood and other organic materials.

After the confines of the room, the expansiveness made everything seem more intense and electric. It gave the Prince something to concentrate on to relieve his paranoia. During the meeting, his brain had been buzzing with thoughts and ideas, but none of them would rise to the surface.

He nodded to the few panic-stricken faces he encountered as he moved slowly down the street lined with cracked and broken shop fronts. Fortunately, no one checked with him the exact time of the cancelled session. Such was their pain, the Children scarcely recognized him. They were hanging grimly to what little sanity remained.

He passed the heap of white ashes in the centre of the street where, every night without fail, the ritual fire was lit. Its cooling surface was criss-crossed with the tyre-marks of the transit, and the odd tread mark of other rare vehicles. Amidst the powdery remains, he noticed with horror the outline of the madman they had seen from the window earlier. It was completely covered-over apart from a piece of tell-tale red hair where the face should have been. The pitiful form still twitched, sinking deeper into its silvery-grey grave, too far gone to be helped.

He hurried past, sliding one of Higgy's downers between his lips to keep down the sudden rise of adrenalin pounding through his veins. There was little time left to hang about.

Further along the street he met George and Maria, owners of the once famous Mountain Grill Restaurant which had been burnt out. The blackened shell was adjacent to the Yellow Van Commune, but had to be abandoned as irrepairable. They were setting up a new shop instead, in the premises once occupied by the old Woolworth's which were still largely intact. He felt a feeling of warmth on seeing them. In the old times, George and

41

Maria had catered for all the group's food needs, and kept a good, plentiful supply of low-cost food going for the many down and out and starving freaks in the area. They had never given in once to the ways of the Establishment, and fought through all the phases of the transformation, standing solidly by the new society of Children. By popular request, they had now been put in charge of Earth City's food requirements.

The present store was already well-advanced, full of sacks and jars containing dried cereals and other foodstuffs salvaged from the abandoned farms and city supermarkets. The huge kitchens, built with the help of an army of supporters, were almost completed, and ready to go into mass production. The normally happy couple, though, shook their heads in despair when the Prince passed. They were still working hard, together with a few Children, but they were noticeably lean and ill, tired with the pressing urgency of the opening deadline.

'Don't worry,' the Prince feigned hopefulness, to cheer them up. 'We're doing all we can to find out what's happening and put it right.'

'Any leads?' the Greek asked.

'No. But I feel confident . . .'

'Christ, I hope you do, Simon, I hope you do. The Children can't take much more, you know. Well, you must come and eat with us again tonight, you know. You haven't eaten properly at all, and our players must have the best, yes?'

'Higgy's been coming to you for the food . . .'

'Not enough, my friend! Not enough . . .' He broke off, attacked by a fit of coughing. Maria held on to him, and started to lead him away inside.

'He's not too well,' she said worriedly. 'I keep telling him to rest, but it's like talking to a brick wall. Now he'll want to get back to his work. Well, we'll be seeing you.'

'Bye, Maria. We'll come over,' the Prince said softly. He touched her arm. 'Don't worry.'

He walked away, feeling upset. Then the downer started to work, and he felt slightly better again. He turned right into Blenheim Crescent and walked up to the house where Moorlock, the Acid Sorcerer lived. He didn't intend paying a visit, mainly because the Moorlock had now decided that nothing could be done to save mankind, and spent most of his days in a black depression. He was rude to his visitors, and unwilling to come outside. The Prince was after something else. Parked in front of the old Victorian terrace of peeling white paint, was the streamlined apricot-coloured Oldsmobile the Moorlock used to get around in during less depressing times. The only concession he allowed his friends during his present mood, was the use of this stunning metal and chrome reminder of the old technology.

The Prince felt as near as it was possible to get to excitement as he pulled out his special key and inserted it into the lock. Then, he was inside the spacious interior smelling of plastic, musty floor upholstery and the stale, acrid cigarette ends he knew to be packed solidly in the ash trays. Lovingly, he felt the controls, and ran his fingers along the smooth, apricot-coloured dash-board. The entire car was tastefully coloured inside and out, in varying shades and hues with this colour. A sense of calmness and order came at once to his mind, as it always did when he sat inside like this. Cars were almost self-contained, private worlds of their own on wheels. They made him feel masterful and safe from the dangers outside.

He stuck in the key, and, with slight hand movements brought the powerful 'Rocket 88' V8 engine to life. The car murmured, and he swung it round into the road and began weaving it dangerously but skilfully in and out of the wreckage. He felt much better. The speed of the car, and the rushing buildings sliding past him somehow counteracted his internal speeding. He was born to the feel of danger, and at times of stress, illogically, he needed it to survive.

As the car bounced and skidded from street to street, absorbing his surface attention, he found he was able to think clearly for the first time in a week. They had been so pre-occupied playing their instruments, and then sleeping for as long as possible, and now suffering the paranoia, that no one had had the time for objective thought.

He allowed the complicated electronic circuitry of their equipment to form free patterns in his mind. He tested and questioned each link. His mental fingers probed in detail the sequence of events that had occurred from the start of the concert up until the present moment. He assembled the instruments inside his head exactly as they were assembled on stage, and played them silently over to himself in the hope of detecting oddities. But each time, the arrangements and sequences worked out naturally, with no abnormalities that he could see. One factor kept sticking in his mind, though. The Delatron – largely because of its newness. So far as he could see, it was the only departure they had made from their older music. He wondered if it contained the answer.

The Delatron was only a modifier. It made the notes cleaner and fuller and gave better separation, that was all.

He had dismissed it a thousand times already. Yet . . . it struck him that the diode arrangement inside the apparatus was unnecessarily complex. He remembered a remark Del Detmar, the group's former electronics wizard once made to him while they had worked together on its prototype.

He had been working long hours and the Prince had come into the workshop late after a party to help finish it off. The satyr-like Del was surrounded by reference books, most of which were technical, but some, he noticed immediately, were books on magical arts, a favourite subject of his. The Delatron's guts were exposed, and inside he could see a straight rod of silver projecting from a parabola of diodes . . . a completely superfluous arrangement.

'Won't hurt the rest of the works,' the musician had said sheepishly. 'Just a bit of fun. I got the figuration out of "Malleus Maleficarum" . . .'

Until the present time, the Prince had not thought twice about the matter. He had never been superstitious and had allowed Del his little indulgence. Now, the memory came home. 'Malleus Maleficarum', by two early Dominicans, Jakob Sprenger and Heinrich Kramer was the most important book on magic and demonology ever written. It almost seemed to demand attention.

He saluted the memory of his old friend, and turned the car around. It was worth giving the idea a try, at least. 'And if your little addition is the cause of all this, you'll go down as the biggest, interfering, meddling prick in history,' he muttered under his breath as he headed back for Blenheim Crescent.

GLINTING JUNKED METAL AND BLOOD

The hot, Indian sun blazed down on the metal and flesh jerking its way across the parched landscape. At the wheel, Rojan cursed and swore as the ancient jeep crashed and lurched slowly over the dry gulleys and channels left behind seven years ago by the last monsoons. The shockwaves rattled the bodywork, and ruined the suspension. They had already lost one of its doors, and now the bonnet was shaking loose.

It had been six days since they had set out from Calcutta, searching vainly in every town they came to for a faster means of transport. At the rate they were travelling, it would take several months to reach London. All the vehicles had been smashed or cannibalised for spare parts, and there were no people left to ask.

Bodies in various stages of decay and dehydration littered the ground, gnawed by rats and other vermin which were pro-liferating in the aftermath. Buildings were mostly in ruins, and food and water were hard to come by. The few airports they managed to locate from maps and signposts, were unusable due to theft of fuel and bomb craters in the runways.

They were approaching the outskirts of Bombay, on the Eastern side of the country, parched and starving, and the jeep was packing up.

The seven alarmed Hindus crammed inside were desperately rocking backward and forward in an attempt to keep the engine turning.

After a while they tired, and Rajan slowly grew more exasperated with them.

'You must keep on rocking, if you do not want us all to die!'

he warned, severely. They were too weak to respond, and the jeep slowed down. He despaired.

'Oh my God!' he beseeched. 'On all sides of me I am surrounded by these bloody fools who will not save their own skin. What am I going to do, God?'

'I cannot go on any more, Rajan,' Kumar, a big weaver said, wearily from behind. 'You will have to understand.'

'Then you are a murderer!' Rajan retorted contemptuously. 'You do not care about anyone but your own big fat self!'

'Don't you call me a murderer!' the big man shouted back hoarsely. He rose from his seat and cuffed Rajan sharply round his ears from behind.

The blow sent Rajan dizzy.

The engine started to cough ominously, and the jerking got worse as he fumbled with the controls. Then he turned round and screamed insults.

'You bloody fucking bastard!' He was beside himself with rage. 'Here I am trying to save you all and you care not one iota. You would not save your own sister, or your own mother, God help her from you you fat, ungrateful, bloody bastard!'

The angry weaver stood up again, and this time made an attempt to strangle the incensed driver, but in the crush of bodies he tripped and fell on top of him instead.

'Look out!' someone cried, as the jeep veered out of control.

'Oh, Holy Mother!' another voice wailed.

There was a sudden uplift as the front end of the vehicle climbed an embankment, and then a heavy, neck-cricking jolt as it crunched into a wall.

The engine stalled.

They were in the middle of a flat, semi-desert of dead and dying vegetation and razed temples, twenty or so miles outside the second Indian city.

From somewhere underneath, came the sound of precious water or petrol, trickling in the silence.

Utterly frustrated by his pursuit of the dream stage, Rajan let go of the wheel and started weeping openly into his hands. The weaver climbed back to his seat, gesturing apologetically to the others. Except for Dachi, they were moaning with despair and the pain from their festering sores and wounds inflicted by the sewer rats.

Dachi, their Holy Man, sat unperturbed in the front seat, nodding and beaming graciously about him with an air of supreme yogic calm and understanding.

THE WAVES OF NEED

The stage was deserted save for one or two Children waiting listlessly among the dead instruments, hopeful that the aura of the music would linger round, and protect them.

Higgy climbed up the side, gasping for breath. He was still groggy from the tablets, but at least they made it easier to cope. At the top, he walked over to where the Delatron lay and started plucking out the wires. Then he carried the black box to the edge. Gently, he lowered it into the compound below. He returned to collect Rudolph's guitar and Thunder Rider's saxaphone. Then he climbed down himself.

He carried the instruments across the compound to the cargo truck and deposited them carefully on the seat inside, through the high door. A glance to the rear of the truck told him that the generator he had attached was still linked up. Satisfied, he walked round to the driver's door and climbed back inside.

The engine roared into life and he set off, bumping across the clinkered ground. A few curious faces peered out at him from behind tent-flaps, and between cracks in the wooden shanties, but they disappeared again when they realized he wasn't Hawkwind returning.

It didn't take him long to reach the Golden Gate, and soon he was turning the heavy vehicle into Lancaster Road only a hundred feet or so away from Yellow Van. He mounted the pavement and pulled up under the vast concrete flyover that spanned Portobello Road.

He jumped out, and carried the equipment over to where the Prince was busy setting the group's standby amps and microphones.

At one time, the spare ground under the viaduct had been used for community recreation purposes, for most of it was sectioned off into a series of large, open rooms, containing stage and various other workings. The air was refreshingly cool in the permanent shade provided by the tons of overhead concrete, making it the ideal location for a small, experimental jamming session. The ideal testing ground would have been the stage itself, but that would attract too much attention from the Children. In addition, the fine weather looked like breaking. Ominous-looking storm clouds were piling up in the north.

By early evening, the preparation was finished. Several puzzled-looking Children had ventured out to help push the heavy generator into position behind one of the dividing walls. Higgy started it up, and began testing the links and checking over the equipment. The first set was to be played without the Delatron being connected, to determine what effect, if any, Hawkwind's live, unadulterated music had.

The Children's response would make the ideal register.

After the sun had dropped below the skyline, the Prince went inside to wake the others.

He shook the Baron first.

'Come on, we're on in a minute.'

The Baron moaned, rubbing his eyes, and then his aching belly. He remembered their arrangements. 'I thought . . .'

'That's all been altered now.'

'You sussed something, then?' He sat up, reaching for his brown leather hat.

'Could be,' the Prince said.

It took them some moments to rouse the others, because of the tremendous resistance they had towards facing the same rotten day twice. Lemmy was the most stubborn, but a can of water soon helped him to orientate.

'What was that for?' he growled, spluttering.

'Tell you outside,' the Prince replied. 'You needn't look so hurt, either. I've not forgotten the time you and Dik Mik carried my bed out into the market and let me wake up in the middle of a blanket auction – only it was my blankets you were auctioning.'

Yawning, and pretending not to hear, Lemmy climbed into his jeans. He pulled on a studded, leather waistcoat and a green neck-tie. The weather had grown too close for his usual heavy cycle jacket.

They woke everyone, except for Stacia, whom they let lie in, and Actonium Doug and the Light Lord. Then they half climbed and half fell down the stairs. They burst out into the street, following the Prince.

'This better serve some purpose,' Thunder Rider warned the Prince, as they listened to his explanations. 'I could have done with a few more hours kip. I feel like a grated cat.'

By the time they reached the temporary stage, more Children had arrived. They were sitting motionlessly, staring at the equipment like zombies. The fight was knocked out of them, and they were faced with the choice of either suffering passively, or going out of their heads.

The band quickly took their positions, and at a signal from the Prince, Higgy started up the generator. The amplifiers hummed to life. Thunder Rider tested the mikes, while Lemmy, Rudolph the Black, and the Baron played with their guitars. Hound Master and Alan Powell were engrossed desperately making the best of a pair of bongo drums and a set of gongs – all the Prince could get together short of bringing over the massive kits.

'What are we gonna play?' Thunder Rider shouted out to the Prince.

The random notes and sounds were smashing into the concrete slabs and pillars, echoing oddly in the vault-like structure of the flyover.

'Doesn't matter. Carry on practising if you want to.' He looked pleased with himself.

'What's the matter with you?'

'Well . . .' the Prince faltered, trying to sense the sounds carefully with his body. 'I don't feel any change in the bad vibes, do you?'

'Come to think of it no – but I'm not very good at feeling right now,' Thunder Rider replied after a pause. 'Anyone else notice anything?'

'Can't say,' Astral Al shouted. 'Try some music, eh?'

'We'll do *Opa Loka* as best we can with what we've got,' Thunder Rider shouted back. 'A one, a two, a *three* . . .'

A terrible, grinding, discordant sound came over the speakers as the stiff players tried to co-ordinate. After a few moments, they gave up.

'Soreeeee!' Thunder Rider waved to the small crowd. He turned to the band. 'That was a fuck-up, wasn't it?'

'Long enough though to prove one thing,' the Prince said. 'I'll connect the Delatron now and see if it makes the difference I hope for.' He put down his electric violin, and together he and Higgy bent over the mica-like cube on the floor.

After a few minutes the connection was made. The instruments' outputs were wired to travel through the mysterious box.

'Now,' the Prince rose to his feet, barely able to hide his excitement. 'I'm pretty sure that if we play, you'll discover what the culprit is. And if my guess turns out to be correct, we've got our magical friend over the water to thank for what's happened.'

AGENT OF DARKNESS

Hot Plate leaned forward, peering through the glass at the two delicate sensors he held between tweezers. A tiny, blue spark crackled across the micro-gap; and he sighed with relief. Anxiously, he reached for the miniature screw driver a few inches away, and tightened the holding screw. Then he sat up, straightening his cricked back. He had been fiddling about for hours trying to get the distance between the rods exactly right. At last the assembly was ready for insertion into the hollowed head of the croquet mallet, ready for the King's practice game tomorrow. If all went well, the equipment would relay information of hitting pressure and estimated putting distance to a meter in the stem of the mallet, and enable the King to develop his stroke to a high degree of accuracy.

The invention had taken weeks of research, on what Hot Plate considered to be a useless and trivial project in these days of global catastrophe. But he could not protest. As the Royal Scientist to His Majesty King Trash, he would run the risk of losing his head.

He lifted the sensors from under the glass and placed them in their casement. Then he screwed down the lid and loaded it into the mallet head. He replaced the grooved cap and stacked the mallet with the others, ready for testing.

The King had been moody lately. The hippy music had driven him into an ever higher state of agony and rage. At the moment, he was resting. But Hot Plate expected the music to commence again soon and he cringed at the thought of what would happen. Strangely, he felt his own 'down' when the music outside stopped, as now. The King, on the other hand, felt elated.

The Royal Scientist had noticed that the music affected different people types differently, and more astoundingly still, it didn't have to be heard to be effective. It seemed to work on a non-sound level – it was like no other emission known to Science. He longed for the opportunity to investigate, but his work at the Palace prevented him.

As he was musing on the prospect the musical effects started up again. A definite wave of pleasure spread throughout his body, tempered by the knowledge that somewhere in the Palace, the King was having a seizure.

Walking cautiously to the door, he closed it, sealing himself off inside his attic laboratory. That should keep the shouts and screams at bay for a while at least, he thought. The King usually went to work on Rastabule, his personal aide, first. Eventually, everyone at the Palace would suffer his moods, as he forced impossible commands on to them, and moaned endlessly. But today, Hot Plate suddenly realized, with trepidation, the pattern was to be reversed.

'Hot Plate!'

A muffled, strangled voice came from the floor below.

'Hot Plate!' the King repeated, louder this time, as he made his way up the stairs. The lifts had long since gone out of action. Hastily, Hot Plate picked up one of the mallets, and took it over to the mass spectrometer, pretending to be working on it. The King wouldn't know that there was very little he could be doing with a mallet and a mass spectrometer.

Eventually, the door burst open. Hot Plate turned round, feigning a sick despairing look on his face. The great mass of the King stood there in his robes, framed in the doorway, his jowled face red and his eyes wild and bloodshot. He had been drinking heavily again, to offset the effects. A sinking feeling gathered in Hot Plate's stomach.

'Y . . . Your Majesty,' he rose from his work, and bowed slightly. 'I'm sorry Your Majesty – I was working hard ready for the game tomorrow.'

'Game!' the King thundered. 'There'll be no game now the way I'm feeling! Get me a chair!' The enraged Monarch waddled into the room, panting from exhaustion. Hot Plate gasped as he saw a strange, box-like structure was attached to the King's posterior, hidden below the velvet gown.

'What are you looking at?' the King shouted at him angrily.

'N-nothing, your Royal Highness.' Hot Plate turned. He procured a soft chair.

'This is my toilet,' the King explained, hotly, patting his rump. 'Rastabule made it to help me fight the terrible noise out there . . . Bugger!' he exclaimed with annoyance. He was unable to seat himself because of the protuberance. 'I'll have his guts for this!' he wailed. 'Why has this happened to me?' he beseeched the walls, flinging wide his arms. He turned on Hot Plate again.

'Hot Plate, my trusted servant,' he put his slug-like arm, fawningly, around the scientist's shoulder. 'You are the only person who seems to have an inkling of what's going on. My Court is at its wit's end with this abominable music. I have decided that you must discover its secret, and build a weapon

52

to defeat its evil. If you can do this, you will be forever in our debt . . . in the debt of England. We,' he corrected, 'will go down in history as . . . bugger that, Hot Plate. Just get it done will you?' He stared angrily at him. 'If I had the men, Hot Plate, I'd shoot them down myself . . .' He started to foam at the mouth. Hot Plate knew the danger signals.

'Your most gracious, generous, venerable, understanding Royal Highness,' he began, speaking the first garbage that came to his head. 'Do not alarm yourself. To see us all so distressed, is a terrible sight. But do not fear! I shall purge the land of this demon! Once more, England will be the proud and noble country that you, in your great and noble wisdom, wish it to be!' Wringing his hands in mock despair, he took the King, who looked somewhat mollified by this outburst, by his shoulder, and led him to the door. He spoke to him all the while to calm him down, hoping the attention would stall the monarch's threatened fit until he was out of the room.

'To combat this hellish enemy, Your Royal Highness, you will see the necessity for me to begin *immediately*,' he added, diplomatically.

When the King had gone, bawling down the stairs for Rastabule, Hot Plate gathered a few papers together and packed a small bag containing his lunch. He donned a suitably hip-looking coat and then, after a last minute glance around the dingy laboratory to check that everything was switched off, he departed through a secret doorway. Known only to him, it led into a maze of hidden passages and staircases that made their way down through the Palace into the Royal cellars. From the basement, it was easy to leave and enter the Palace undetected as the Royal Guards were thin on the ground. Most of them had been killed off in the troubles.

It felt good to get out of the Palace again, more so because he was able to express his true feelings openly, without fear of reprisals.

He skipped and sang on his way to the park, but then remembered the King's high-powered telescope, and thought better of his behaviour.

When he reached the roundabout not far from the gates, it

began to dawn on him that the hippy music, wherever it was, was not issuing from its usual source. For one, he could not hear the sounds. Secondly, a great crowd of hippies and similar kinds of people were on the move. They were walking past the fractured, defaced, Queen Victoria monument, heading up Constitution Hill.

Hoping they would lead him to the concert, he joined the streaming, happy throng.

The hippies were not a bad sort of person really, he thought to himself, remembering the severe beatings and humiliations he had received at the hands of King Trash, and the tightness of relationships generally at the Palace. There was just no comparison with the warm, friendly mood of the crowd.

They turned up cracked, weed-infested Park Lane. On their right were the burnt-out ruins of the London Hilton, together with other one-time famous hotels.

They turned left into the Bayswater Road, and at length the crowd reached the decay of Notting Hill. Soon the scientist could hear the strains of the music drifting through streets. The congestion got worse as he threaded his way forward through the bodies, trying to find a satisfactory vantage point. The still, close air reeked of unfamiliar smells he wasn't used to. He wrinkled up his nose, and tried to think of the unpleasant odours objectively, by their chemical names, to avoid being sick.

By sliding his thin frame through endless groups of people, he finally managed to reach the viaduct and without thinking, exposed himself directly to the massive volume of sound. Involuntarily, he cupped his hands over his ears, and went to lean against one of the huge, grey pillars for support.

Then, overpowered by the feelings of extreme elation, he collapsed and fell unconscious to the ground.

THE STRANGE, HOT RAINS OF EARTH

The pin-ball table at Yellow Van shuddered under the impact of Lemmy's weight. Quickly, the guitarist slipped the freed ball into a corner with the flipper controls. An astronomical total clattered up on the brightly coloured indicator panel. He wasn't really playing his best.

'Here it comes,' he said, referring to the Horrors which were starting to build up again. He gritted his teeth. They had stopped gigging after a few hours, and had returned to the Yellow Van. They were in the kitchen.

None of them had managed to get into the numbers properly, and they had only persevered for the sake of the Children who appeared in droves as if out of nowhere as soon as the Delatron had been put into use.

'At least the experiment was a success,' Stacia commented. She and Liquid Len, less tired than the others, were fixing a huge, collective meal for the group, prepared from wholefoods obtained at the New Mountain Grill.

'I still don't understand what the Delatron does to make our music so potent,' the Sonic Prince repeated for the tenth time. 'Unless you want to believe in all that magical stuff.'

'There's nothing wrong with magic,' Rudolph the Black spoke lazily. 'I used to read my horoscope every day.'

'Astrology isn't magic,' the Prince groaned, '. . . though it's just as funny. I'll tell you what's wrong with it – it doesn't prove anything, that's what. If you follow a scientific experiment, you can prove things work. You can see how they work. Try to make a magic "spell" work though!'

'Hear, hear!' A strange, high pitched voice came from the open doorway.

Everyone stiffened and stopped what they were doing. They turned, to see who it was.

A pitifully thin, gangling figure emerged from behind the door. He had black, curly hair, and a long red nose, and glasses. He wore a heavy, blue trenchcoat – far too long and heavy for comfort in the humid heatwave. Beads of sweat were rolling down his spotty face.

'You OK?' Thunder asked of it. The figure tottered slightly, and then steadied itself.

'Fine now, thanks.'

'Who are you?' Stacia asked, stopping the dinner. 'You don't look like one of the Children to me.'

'Name's Hot Plate,' the stranger replied courteously. 'Scientist to His Royal Highness, the King – or so I am in-formed,' he bowed stiffly.

'King who?' Lemmy asked. He let the pin ball roll down the table into the 'lost' hole. With his regalia of leather and studs, and the bizarre tattoos covering his bronzed chest and arms, he did not give an exactly friendly impression. But Hot Plate seemed not to have noticed.

'Trash – at the Palace.'

'I didn't know ye had a King!' Higgy looked amazed, ruin-ing the effect of cautious hostility that had been instinctively created. Rarely had such an obviously straight-looking charac-ter as Hot Plate been admitted to Yellow Van before.

'Nor did I, until one day I was working in my lab and I found myself press-ganged!' Hot Plate complained, grinning. He decided to come clean with them. 'Mind if I take off my coat?' he asked. When he got no reply, he decided it would be all right. He struggled out of it, and folded it over the back of a chair. Then he continued: 'I was sent to spy on you, to find the secret of your music . . .'

They were silent, waiting for him to elaborate.

'On the way . . . I experienced something of a conversion to your . . . "sound". I realized I actually liked it. It made me feel good.' He paused, and looked around again, to see whether his words were being taken sincerely, as he intended.

'Why should your King, whoever he is, want to spy on us?' Stacia asked, indignantly. The word 'spy' had got her back up. 'We mind our business, why can't he mind his?'

'Yeah, we're minding our own business,' Astral Al repeated. His white hat was tilted down slightly over his face, and he was slouched against the pin-ball table, staring at the intruder.

56

'Because your music makes *him* feel *bad*. Not only him, but everyone like him.'

'The straights, you mean?' Lemmy asked. Before Hot Plate could answer, he continued: 'How come you're any different to them? You look like a straight to me.' He disliked and admired Hot Plate's boldness at the same time, and didn't know which way to take him. Nevertheless, if the man proved to be truthful he would take him as his friend.

'I . . . I can't answer that one,' the scientist stammered, as his courage began to crumble. 'But you can judge for yourselves. I've told you who I am, and what I was supposed to be up to . . . I don't want to go back to the Palace,' he added gloomily, looking at the floor.

'How do we know that's the truth?' Hound Master asked, more gently.

'You'll have to trust me!' Hot Plate looked up, imploringly.

'Ye've come tae escape the wicked bastard and li' wi' us, is that it?' Higgy asked, reading the future already, worrying about the extra mouth.

'I've come to *help*.'

'Help?' asked the Prince, showing interest.

'I overheard what you said about the Delatron just then, and it struck me that I have the knowledge and the instruments at my disposal to make a proper investigation . . .'

'We don't need an investigation now,' interrupted Stacia. 'We know that it works; that's all that matters. The Prince can fix us up with an automatic system to combat the Horrors.'

'The what . . .?' Hot Plate looked confused.

'You know, what we're feeling right now.'

Hot Plate nodded unhappily. Since the impromptu concert had stopped, the Horrors, if that's what they were called, had got worse. Away from the Palace, he seemed to be more vulnerable to them.

He shivered.

'Actually, we could do with Hot Plate's help,' the Sonic Prince spoke excitedly. 'If everyone's agreeable, I'd like to propose he stays, to help me find out how the Delatron works.'

'But we don't need to find that out!' persisted Stacia.

Like Higgy, she was concerned with the group's welfare. There was still no concrete proof that Hot Plate was who he claimed to be.

'But that's precisely what we *do* need to find out!' the Prince cried out. 'More importantly than anything else. We can go ahead and build any number of music broadcasters, but unless we know what's behind the effects – which, may I point out, are getting stronger all the time – we've got no real, lasting defence at all. What happens if the bad effects get so powerful our music no longer counteracts them? I need all the help I can get. We'll just have to trust Hot Plate.'

Before anyone could answer, the deathly feeling inside their bodies and minds had reached a new and frightening intensity. It gripped them all. Outside, the heat began to break and a cold, fierce wind beat against the windows. A dark malign shadow crossed over the sky. A thick ochre liquid began splattering down, stinging the earth. The rain gave off an acid sulphurous vapour, which gradually pervaded the room.

Once more, the inner landscapes of their minds started to crack. From the fissures poured the hideous satanic creatures of their nightmares. They battled for the control of their minds, clutching their heads and swaying about in pain. From outside came the shrieks and screams of the Children trying desperately to escape the burning rain.

Thunder Rider was the first to regain his sanity and forced his body across the room stowards Hot Plate.

'That settles it, then,' he gasped, his face white and contorted. 'We do need all the help we can get.' He turned towards Hot Plate. 'If we are to save Mankind, you must help the Prince to build the equipment we need to counteract the effects . . . do it now and help us . . . friend . . .'

Satisfied at the outcome of the talks, the Prince rose to his feet. But his face was ashen. With his usual iron control, he disappeared next door into the living room to disconnect the record deck and collect the Hawkwind albums.

Then he returned to the kitchen.

'Sorry, I couldn't eat a thing,' he said to the cooks. He motioned to Hot Plate. 'You coming? We might as well start right now.'

With Hot Plate's help, he began carrying the deck and the records downstairs. They grabbed some umbrellas and Wellingtons from the old rack in the hall and walked out into the hot, chemical miasma that was pouring down out of the sky.

FIERCE SOLAR FLARES

Lance Corporal Burk let the needle drop heavily on to the record. He felt more than usually unsettled in his bowels both as a result of the rays and of his newly deputed job as Camp DJ.

A loud, fuzzy shriek rent the speakers above him as the diamond stylus gouged into the fine grooves. He felt a vicious satisfaction, sufficient to get him through the next number: 'Mary Had a Little Lamb' by Paul McCartney and Wings.

The twin decks were installed in the back of one of the hot, dusty Bedford Cargo Trucks that was slowly rumbling its way along the perimeter road of the abandoned SOB Garrison.

An elaborate arrangement of suspension springs absorbed the constant shocks delivered to them. The speakers were mounted outside on the roof, broadcasting the pop music to the convoy, and keeping the troops inside relatively free from the crippling symptoms of the Enemy music.

The Music Carrier was a special vehicle. It had a limited broadcasting range compared with the ubiquitous Hippy rays. Therefore it was positioned closely behind Colonel Mephis's Land-Rover and the Fit For Roll vehicle at the front of the column. In its wake trailed the other sixty-eight vehicles, as they came off the perimeter in a long, straggly line.

The convoy started out across the hot, shimmering desert, leaving the tall distillery towers of the massive oil refinery far behind. They set course for Kuwait, on Saudi Arabia's Western border.

Much mysterious manoevering had taken place of late in the Garrison. Old traditions had been changed. Troop behaviour had been altered – so had its attitude. At one time soldiers had been trained to think of themselves as aiding Civvy Street in times of emergency. Now, puzzlingly, they were being told that it was better to let civilians perish.

The truck lurched to a halt, shattering the DJ's reverie. The needle screeched off the disc. Alarmed, he climbed up to the forward-looking window to see what the trouble was.

The entire convoy had come to a halt. At its head, the Colonel's Land-Rover and the FFR vehicle were parked together. In between them, lying on the sand was a body. Evidently, it had been flung there from the Colonel's vehicle, for the tall, thin figure of Mephis was standing over it. His pistol was drawn, ready to shoot.

The figure squirmed. It got up on its knees in a begging posture. It was the Garrison's Padre, Captain Makeson, the Lance Corporal realized in horrified puzzlement.

'God in Heaven, have mercy Colonel. Not on me, for my body is worthless, but on the civilians! Don't do this dreadful thing!' The Padre's idiotic face was screaming at him. Mephis felt a sudden compulsion to still him now. He gritted his teeth instead, uncertain of the consequences.

'You are a fool, Padre!' he shouted, bringing the special Magnum revolver he possessed into line with the Padre's temple and loading the chamber. 'God is no longer alive . . . how can he be in all this anarchy . . .?'

'God *is* alive here, even now . . . listen! I swear . . .'

'Leave me alone! Leave me alone!' the Colonel shrieked. Something snapped inside his head. He jerked and trembled spasmodically. Then, a cruel smile twisted his lips. His grip tightened round the gun and he pressed it closer to the trembling man's temple. A pleasurable feeling came over him. The fear in the other's eyes brought immediate release from the emanations. Sadistically, he pulled the trigger. The kneeling figure reeled backward. Bits of its head flew like turnip peelings over the sand.

'Ha, ha, ha, ha, hahahahahahahahahaha . . .' the Colonel fell to his knees, laughing. 'Hahahahahahahahahahahahahahah . . .' He staggered to his feet. He composed himself. With a hard, austere expression he marched abruptly to his Land-Rover, and climbed inside. He signalled to the FFR to drive on.

Back in his seat, he felt a catatonic, trance-like thrill settle over him. During the last few days, he had worked feverishly at the departure preparations, trying to prevent the mounting feeling of uncontrollable hatred from consuming him altogether. He had managed to fight it off, knowing that he had to keep a cool, ruthless head to satiate his desires. Out there on the sand, he'd let it all out, and it felt good – better than he had ever imagined.

He had changed. In that glorious instant, he had lost his petty human attachments and the ridiculous sentiments that had bogged him down all his life. He sensed victory.

As the search and destroy mission got under way once more, he felt collected, all-powerful. The smile played evilly over his devil face at the thought of the blood bath to come . . .

High above, as they journeyed onward, the fierce solar light began pulsing madly, as the fiery chambers at the sun's mighty atomic heart gradually became unstable.

The light dimmed, and then brightened, as the desert landscape all around them was plunged into a flickering, unearthly lightshow of hellish intensity.

THE ACID SORCERER

'What was that?' Stacia jumped with fright as the leaden, black clouds outside the living-room window suddenly lit up with a series of vivid, orange-red lights. Her nerves were still badly shaken. They had abandoned the food. Now she and Thunder Rider were trying to get the prone figure of Actonium Doug into a sitting position.

They ran to the window in time to see the last pulse of

light illuminate the gaping ruins and towers in the distance with a ghastly, lurid glow. The roadways were deserted, running with the yellow, pus-like water. Hot steam clouds were rising in coils and wreaths into the bellies of the storm clouds that imprisoned London.

'God knows what it was,' Thunder Rider shivered. 'I thought it was the Horrors. Maybe it was an explosion of some sort,' he said vaguely. 'I hope the Prince and Hot Plate are OK.'

Shaken, they turned away and started once more to raise the lifeless figure on the floor. They lifted him on to the old psycho-analyst's couch. Stacia started to revive him by slapping his face. The ex-manager stirred, and groaned.

'Pass me the water, will you?' she asked Thunder Rider. Thunder Rider handed her the tumbler of water he had left standing in the fridge, and she splashed some of it into the unconscious man's face. His eyes opened, revealing glazed, blood-shot whites that stared listlessly out at the world. Then his lips moved.

'Bloody interfering fools! Leave me alone!' he grunted harshly at them. 'I keep telling you its no use . . .' He trailed off into nonsensical words and closed his eyes again.

'Doug! Wake up!' Thunder Rider pushed Stacia aside, and started to shake Actonium Doug by the shoulder. 'You can't cop out like this. We need everyman's help now . . .' He let the man fall back and stared helplessly at Stacia. 'What can we do to make him realize?' he asked in exasperation. 'There must be a way of appealing to him.'

Both were silent for a moment while they tried to think through the jittery, psychic horror film going on inside their heads.

Moorlock, the Acid Sorcerer, was languishing in a similar depressed state at his headquarters in Blenheim Crescent. His acid-rock band, *The Deep Fix*, had flourished back in the mid-seventies, but had split up shortly before all the trouble. Its members, with the exception of the Acid Sorcerer himself, were probably dead. It was a slim chance, but Thunder Rider felt that if he could rouse the Moorlock, Actonium Doug would listen to him.

He told Stacia of his plan. They both went upstairs to the room where they kept their clothes and costumes. They selected two PVC stage outfits and clad themselves in the garish, dayglow colours – one orange, the other green. They found two pairs of underwater goggles and strapped them on.

'Let's go,' Thunder Rider urged as they hurried out of the room.

Outside the air was foul and acrid with the curling, damp fumes, and they coughed as the vapours rasped against the back of their throats. The buildings were scarcely visible. Covering their mouths with their hands, they started to run along the pitted pavement.

Eventually they found their way through the lurid mist to Blenheim Crescent. The pale hump of the Oldsmobile gradually became visible as they drew closer and the reeking curtains dropped away. They climbed up the crumbling, acid-eaten steps to the house and rang the bell.

There was no response. The vapours were denser and they were scarcely able to lash out as the acid forced its way into their throats and began slowly to asphyxiate them. Desperately, Thunder Rider pressed the bell once more. This time he kept his finger on it.

Eventually, a curtain was drawn fractionally aside behind the armoured plate glass window. Amidst the gloom in the room behind they made out the face of the Sorcerer. The face disappeared, and a long moment later, the door opened electronically. They fell through it into a long, spacious hallway. Immediately, the door closed again behind them. They lay on the floor, breathing in lungfuls of the pure, clean air. From somewhere in the passageway, came the familiar hum and crackling of a loudspeaker being switched on. The Sorcerer's voice came over the air, reverberating deeply against the walls.

'I can't let you in like that. You'll have to undress.'

They looked at one another in amazement. Then Stacia shrugged. She climbed to her feet. She started to strip off. Grudgingly, Thunder Rider followed suit. Soon they were both standing naked, shivering in the cold. From somewhere came a blast of heat. Then, a door opened by their side.

'You might as well come in,' said the amplified voice again. Thunder Rider took the lead. He walked slowly into the room. The door closed behind them. Inside, the room was just as he remembered it – full of gadgets and lined from ceiling to floor with books.

In the corner, a massive leather armchair seated the heavily built frame of the Moorlock. He was wearing silk, Indian robes, patterned with coloured scenes of Eastern mystic life. Down its smooth, golden front fell long, silver hair and beard. Under the robe, his feet were shoeless, and crossed. His hands were clasped neatly on his lap in front of him. By his side stood a control panel, with microphone.

'What was all that for?' Thunder Rider complained, glancing down at his nakedness before the Moorlock could speak.

'You were filthy!' the Moorlock retorted, sitting quite motionless. 'I'm not having you contaminating the atmosphere in here. What've you come filching round for, anyway? I wouldn't have let you in had it not been for the, shall we say, adverse weather conditions. You were lucky.' He was silent for a moment. Then he seemed to relent. 'You better wrap those covers around you, seeing you're here.' He indicated the silk settee coverlets with a long, manicured finger. There was a faint tone of amusement in his voice. A slight surge of hope rose in Thunder Rider. The Moorlock was usually fairly humorous. It seemed he might be reverting back to his old self. He said nothing, but did as he had been directed. He offered a coverlet to Stacia. Then he sat down again and faced the Sorcerer.

'We've come to try to get you to join us,' he began, staring the Sorcerer challengingly in the eye.

From the shadows in the room, the bright, beady eyes of the Moorlock fixed him back. On the surface, they were bright. But they danced on a grey, gloomy sea of thoughts – a weight so heavy with secret knowledge they had held the man down for more than a year, imprisoned in a dingy cell of their own making.

Now the two pairs of eyes met, and sparked. The thoughts began to flicker and turn. They began to cry out with futility and hope behind the mask of eyes.

MIRROR OF ILLUSION

Fully automatic Hawkwind music began to explode into the air below the flyover, blasting out the futuristic notes of *Spiral Galaxy 28948* over the roar of the generator.

The first, fully automatic Hawkwind Music Broadcaster complete with Delatron was a reality.

The Sonic Prince and the small group standing round gave a whoop of joy, despite the choking mist that swirled beneath the concrete roof of the motorway.

The cramping sickness left them. Hot Plate stopped trembling. His skin gradually assumed its normal, ruddy complexion.

They celebrated with a bottle of Bells Whisky Higgy had miraculously managed to save from the last Earth City Party by stowing under the seat of the truck for a special occasion. Then leaving Higgy temporarily in charge of the broadcaster, the Prince and Hot Plate set out to the Palace in the transit. The trusty vehicle seemed to be standing up to the acid attack fairly well.

As they drew further away from the broadcaster, they began to notice the effects of elation wearing off.

'Unlike live music, canned music must have a short-range effect,' Hot Plate observed.

'First priority, then, is to build as many Delatrons as we can!' the Prince remarked.

They ploughed along in silence, through a continuous lake of the yellow fluid. The city's drains had blocked up, and flooded the streets.

They arrived at the side of the Palace in Buckingham Palace Road. Hot Plate took the lead, splashing through the muck, coughing and spluttering beneath his umbrella. Not a guard was in sight, and visibility was low on account of the vapours. They hurried across the concrete expanse of the car park, and made their way around a gate leading to the Palace itself.

The stone bastions of the royal abode loomed ahead. Hot Plate moved stealthily along the pitted surface of its ornate south-westerly face which overlooked the flattened flower gardens and the drooping ornamental trees and shrubbery. He reached the narrow rear entrance which he used as his escape route, and he beckoned the Prince inside. They entered the cold but dry cellars and walked across them towards the secret staircase. Soon, they were standing, out of breath, at the top of the endless flight of stairs. They climbed inside the cramped attic laboratory. In here the symptoms were more or less back to normal, and the first thing Hot Plate did was to reach for a jar containing pink-coloured tablets from one of the numerous dusty shelves. He opened the jar and gave one of its contents to the Prince.

'Here, take this. It'll help you. I use them myself to calm the effects and they work quite well.'

The Prince took the proffered tablet, and swallowed it. Hot Plate did likewise, and replaced the jar on the shelf. Then they took off their Wellingtons, and put them with their umbrellas out of sight behind a bank of instruments.

'First, I'll show you around,' said Hot Plate. 'Then you can get to work on the Delatrons. I think you'll find everything you're likely to need. That's one thing the King's good at – he spared no expense equipping the lab.'

The Prince began to feel slightly pleased with the array of equipment. He recognized some of the complicated electronics apparatus – the very best. It was ages since he had got the chance to work with equipment of such calibre. Providing the scientist stocked some of the smaller parts he needed, he would have no trouble at all building and testing the Delatrons.

'By the way, you'll have to fill me in on the circuitry side,' Hot Plate said, when the tour was over. 'I'm hopeless at your side of things.'

'Whatever you want to know!' the Prince grinned, obligingly. 'I suggest we talk it over first, before I begin. Then you can let some of that pure science whizz-kiddery of yours loose and find out what's causing our music to behave the way it does!'

While the Prince talked, Hot Plate began taking out relevant pieces of equipment. He placed them on a bench in front of him, and connected them up.

He set up an experiment he had first vaguely thought of trying earlier during the day, when he had been pondering on the effects of the music. The information the Prince fed to him on his home-made detectors, enabled him to construct a more accurate and sophisticated apparatus. By the time the Prince had finished telling him all the details, a complicated arrangement of dials, meters and boxes was humming and flashing on his work bench.

The scientist now became totally engrossed in his work, and seemed to ignore his companion completely. Feeling slightly put out, the Prince started to collect his own equipment together.

Soon, he too became absorbed. Time passed.

They worked on until nightfall, and well into the night without speaking. At last, the Prince had the basics of a dozen Delatrons laid out in front of him, their jumbled guts sprawling in all directions. All they needed was to be tidied up and tested. Then they could be inserted into cases and put into use. As he laid down his soldering iron to rest and stretch his back, an excited shout came from Hot Plate.

'Well, well!' the scientist exclaimed, peering at one of the meters. The Prince joined him. The meter needle was fluctuating beserkly.

'I can just about pick up Higgy's broadcast from here,' he continued. 'Look, you can see it registering now. But over here, my friend, you will see something even more amazing.' The Prince followed the scientist down the full length of the bench. At the bottom, was a peculiar looking instrument with a part that revolved. It had a screen on the front that flashed brilliant, metallic colours.

'This is what I call a bio-simulator,' Hot Plate explained, noticing his puzzled expression. 'It simulates the exact nervous function of the human body. It also tells me what effects outside agents can have on it. I've been using it to try to match bodily sensations with those produced by your music, and it would appear that the nervous condition most resembling it is one normally brought on by acupuncture . . . in fact it appears that your music works by giving human beings a total acupuncture effect. Fantastic, isn't it?'

'But how . . .?' the Prince asked, incredulously.

'Don't ask me that!' the other replied. 'If I knew, we'd have solved everything! It isn't going to be so simple.'

'You mean, because our music has a different effect on different people . . .'

'Exactly. It's too simplistic to conclude your music is acupuncture.'

'But couldn't the acupuncture have a bad effect on some, and a good effect on others –'

'Possible, but unlikely. My bet is that we've only stumbled on half the answer. The other half is going to take a lot more digging. Rest assured, I'll find it!'

'You mean now?' the Prince asked. His normally resistant body was ready to drop from exhaustion and from the effects of the Horrors kept at bay on the end of a slender chemical thread. 'You're going to work through the night?'

'If need be. Don't forget, this is my line of work! I'm built to take it!' he grinned again, a shock of curly hair falling in front of his eyes. He shook it back. 'I suggest you get some sleep over on the couch.' He indicated a dark shape in a cluttered recess. 'You'll be safe there. Here, you better take another of these.' He offered the Prince the jar of tablets.

It was no use battling with his feelings. His legs felt ready to collapse. His mind felt like a leaden, thoughtless block. He took the tablet, and went to lie down, leaving the scientist to get on with the research.

When he awoke, it was morning.

He felt groggy with a hangover, caused by the Horrors. The events of the previous day still swam in his mind. Slowly he re-orientated himself amid the strange scenery of the laboratory. It was much brighter now. The storm must have passed over.

He stood up and glanced towards the work bench where Hot Plate had been engaged. Now, there was no-one there. He noticed a pungent aroma in the air. His heart raced with alarm. It was not the acid tang of the sulphur dioxide, but the acrid smell of burnt plastic and wires. From long experience, he knew what had happened.

A quick glance at the badly scarred bench and fused equipment confirmed his fears. Scarcely daring to, he lowered his eyes to the still form lying humped on the gangway between the benches. Moving as fast as he could, he reached the body and knelt down. The clothes and skin looked intact. Gingerly, he placed his palm to the brave scientist's heart. He swallowed. There was a faint beat.

Quickly, he began to massage the chest. Then he slapped the whitened face. He looked around for something of use and spotted a bottle containing ethyl alcohol. He brought it to the dying man. He removed the stopper and pressed the neck to the purple lips, while pumping the heart back into action.

Gradually, the pallor on the face departed, and a flush of red infused slowly back into the skin.

After a while, the prone scientist's heart rate returned to normal. The Prince dragged the stirring figure to the couch. He got some water in a beaker, and placed it against the dry, eager lips.

When the scientist recovered sufficiently to speak, he launched into a detailed description of the night's work. The Prince propped him up as he continued to whisper in urgent, gasping jerks.

'Let me see . . . let me see . . . you must listen carefully . . . we were completely on the wrong track . . .' he smiled weakly, then gained momentum. 'So far as I can see we are, as you suspected, under some sort of attack . . . by what . . . from where I still have no idea. It isn't the music that's causing either the pleasure or the pain . . .'

A perplexed, incredulous look registered on the Prince's

face. He felt irritated. 'Then what . . .?'

'. . . don't worry yourself. Simple really . . . we've been looking at it the wrong way. Your music doesn't *produce* the rays that do the work . . . it appears that it acts by neutralizing *another* ray . . .'

'An attacking ray?' The Horrors grew worse inside the Prince as he thought about the implications.

'. . . that's right,' Hot Plate spoke with great effort, as though from across distant reaches of space. The Prince leant closer to catch his words. '. . . I've analysed the attacking ray . . . it's no saint . . . in fact it's the most lethal concoction I've come across . . . it seems to be a virulent admix of high energy waves propogated in some non-Newtonian manner . . . completely undetectable on conventional equipment . . . the only reason we aren't all dead is that it's still being transmitted at a fairly low intensity . . .' The scientist coughed and spluttered, half choking over his own saliva. 'You must tell the others,' he gasped urgently. Then his eyes closed again. The Prince let him rest.

Confusing, nightmare thoughts jumped around inside his mind. He couldn't collect them together in his present condition, so he took some more of the pink tablets and sat down. It wouldn't be wise to contact the others, he thought suddenly, until he'd completed assembling the Delatrons. They were certainly going to be needed now, and if he left the Palace prematurely he might never get back in to finish them off.

THE WATCHER

Long before the final collapse, the Moorlock had known what would happen to Humanity. His peculiar sensitivity had seen in advance the outcome of the recklessness and the greed. He had seen the cities collapsing, and the men running like frightened ants across the wasted deserts. He had seen the bombs dropping. He had seen the pesticides and the smokes gradually maim and destroy. He had seen the children of the future lying battered and dead in their cots. He had tried to warn of the silent holocaust, and the bitter fighting and rioting, as the survivors fought for control of the last remaining pieces of greenery. He had written books about it. He had spoken on television about it. He had made a film about it. Finally, he had sung about it. He had formed his own group, *The Deep Fix*, and played at concerts and outdoor festivals. But no-one had listened. The game of death had blindly continued. Gradually, the prophecies had come true. Prophesies that not only he predicted, but also the ancient books of lore.

Disillusioned, and scornful of his selfish fellow men, he had decided that the outside world and all it contained was no more than a grisly cosmic joke perpetuated by sick-minded Gods. He built a thick, protective shell around him, and locked himself away.

For months he brooded, absorbing the knowledge from his books. Even inside his electronic fortress he was unable to escape the events outside. Man's follies haunted him – he was of the same race, he could never escape. Many times he had almost given up, and opened the doors to the marauding gangs and the self-styled militia. But he had held out. Now, after the final death, they had come in from outside to tell him that a new race of Man was being born out of the ruins. Now they were telling him that the whole rotten show was trying to start all over again.

Now, he stared through the shadows of his cell at the two intent figures sitting on the sofa opposite him. They were man and woman. They were Stacia and Thunder Rider. They were a part of the new men he dared not belong to. Finally, he spoke. 'You've come at the right time,' he told them. 'I'll help you.'

The Acid Sorcerer leant his head thoughtfully against one of his ringed fingers as he listened to the Prince. Thunder Rider and the others were sat forward, speechlessly, in their chairs as the horrifying news and its even more terrifying implications were being announced.

They were inside the Moorlock's room. After he had finally relented he had invited them there. But he made it abundantly clear that he would only spare time to help his friend Actonium Doug.

As if by magic, the ex-manager had made a startling recovery, as though he had been waiting for the Sorcerer to make the first move. Now he and Higgy were discussing plans to form a work crew specifically responsible for security and maintenance. Their first task would be the distribution and erection of larger music broadcasting equipment and the commandeering of the parts they would need.

Over the Delatron attached to the hi-fi in the Moorlock's room came the sound of *The Golden Void*, raising their spirits in the close confines. Outside, under the viaduct, a looped tape was playing parts of *Goat Willow* to the survivors of the storm packed in the streets.

'My bet is that the ray or wave, whatever it is, has been there since time immemorial,' Hound Master commented, after the Prince had finished bringing them up to date on developments. 'It's just got steadily worse and worse, enslaving humanity in its evil grip. All along we've been putting up with our miserable lot, thinking life's a burden, when in fact it's not.'

'In fact, life is happiness and joy, as the Delatron music shows when it momentarily banishes the Ray,' Thunder Rider continued. 'Only a few people in every generation have the vision to see through, and the guts to persevere catching rare glimpses of the beauty . . .'

'. . . Inventing elaborate psychological and mystical lifestyles to overcome the boredom and depression,' added the Moorlock cynically, pleased to be proved right at last. 'Taking drugs . . .'

'But why? And who's doing it? Why are straights affected differently? How come they actually *enjoy* the Ray?' the Prince asked.

'I'd like to know,' Lemmy said threateningly, 'the time I've had on it.'

'Wherever it's coming from, the sender must have heard your music and not liked it, because it started escalating when you first used the Delatron,' Hot Plate observed. 'Our main worry now is how bad is it going to get? Can our equipment stand it? If it can't we won't last out longer than a week. The stuff goes for our nervous systems and it won't take much of a rise to kill off the most vulnerable of those tissues – our brain cells.'

The assembled Hawkmen shuddered.

'We've got to stop it getting any worse!' Thunder Rider stated. 'Our first concern must be to get those Delatrons assembled,' he looked at Doug, 'and to make as many more as parts exist for – raid the universities and hospitals if we have to!' He glanced at the Prince, and Hot Plate. 'The rest of us, now that we've got cover from the Delatrons, will have to try to boost the morale of the Children, and get Earth City back on its feet.'

'True,' said Baron Brock, holding himself powerfully erect, 'we'll not die, Hot Plate. We'll scour the entire universe for whoever or whatever's responsible, until we've banished the Ray once and for all!'

'Earth must not die!' Stacia agreed. She stood up and saluted Lemmy with clenched fist. 'And the new breed of man must be allowed to continue!'

'Aye, think o' th' stock ye co' fro',' Higgy said proudly. 'Ye all know th' Hawkwind legend.'

The room fell silent as the words of the ancient prophesy ran through their heads.

'And in the fullness of time, the prophecy must be ful-

73

filled and the Hawklords shall return to smite the land. And the Dark Force shall be scourged, the cities razed and made into parks. Peace shall come to everyone. For is it not written that the sword is key to heaven *and* hell?'

It was a psalm from one of the ancient lore books in the Moorlock's library. The book was called *The Saga of Doremi Fasol Latido*. The group had made an album of chants taken from the work many years back, but no-one had really taken the legend completely seriously. The book itself, although undoubtedly ancient, and based on a script known to have been in the possession of King Arthur, had seemed an improbable object in the days of technology and reason and logic – to all but Hound Master, and Del Detmar, that was. Thunder Rider had a streak of mystical curiosity in him too, but he had always agreed with the Moorlock that the book was probably a clever fabrication – that the name 'Hawkwind', referred to many times in the text must have been noticed by Baron Brock and Thunder Rider who had originally given them their name. The Acid Sorcerer had once explained that magic books and ancient records often proved to be fantasies invented by monks and other authorities of old as a means of securing power over gullible peasants.

Now, at the end of another cycle of man, in the ruins of his civilization, the book seemed more believable, logical. They could well imagine it to have been written during a similar period of change in the past . . . perhaps, even, in another age of magic – if the present could be viewed as being magical, as Hound Master kept insisting that it was.

Whether or not is was true, they felt themselves being collectively influenced by the words. The room grew lighter, yet more indistinct. New energy flowed through their veins as the inspiration to fight came. Phantom warriors of old, their armour cold and hard, their swords clanking at their sides, seemed to stand in the room with them, their presence felt but not seen. A slight, mild breeze blew, and they had the impression they were on horseback on a cliff-top, on top of the world, overlooking with longing the white, endless vista of time.

Their old, mortal selves peeled away. They were becoming the true Hawklords of the legend.

CIRCLE OF POWER

The acid rain clouds rolled back. A curtain opened up on the scarred and beaten landscape. Sun glinted on jagged metal and glass as the blue skies returned.

Earth City lay battered and broken in the wake of the acid techno-storm. Most of its tents and shelters had to be remade, and many human casualties needed treatment.

But the Children of the Sun fought bravely back. After the news that continuous Hawkwind music could now be broadcast to combat the Ray, the mood in the first real people's city was one of grim determination to regain their hard-won foothold.

They set to work where they had left off, organizing the thousand and one necessities that were needed for human existence – doing in earnest what they had practiced unwittingly so many times before in earlier days, at so many different music festivals.

Actonium Doug and Heavy Gang started work on the tall, Hawkwind music towers that would be used to fight the Enemy radiations. They roared about London in a small army of commandeered trucks and lorries, looking for scaffolding, electronic components and any waste metal they could lay their hands on. They were racing against time, before the Death Ray escalated to such an extent that the intervals between live gigs would become too much to bear and send them all mad . . . or dead.

The population continually swelled with the influx of shattered Humanity still arriving in boats and planes. The boundaries of the new City had been forced to widen to encompass adjacent parkland of St James' and Hyde Park. But in only ten days, the whole of this large, West Central area of London was covered by the music beams of the magical towers, forming a huge, elongated circle of Hawkwind power that protected the inhabitants.

Finally, the task was complete. The taped music began to play. Cautiously, Hawkwind left their positions on stage. A slight drop in protective power was experienced as the switch-over took place. Then, gradually, the new level became accepted as normal.

Earth City heaved a collective sigh of relief.

For the first time since the rock festival began, the survivors were able to relax without worry, sleep without the fear of the delirium. A healthy look returned to their faces as they went about their daily business, cleaner and better fed. Some people even dared to be happy . . .

The first stage in the battle against the powers of evil that were beginning to threaten mankind, was over.

But then a deadening tiredness came over Hawkwind. Their minds and bodies were worn out from playing, from the combined effects of sleep loss and the Horrors.

They were sick. They knew that death was close at hand if complete rest did not come soon.

Insensible, they were carried bodily back to the Yellow Van, and left there to recover.

BOOK TWO

'THE TIME OF THE HAWKLORDS'

WAVES OF THE DARK CULTURE

Moodily, Seksass, the Press Reporter at Control, sat hunched over his desk, clutching at his stomach. His face was drained of blood, and his body was visibly shaking. Once again, the day had been claimed by the toilet and the sick bay, and his work was getting badly behind.

Thankfully, it was the same for everyone at Control since the disgusting Hippy music had started up. Why on earth their own guard of soldiers couldn't have stopped it all happening in the first place, he would never know. The opportunities had been there, and now they had mysteriously been lost.

The Press staff at Control, of course, could never leave their posts and take up arms. They could never leave the computer. Too many millions of lives were at stake . . . minds that, one day, might live corporately again, and serve to repopulate the country when the New Order emerged.

He sighed and belched sickly. It was time to check on the Twinny Triad Case again, and he didn't feel like going in today. What had started out as a revolting case of sex between two deviant ghost minds who lived inside the computer, had now turned into one of the most lengthy, difficult assignments of his career. Normally, it was fairly easy to track guilty partners down on account of their ostentatious behaviour. But in this instance, the third woman – in, of all the possible terrible things, a *triad* relationship – had proved extremely hard to catch. She was an expert in mental camouflage, and being the instigator, had to be caught. The other two, a man and another woman had been kept under observation, but couldn't be brought to justice until they had unwittingly incriminated the third.

Seksass belched miserably again as the nauseating juices in his stomach heaved and bubbled.

He rose unsteadily to his feet and left his office. Soon, he was travelling down twenty odd flights of Control on to the second floor where the entrance booths were. He stepped out of the lift, as smartly as he could in his regulation grey uniform and set off across the polished marble floor of the hall towards the registration hatches on the far side. Soothing music, the *Sounds of Silence* by Simon and Garfunkle were playing out here, and he wondered grudgingly why they couldn't have their own music source installed upstairs in the offices.

He stopped at one of the hatches and spoke his voice print to the Clerk behind the window. The Clerk weakly took his particulars and handed him his access token and pill, before hurriedly taking another sip of a bicarbonate of soda drink he had mixed. One look at the fizzing drink made Seksass's bowels lurch again, and he was glad to get away.

Next to the hatches were a row of booths with glass doors. Most of them were already occupied with still, pallid looking bodies attached to the wiring. He found a vacant booth and slid inside.

Once the door was shut, the booth was perfectly quiet. The air was fresh and cool, being constantly renewed to ensure the best possible revival conditions for the bodies when their owners' minds returned.

He inserted his token into the slot in front of him. The machinery hummed and clicked as his identity was confirmed. Then he took up the rubber skull piece with the maze of wires attached and placed it on top of his head. He sat down on the specially wired chair and strapped himself in. Finally, he took the minuscule blue pill he had been given and closed his eyes.

WHITE BONES, SOFTLY BLEACHED SAND,
A FEW CAR WRECKS...

The M23 to Brighton was an endless ribbon of crashed and parked cars in both directions. A loose scree of glass, white bones and other debris was strewn across the surface, making it hazardous to drive on. They had to keep stopping every so often to push aside the wreckage and forge a way through.

Higgy rammed his foot down hard on the accelerator. With an angry snarl, the Mercedes jerked clear of the last entanglements of London's stilled, crashed traffic.

Hawkwind had slept for two days and nights, and now they were taking a well-deserved holiday – not that they expected to find much in Brighton. It was just a place they felt drawn to for some reason. All of them had holidayed there on occasion in the past. It was somewhere they could retreat to.

They had left Doug and the Roadhawks in charge of operations. Hot Plate had had to stay behind to continue his vital research into the origin of the Death Ray. But before they had set out the friendly scientist had slipped them a surprise set of armoury he had been working on. They were the prototypes of pistol-shaped music guns which he eventually intended to issue to everybody. They worked by sending a battery generated supply of taped Hawkwind music through miniaturized Delatrons in the nozzles.

As they drew away from the City and the safety of the music towers, they felt the first sign of the Horrors returning. Since the eerie conversation in the Moorlock's room almost a fortnight ago, their bodies had somehow built up a better resistance to the effects. But the improvements had only been slight. The magical metamorphosis that had commenced after they had conversed had just as mysteriously stopped, uncompleted.

Higgy leant forward and pressed a cartridge into the modified portable player on the dash panel in front of him. Soon, an old Brock composition, *Lord of Light*, was being transmitted through the air of the cab, and they began to feel better.

Outside, the fields were bleached yellow. The trees of the once beautiful English countryside had turned prematurely brown – a sickly yellow-brown, and black. The rivers foamed white. There was no life in any of the farms or villages they passed.

They felt wretched inside. The acid techno-storm had done its worst. They wondered forlornly how wide the stricken area reached. They cried as the vision of a dead planet gripped them with fear and loneliness, as they realized now that Earth could probably never be saved. It would take years, probably for ever for its precious soil to be rejuvenated once more. Without any help from the Death Ray, Mankind might have sealed its fate years earlier, when the lethal chemicals had originally collected in the atmosphere.

No one knew what to say or do.

They sat speechless as the ghastly scenery passed. There was no room or place for hate of their race. It had developed too far for that. Mankind's selfish and aggressive nature had been in-built from an early stage, originally as a survival drive. Now, unable to adapt to changing conditions, his violence had turned inward, and devoured him. Next in line in the evolutionary scale upwards were the Children of the Sun. What was left for them? How long could Earth City last out?

The vehicles continued to nudge their way along the cracked and weed-grown roadway. Occasionally, gaps in the stilled traffic allowed them to put on a burst of speed, and the moving, real-life drama film viewed from the windows, speeded up.

Eventually, they left the motorway and joined the A23. The winding road passed through innumerable small townsteads and villages in which they looked vainly for signs of life. When they had last toured the country, what seemed an age ago, Britain had seemed as though it might be able to get back on its feet. Survivors were dotted about everywhere. Hawkwind had gigged to them in an attempt to attract them to the concert in London. Some had resisted the urge, but now there was no sign of them. They had gone elsewhere, or perished.

The outskirts of Brighton came into view, raising their hopes. Here at least there ought to be some sort of bringing

together of the isolated survivors. But they were quickly disillusioned. The buildings were mostly completely burned out or
smashed down. The sea looked rank and oily. It heaved rottenly, disgorging a rancid grey sludge on to the beaches.
Strangely, the only intact structures were the numerous amusement arcades, and the vast fair-ground complex. It seemed
almost as though these had been religiously preserved by the
warring sects and gangs who had once terrorized the seaside
town. Most probably they had been used as areas of mutual
truce where the protagonists could escape from the tension.
Perhaps they had been the privileged leisure grounds of the
dominant fighters. Now they were the silent, deserted machinery of ghosts and the wind – and rats.

Higgy stopped the van. They looked through the side windows at the outlines of the corroded Ferris wheel and the Big
Dipper.

'Might as well see if any of that junk is still workable,' Lemmy
broke the awed silence. 'Anyone for a stroll down the amusement arcade?'

'You're joking!' Stacia retorted. 'Maybe you want to end up
as dinner for the rats, but not me. Look at them . . . !' She
pressed her face to the window. Looking like tattered rags
amongst the debris sat the over-sized hungry-looking rodents.
They were lean and perfectly motionless, as though waiting for
edible life to stumble along.

'Good excuse to try out the music guns,' Astral Al muttered
under his hat.

The cartridge player had stopped. Intrigued, Lemmy drew
out his gun and lowered his window. He pointed its snub
nozzle outside and pressed the play button. Instantly, a
transistor pitch version of *Master Of The Universe* began to
issue forth.

The rats twitched, as though uncertain of the new threat.
Then, shrieking, they kicked out their hind legs and fled.

Lemmy opened the door and climbed out. He turned up the
volume control of the gun and sprayed the sound all around
him.

He looked in at them and grinned.

'Not such a bad guy that Hot Plate fellow,' he said, fondling the gun. He slid it back into its breast holster inside his jacket. 'Anyone still care for that stroll?'

Gingerly, they all stepped out, glad of the opportunity to stretch their legs.

'Maybe if we can stick the scenery our holiday won't be too bad after all,' Rudolph the Black smiled laconically about. He sized up the landmarks.

Music guns drawn, they walked towards the fun-fair entrance. It seemed odd to be revisiting their childhood venue now, in such altered circumstances.

Inside, the rifle ranges and the penny arcades were open and intact. Nothing had been disturbed. The rifles still lay chained to their shelves. Only the dust told that they had not recently been used.

The floor was littered with the tiny bones of fowl and rats, grease paper and rusty drink cans, signs that indicated that the mobster lords who once resided there had enjoyed their stolen comforts to the full.

The group moved warily onward, towards the Big Dipper. A sudden scream from Stacia brought them to an abrupt halt. The lady dancer was gazing frozenly behind them, a picture of stark terror on her face.

The group spun round in the direction of her gaze. The fun site's entrance lay a few yards away. In front of the open gates the dark shape of a figure was materializing. It shimmered before them, hooded and sinister, its arms raised out as though to engulf them. It seemed to be trapping them inside.

They stared, rooted with fear. It seemed improbable. Only in dreams had they seen a creature of such deathly substance and proportions.

The apparition grew in intensity. Now it was oily black. They could see the glimmer of a force field surrounding it, keeping it stable.

'Fire the guns!' Thunder Rider yelled out. As one, they raised their music guns and played them at full volume. A loud, jarring mixture of Hawkwind songs burst out and leapt at the ghostly form.

Momentarily, the creature withstood the onslaught. Then its edges glowed and the white-hot fire burned in and consumed it. Soon, the still claustrophobic fair remained again.

They ran through the gates, guns still blaring toward the Mercedes bus and piled inside. Higgy let the handbrake down and they shot off down the road.

'What was it?' Lemmy asked, shaken.

No one answered him. They did not know.

'It seemed to be telling us something,' Stacia spoke, her voice trembling.

'I thought it was trying to kill us,' the Baron scowled. His hunched form glowered in the back seat. 'As if we don't have enough to put up with . . .'

They recovered slightly from the shock. Higgy drove straight ahead with the intention of putting as much distance as possible between him and the haunted fun fair. Now they found themselves following the coastal route leading out of the old resort town.

'There's nothing for us out here . . . we should never have come away,' Stacia complained.

They journeyed on, unable to understand the hellish vision. Their instincts screamed out for them to stop and return to London – but a strange desire compelled them not to.

They sped down the road. It was mysteriously free of wreckage, cleared away perhaps by the last inhabitants. There were numerous small fishing towns along the coast, and possibly one of them may have escaped the mass insanity. Already there was a marked difference in the landscape. Intact houses began appearing again. There were fewer signs of overt violence. Their hopes were raised again.

Stacia leant forward and pointed over Higgy's shoulder.

'A green tree,' she observed, still too shaken to be excited.

'Bloody incredible!' Thunder Rider breathed as his eyes followed her arm. 'Stop the bloody van, Higgy!'

The Scot braked the bus hard. When they were stationary, they craned forward in their seats to see.

Above the rooftops on their left hand side rose a line of blackened, skeletal trees. Unbelievably, the centre tree was daubed with a weak slash of green. It stood perfectly still in the windless air. They could clearly see the leaves hanging.

Slowly, their hearts responded with warmth and gladness at the sight of green amidst the drab colours of death and decay.

'Where there's a bit, there's probably a bit more!' the Light Lord called out enthusiastically from the crush of straining forms on the back seat. 'I suggest we take the next turn off to the left.'

Heeding his advice, they set off once again, jerked back in their seats. Soon, they came to the Rottingdean turn-off. Higgy braked and swung the yellow bus down its new course.

Almost immediately more greenery began to appear – first, a few isolated patches on trees swept bare by the strong sea gales, then clumps of grass, and whole lengths of hedgerow. Soon, to the amazement and disbelief of everyone, they were riding along verdant roadsides, beneath avenues of over-hanging trees richly cloaked with greens of delicate summer hues.

After a short ride, they arrived at the quaint country village of Rottingdean. Its old world cottages and public houses were unbelievably intact. The village was deserted, judging by the overgrown gardens and the weed-cracked surface of the pavements and roads.

They drove into the picturesque square, their engine noise shattering the grave-like silence, and pulled up outside the Red Fox Inn. Immediately, the stillness returned, save for the small cooling sounds of the engine. It was an eerie silence which at first they couldn't understand.

Liquid Len opened the door, and stepped out cautiously. No visible signs of danger manifested themselves. The others followed him. They stood outside, stretching their legs and looking around them.

'Got it!' Stacia exclaimed. 'I know what's wrong – there's no birdsongs.'

'She's right,' the Moorlock said, examining the crumbling stonework on the inn. 'This place hasn't been touched by the storm. Maybe, the whole of the East part of the country escaped it.'

'Might just have been a freak weather condition,' the Prince put in. 'We can drive back inland from here, when we leave, and we can see for ourselves.'

'Good idea,' said Thunder Rider. 'There might even be a case for moving Earth City down here.'

'Through all those rats?' the Baron retorted, disgustedly.

'This time next week, they'll be dead,' Thunder Rider replied. 'They've got nothing left to live off.'

'No one knows what will happen in the future,' the Moorlock said philosophically. He had remained silent for most of the ride, observing the disturbing events that had taken place with a thoughtful mind.

Now he looked equally thoughtfully at the Inn in front of them.

'We'll sort things out as we come to them,' the Baron agreed. ' 'Ain't no use making plans.'

Thunder Rider shrugged. 'Let's look in here for somewhere to crash then.'

THE PHANTOM INN AT ARRANAR

'This is more like it!' Thunder Rider pronounced, tucking into a large ham sandwich and knocking back a glass of wine. He burped. 'Pardon me.' He wiped his mouth with a corner of the table napkin which he had stuck down the front of his painted leather shirt. He set to once again.

The fire crackled cheerfully in the grate, sending warm orange lights dancing and flickering round the oak panelling of the Red Fox lounge. A long dining table was pulled up in front of the fire. It was lit by three silver candelabras, each with six heads. On it, was lain a pure white table cloth, and the best silverware the Inn could afford.

The Hawklords and the Hawklady sat round the table, eating the biggest meal they had consumed since the Disaster.

'You've got the manners of a pig, Thunder Rider!' the

Moorlock commented. 'Allow others to eat their meals in peace, will you?' He poured more wine from his bottle into the tall glass by his side. Then, delicately, he took the glass by its stem, and put it to his lips. 'Ah! The magic of Aphrodite!' he exclaimed, closing his eyes and drifting off.

'Christ, he's on one of his bloody aesthete trips again!' the Baron said, rocking back on his Queen Anne chair. The legs creaked, ominously, and he righted himself. ' 'Course I might have expected it in this toffy's place. It's just up his street.' He leant forward and crammed some more cheese and pickle into his mouth.

'Bloody wine tastes like water!' Lemmy said, pulling a face. 'Give us a scotch, anyday.'

'What do you mean?' the Moorlock asked, in an insulted tone. 'This "water" happens to be a very good year! I got it myself!'

'He probably pissed in the bottles!' Astral Al laughed.

'You stuff yourself!' the Moorlock retorted, opening his eyes again.

'A think ye've all got foul table manners!' Higgy was the next to speak out. His bottle was already empty, and he was reaching drunkenly across the silverware for Stacia's. 'Yer forgettin' who made ye this wee feastie whilst ye were al' messin' about lookin' fer things yer could loot, ya thievin' English swines . . . near one a' yer has breathed so much as a thankye.'

'Aye, that's true,' the Baron said, raising his glass. 'Come on you blaggards. A toast for Higgy.'

As though from one arm, the drinks shot high into the air, and crashed together. 'For Higgy!' the chorus of voices all agreed.

'May he live on to make many another good feastie!' Thunder Rider shouted, approvingly.

They returned to their seats, and for a while they were preoccupied with eating. Then Stacia lowered her glass from her lips, thoughtfully. Something ponderous had been on her mind.

'I suppose no one's noticed,' she said at last, 'how happy we suddenly are again.'

'I think about it every minute!' Thunder Rider joked, swigging back his bottle.

'You know what I mean,' she persisted. 'I'm not getting a screw loose or anything. I mean, why aren't we feeling bad?'

'What's happened to the Horrors, you mean?' the Prince asked.

'Right, what's happened to the Horrors,' she repeated, looking round the table, and nodding.

They all fell silent for a while, reluctant to be reminded of the outside world.

'There's no Horrors because our music's still playing in the . . .' began Thunder Rider, his mouth full of food. Then he stopped chewing as he realised that the cartridge they had left playing in the kitchen must have stopped about an hour ago.

'Precisely,' Stacia smiled.

'Then . . .'

'Either the Death Ray's stopped, or else we really are getting immune to it,' she continued. 'The metamorphosis must be starting up again.'

'Don't kid yourself for one minute that the Death Ray's stopped,' Hound Master muttered into his glass.

'I agree,' the Baron said, 'It would be too much of a co-incidence to suppose it stopped at the exact moment the tape ran out.'

Tall, smiling Rudolph the Black rose smoothly from his seat, glass in hand. He walked across the thick, maroon carpet and sat in one of the luxurious easy chairs in front of the fire. He looked up at the black beams criss-crossing the ceiling. 'This place is bewitched,' he said laconically.

'A felt that too!' Higgy cried out. 'But a thought ye'd all think a was touched if a told ye.'

A strange tingling sensation began in their minds. They had all thought the same thing – but they had been too hungry and starved of the simple luxuries of life to worry about it.

Astral Al poked about with his knife in his food, his appetite gone. The brief respite they had earned away from the nightmare apocalyptic landscapes outside the inn, their so-called holiday, was over.

'I've been feeling kind of . . . odd,' he admitted. 'Thought it was just me. That sudden greenery, in all the deadness . . . and this inn, stuffed full of food that ought by rights to be rotten by now . . . It stands to reason, that something's wrong . . .'

A log cracked loudly from the fire, and a sudden fierce flame hissed out of the fissure. The extra fire-light flickered over the shiny, teak bar behind them where the ghosts of the old locals still drank. It glinted mysteriously off the hunting ornaments arrayed on the walls. The room seemed suddenly mediaeval in atmosphere – and sinister, as though at any moment its walls might dissolve away, and take them with it.

The agitated voice of the Light Lord burst out.

'What you say can't possibly be true! You're taking leave of your senses! All this rubbish about magic . . . !' He snorted disgustedly. He left his place and began pacing up and down the lounge, his gaunt frame stooping under the low ceiling.

'I sympathize with you,' the Prince said, 'but there's just too many strange things happening to say with certainty what's real and what isn't, anymore. And I'm afraid I'm inclined to believe the magic, now. I really do think this Ray or whatever it is, has triggered off something inside us . . . the thing in the Hawkwind legend – I reckon we *are* evolving into Hawklords. Rest assured, though, one day you'll see there's a scientific explanation for all this . . .' He trailed off. A vague, unresolved thought had entered into his head. He couldn't for the life of him remember what it was through the hazy effects of the wine, but he searched around inside his mind.

'I'll get us some more o' the Aphrodite,' Higgy offered, sensing that another long conference was about to start. He rose from the table, and disappeared out of the room.

Liquid Len groaned with exasperation. 'If you start to put weird ideas about you'll eventually start to believe them. Then, the facts will start to fit the fantasies. Suggestion. That's what magic is all about, can't you see that? You're all searching for simple solutions, which is what people do when they're in an unfamiliar, confusing situation – in deserts, for instance,' he added sarcastically, throwing his hands in the air. 'I give up, I really give up.'

'All right,' Hound Master said to Liquid Len, somewhat hurt. 'You provide us with an alternative explanation.'

'Delighted to,' the Light Lord replied. 'I suppose it's not occured to any of you that we might all be the victims of a mass delusion? That all we really are is a bunch of survivors trying to get it together, going slightly potty under the strain, imagining, like our primitive ancestors once did, that the great strange unknown outside our rabbit hutches is the territory of gods who we have to appease? All this rubbish about the Death Ray, and its superstitious implications, and the fantastic notions about evolving into Hawklords. Shit, the kids like our music because it's what they're used to! They need it – we all need it – to help us stabilize in a wrecked world. It's what we're used to. The Straights don't like it purely and simply because they never have done. Remember, their kicks are strictly jingles and Frank Sinatra, and anything more adventurous would disturb their minds . . . just like their music disturbs ours. No. I say the dreams, the Horrors and all the other manifestations are products of a mass psychological hallucination we've been stupid enough to devise for ourselves . . .' He finished his tirade, and looked around to see if his words had registered.

'You obviously don't *feel* what's happening like we do, Len,' Thunder Rider said after a while, shaking his head sadly. He spoke for everyone. 'If you did, you'd know . . . and then there's all Hot Plate's research . . .'

'But I do! I *do* feel!' The Light Lord replied, with irritation. 'But I don't blindly accept. As for Hot Plate, he could be what we first suspected – a misinforming spy from the Reactionaries or the Straights.'

'No way!' The Prince objected, remembering the laboratory accident. 'I'm no occultist, Len. Nor do I see things through rose-coloured spectacles. I saw what happened in the lab, and it's all correct. You'll just have to believe that.'

'Well, what about the Moorlock, Higgy, Stacia and myself, then? We're not strictly speaking part of Hawkwind, yet according to all that's crazy we're changing too!'

'You're not original members, true,' Thunder Rider replied. 'But then many of us aren't. Besides, you're all more or less indispensable now. And who's to say who the real Hawklords really are anyway?'

'There you go again!' Liquid Len accused, hotly. 'I think I'll leave this madhouse and retire. Good night, fellow humans!' He picked up his glass and collected another bottle of wine from Higgy who was standing in the doorway holding a fresh crate, listening to the discussion. Then he stalked out, and stomped upstairs.

The room was silent for a moment.

'Don't worry. He'll be okay in the morning,' Thunder Rider said. 'I have a funny feeling though that things are going to start speeding up now, and pretty soon it'll all be crystal clear to everyone. What say you, Prince?'

The Prince nodded. 'I think you're right, Thunder Rider,' he said mysteriously. He had regained his memory, and realized what it was he wanted to say. The key to what was happening to them, lay in the *Doremi Fasol Latido* psalm book that the Moorlock kept in his possession. He had once read passages out of the book many months earlier when he had been researching musical ideas in less incredible times. Some of the mystical journeys of the old Lords the book described seemed now to be more than familiar, as though . . .

'Moorlock?' he asked, looking to the head of the table, where the Sorcerer had sat. But his chair was empty. Puzzled, he looked around the room.

It had grown quiet again.

The transforming energy from beyond space and time began manifesting itself. A ghostly breeze fanned the fire and set the flames crackling higher as the surprised Hawkmen stared at one another.

Then, the large figure of the Moorlock appeared reassuringly in the doorway.

'I think you were going to call for this, Prince,' he said, holding up the ancient book with both hands. 'I slipped out whilst you were arguing, and got it from the van.'

He walked slowly, exaltedly into the room. He placed the heavy tome on the table in front of the Prince.

'Page 3,784,' he said. 'Under the section dealing with Magical Transmutation.'

Hurriedly, the Prince pulled open the book. The cover fell back with a thud onto the table, and an old, musty smell rose off the yellowed pages inside. He turned over the pages as fast as he could without damaging them, while his eyes scanned the columns of ancient text, searching for the reference he required. After several tense moments, he stabbed his finger excitedly on the parchment.

'There! I knew I was right! Now we have the answers . . . how did you know?' he asked the Moorlock, puzzled.

'The same way as you. Don't forget, they're my books. I've made a special study of them, though I admit I'd got a little rusty . . . do you want to read, or shall I?'

'You can read,' the Prince said, and turned the book round. The Acid Sorcerer leant over the table, and began to read in his strong, emotive voice. He was familiar with the old language, and read easily and faultlessly.

'When the Persons do reach the Machineries of Joy in Barlehaman, that is the second completement of their Transmutation after they have ordered the Lost Souls at the City of Menzaire. They will bear Parahalsys, and other divers illuminations of the Dark One, until they know Him more, and will never forget except on Death, and they will receive also the honoured Shield of Atmar. When the same Persons do reach the Phantom Inn at Arranar, that is the Third and Final Completement. Know then their Power, and receive the Bowl of Void, and the Sword of Life, and be then prepared to order the Psalm XIV of the Saga, and the will of Hoart Aire in the Third Age of Magik . . .'

The Moorlock broke off, and looked around him at the uncomprehending faces.

'Shall I go on, or will that do?' he asked.

'Tell us what it all means, first!' Astral Al demanded, nervously. Like the others, he had sensed a vague meaning to the words. Now they had been uttered, it was as though their sound had acted as a catalyst from the beginning of time, and somewhere deep down inside themselves, they knew everything. They felt a strange awe and fear enter into them. A feeling of pleasure, at the same time of pain. It was like the honed edge of a glinting knife.

The Moorlock too, felt the change, and he became less flamboyant.

'Very well,' he said. 'I will perform the honours. "Barlehaman" was the Ancient World, destroyed by excess and greed. The "Machineries of Joy", I believe mean the instruments of excess. In our modern Armageddon these correspond to the Fun Fair at Brighton. The "Lost Souls at the City of Menzaire" refer to the survivors of the Ancient World, squatting in the ruins of one of the famous cities of that age. This, of course, corresponds to the Children of The Sun, and the City of London. The bringing together or "ordering" of the "Lost Souls" represents the "First Completion" or phase in our evolution into Hawklords. "Parahalsys" is the old word for a condition of hallucinations, or visions which have been planted as knowledge or messages from the Gods – or from sufficiently powerful Devils. In this instance, the messages cause one to "know the Dark One fully", or know their Enemy – the apparition at the Fun Fair was a messenger. The Shield of Atmar, is symbolic for protection from the harmful rays – Atmar was a God of War who fought particularly bitterly against the Dark Forces of the Old World. The "Phantom Inn at Arranar", arrival at which brings about the "Third Completement", was the Inn where Mephistopheles was finally tricked by Atmar, and his satanic influence overthrown. "Arranar" is the country where the Inn stood, and which ever since has been lost to Man. Presumably, the Inn corresponds to this place . . .' He cast an awe-filled gaze over the walls of the room. Now they seemed to be a roaring mass of cold flame, totally obliterating the woodwork. The room had become almost hallucinatory in its intensity of presence. The air crackled with electrical charges, and the Hawkmen looked as though they were cast from marble. Their eyes gleamed with an unnatural intensity. '. . . this being the place where they

94

receive the "Bowl of Void",' he continued uncertainly, 'and the "Swords of Life", which are symbols for Universal Energy – not eating, and Immortality, in other words. The "Psalm XIV" is, of course, the legend we've already encountered about the Hawklords. The "Will of Hoart Aire" roughly translated, means the "Will of the Hawk Wind God" . . . "Hoart" means "Hawk God" and "Aire" is the old word for "Wind". As for the last reference, the "Third Age of Magik" – that self-evidently refers to the present, to the first note we struck that went through a Delatron, to right now, to this very room.'

He was silent.

Now there was no disputing the parallels between their own, unconscious journey to the Inn, and the stages of War enacted thousands of centuries ago. It was too much of a coincidence for even Liquid Len to dispute, were he present.

Then Higgy spoke.

'Presumably the legends of King Arthur co' fro' the Second Age, then,' he stated, fascinated by the history. Then he looked downcast. 'Bye th' way, arve got somethin' ter tell ye, i' th' way o' a confession. A notice now, ye really are changin', there's nae disputin' that . . . lads, arma not changin' with ye. Here . . .' He reached inside his pocket, and pulled out a bottle of tablets. 'A hoarded them for meself, an a bin takin' them ere since . . .' Guiltily, he layed the bottle down the table, and walked out of the room before any of the stricken assembly could halt him.

ACROSS THE DEATH TEETH

From out of the merciless steel sky, the black disc of the sun blazed down on the Hindus in the wrecked car.

Dachi, the Holy Man, was still smiling. He was very old, and had lost both his legs from the thighs down. They had found him propped up against a tree by the roadside near a

Hindu temple and had taken him with them into the sewers. Since then, he had pacifically refused all food rations, preferring to leave his share for others. Somehow or other, he still survived, and managed to retain a surprising stamina and reserve of energy – a feat which caused him to be held in awe.

'Do not doubt yourselves,' he told them kindly. 'The Mother Durga is powerful and will save you.'

His words cut dryly through the hysterical shouting and sobbing, and had the effect of instantly soothing them.

Rojan looked up imploringly. 'What is going to happen to us, Dachi?'

The Holy Man smiled wordlessly. Then, holding on to the jeep framework, he swung himself out through the broken door. His stumps landed with a slight thud onto the baked earth. He indicated the road ahead with his thin, brown arm.

'He wants us to walk, bloody hell!' Rojan shouted excitedly, his feud with the weaver forgotten. 'How does he think we will carry him?'

A furious debate started up again, but eventually they dismounted, and prepared to follow the old man's advice. They needed him like they needed religion. Two of them picked up the surprisingly light and frail body, and together they set off, bags and bottles swinging at their sides.

'Are you hungry yet, Dachi?' Rojan asked the ragged, hairy old man, after they had travelled some way.

'I have food – the food of God! I still have no need of mortal food!' replied the Holy Man, supremely. 'But listen to me, Rojan. I had the most remarkable vision. In it was explained to me the nature of the terrible catastrophe that has befallen all Hindus and Mankind – and the new beginning God has planned for those of us who remain alive and faithful to his cause.'

'That must be the same vision I had, Dachi!' Rojan cried excitedly. He turned to the others. 'Now, you bloody liars, you will see that I've been speaking the truth! I've been trying to help you!'

'Can you not feel the vibrations for yourselves?' the Holy Man asked. His words were gentle and sweet, sustaining them as they staggered onwards. 'They are very strong, like a sound-less music. Listen!'

'Oh, yes! We hear them!' cried Rojan, ecstatically.

The party halted. They could feel the goodness seeping out of the dereliction of the blasted landscape. They felt happy and content, and smiled at their own stupidity as the feelings washed over them. Then Rojan grew doubtful again.

'If God is so obliging, Dachi, why has he given us a useless old jeep to make our pilgrimage in? We seem to have the luck of beggars, when we should be riding around like princes!' he declared, miserably.

The old man did not answer. The party had set off once more, and he had fallen asleep with the jogging. Tantalisingly, a smile played on his lips.

They forced themselves on, taking it in turns to carry him, moaning and complaining.

Then, as one, they started to tremble and shake. The day went cold, and they began to shiver and vomit.

'Now we are done!' Rojan shouted, stumbling in a circle. 'God has deserted us again!' He closed his eyes. The stage in his vision was still there, but now it was crawling with monstrous, black insects that ran with great speed among the fleeing crowds, gobbling them up with glittering black claws. The ground round about opened and cracked, and out jumped the demons and other un-namable creatures that froze him to the bone. He opened his eyes in stark terror. Then, he lay down on the ground with the others until the nightmare passed away. Eventually, it would; just as it had come a dozen times already.

God was testing them for their faith. Deep down, he was not afraid. Throughout the worst, he would always retain the image of the stage as it had been, and he knew that they must still persevere to reach it, whatever the cost.

One day, that moment would come, he told himself.

Then, he felt a strange hardness about the ground beneath him. It was an unusual texture, hard like concrete. Curiously, he fought down the nightmare effects. He looked around him.

With a jolt of excitement, it dawned on him that they had

97

wandered on to a massive airport runway. In the distance, were the line of black hangers and the crumbling, white finger of the control tower.

VISION OF THE SKULL

The Light Lord slept badly in the tiny, loft-like room he had chosen at the top of the Inn. The first twinges of the delirium had begun immediately after he had stormed out of the lounge. Angrily, he had cast the unpleasant thought out of his head, as he mounted the stairs, dismissing it as being brought on by suggestion.

Then, when he had got upstairs, and thrown down his leather jacket on the side table, he felt the stale air in the old room grow suddenly chill. Alarmed, he lay down on the bed fully clothed, and drew a cover over him. A pain filled his head. The hideous thoughts sprang at him again, as though from somewhere outside his mind.

He closed his eyes to escape them, but instead he fell deeper into the horrifying scenes of butchery and torture they evoked.

He had seen the sick, broken landscapes before – the rent earth fuming, and the creatures pouring out – during an attack of the Horrors. Now, the pictures were more detailed and explicit. The gaping vents changed into seeping wounds on the bodies of the Children. The humanoid creatures from inside the Earth sprang on the dead and the dying, sucking their blood and eating their flesh. They dragged down the living, while soldiers in modern dress shot and slashed them where they lay. The soldiers marched across the corpse-strewn ground – land which the Light Lord now recognized as being a part of Earth City.

He moaned and writhed in his bed, breaking out in a cold sweat. At intervals throughout the night, as the visions assailed him relentlessly, unmercifully, he awoke screaming in the soaking sheets. Then, he drifted off again – a thousand times, and each time he relived the nightmare again.

Eventually, a weak and watery dawn broke, and the delirium passed away as suddenly as it had come. He dressed quickly, to wake the others. Now he had felt. Now he had known the feelings.

Deep in his heart, he knew that the knowledge had come too late . . . that already, Earth City was in serious trouble. His boots slipped on the crumbling wood. As he raced downstairs, the Phantom Inn began to decay. He hammered on the doors of the other bedrooms. They broke as though paper under his assault. Inside, the rotting rooms were empty.

In desperation he ran outside. Vibrations caused the ancient building to collapse in a heap of beams and dust behind him.

In the little square ahead of him, he saw the Mercedes. It was alight with chromatic colours crackling across its body-work, and an outline of pulsating orange light, as though at any minute it would disappear.

The door opened, and the ghostly figure of the Prince beckoned him on with frantic gestures.

'Come on!' he shouted. 'Get in, quick!'

The Light Lord moved across the space with a burst of in-human strength and soon was being helped through into the cab.

The door slammed shut behind him. Rudolph the Black released the clutch. The van bumped away out of the heavily charged area.

'We thought you'd had it,' Rudolph turned towards him after they were back on the road. Now, the trees outside were withered and dead, and skulls littered the ground. 'We tried to get you out, but your door was stuck. The handle refused to move. At first, we thought you had been singled out to perish . . .'

'On account of my beliefs!' the Light Lord asked. He shud-dered. Then he smiled, grimly. 'I got myself converted.' He remembered the visions. A look of alarm sprang to his face. 'Earth City . . . we must get back . . .'

'We know,' said smiling Rudolph. 'We all of us know. What

do you think we were doing up at this time?' He managed a weak, sardonic smile. 'It all happened last night, while you were rocking in that pretty bed of yours.'

'Where's Higgy?' the Light Lord suddenly realised.

Rudolph explained what had happened. 'He's in the back, unconscious. His system couldn't take it . . .'

'What, you mean we are now . . .'

'Yep, that's right. Fully fledged Hawklords. Nothing else could have come out of that inferno behind us, and lived . . . except Higgy, of course. Strong as he is, he's only just alive . . .'

The Light Lord was silent for a moment. Then he said: 'I hope he lives. Higgy, I hope you live.'

Then he felt the power of the Hawklords possess him. He felt it ripple through his body. He felt every cell of his mind expand. It was a super, powerful computer. He felt he was able to perform impossible tasks – squash metal with his bare hands, melt rocks with the concentration of his mind. When the van sped beneath the shadows of tall buildings, and the cab grew dark, he could see his tough new skin glow, faintly, with phosphorescence.

Suddenly relaxed, and confident, he lay back against the seat, watching the ruins of Brighton town sliding past him. They made better speed now that they were able to re-use the pathway they had cleared yesterday, a time that now seemed a hundred years ago and an earlier and immature stage of their lives.

Only the memory of the nightmare vision kept the Light Lord from becoming too peaceful. It burnt in his brain. It burnt in the brains of them all, as Rudolph desperately manoeuvred the vulnerable van nearer to its bloody destination.

THE HAWKLORDS RIDE

As they crossed the Chelsea Bridge over the River Thames, they began to see signs of the massacre. A few bodies lay motionless on the grey rubble and rubbish. They were brutally stabbed and slashed, some of them shot. A boy, whom the Baron thought he recognised, was bent face down over a window ledge. A tracery of bullet wounds had cut right across his back, as he had tried desperately to climb through the broken window in the last seconds of his life. A pool of blood had trickled away into the gutter.

The Baron got out of the van for a closer look. He leapt inside the window and lifted the head. It was the son of a Jamaican family who lived in Portobello, next door to the commune. The clear, brown skin of the slender youth was quite cold and smooth. The Hawklord gritted his teeth, and made his way back to the waiting Mercedes.

The Boy would not have hurt anyone. He was totally innocent of all crime . . .

'Right, that does it!' he said to them when he returned. His face was angry and red with rage. 'So far as I'm concerned, this means all-out war – and I won't stop until every last one of the bastards responsible is lying in the same position as that poor kid. Come on, let's arm ourselves!'

'I'm with you,' Thunder Rider said. He pulled his music gun out of his pocket and tested it. 'What else do we use?'

'Lengths of piping, if necessary!' the Baron replied, holding himself powerfully erect, and already scanning the dim outlines of the ruins. Dark, sullen clouds had returned again, and covered up the sunlight. 'Anything we can lay our bloody hands on!'

'Come off it, we can't fight bullets with piping!' Stacia retorted from the back of the van. She was lying by the side of Higgy, helping him to recover.

'Look madam, we're Hawklords aren't we?' the Baron said, acidly.

'Stacia's right,' said the Sonic Prince. 'We might have the powers of Hawklords, but we don't even know yet who or what we're up against, or how many. If it *is* an army, they could shoot us to bits. We need protection first, like a good dose of our music to send them scattering. Then we can move in for the kill with the help of the Children, if there are any left. I vote we get our instruments – they're our best weapons.'

The Baron looked half-strangled, first at Thunder Rider and Liquid Len who were sat on the front seat, then at Stacia and the others behind. The Hound Master and Astral Al were in the process of opening the sliding doors in the side to join him, but the rest were holding their ground. He held the stare for a few moments, and then let it go. With a snort of contempt, he reached for the open door and hauled himself in next to the Prince.

Wordlessly, Rudolph the Black started the engine and they set off again. He stared tensely through the windscreen. The land ahead was full of shadows, and at any moment he expected to take a burst of machine-gun fire straight in his face.

'The kid was cold,' the Baron stated, after a long silence. 'Must've been done in last night while we were noshing at the Inn.'

'That means we may be safe for the moment,' Thunder Rider said. 'But sooner or later we're going to drive smack in the middle of whoever's to blame.'

Hound Master shuddered. His long, straight hair quivered in the bad light. 'We'll have to take that chance,' he said. 'I don't fancy finding my way back on foot in this lot.'

The uniform grey cloud grew denser the further into the City they went. It was the normal, drab, grey-black sort, only deeper and dirtier than they had ever seen it before. Visibility went down to only a few yards, and Rudolph had to switch on the headlamps.

'With any luck, they won't spot us. If they do, we'll have as much chance of being hit as a duck in a . . .!!'

As he spoke, a fork of jagged lightning ripped across Sloane Square ahead of them, and they all jumped. It lit up the gaping shop fronts, and skeleton trees with a brief brilliant flash. It made no sound. The dismal air was perfectly still, and heavy with heat. Then the square was plunged in darkness again, blacker than before as their eyes strained to adjust.

'Must be some sort of electrical phenomenon, brought on by these clouds,' the Prince observed. 'Potentially very dangerous. Can't you go any faster, Blacky? There's a chance of finding survivors while it lasts, and under cover of darkness we can get our equipment together.'

'Sorry, mate. We're going as fast as we can. I daren't push her. If we hit anything, we could be stuck out here for hours.'

Slowly, the Hawklords journeyed up Sloane Street. After what seemed an age, they reached Knightsbridge Road, now scarcely recognisable in the dimness. When they got to Kensington Gardens, they were brought up again as more signs of the slaughter appeared.

Looming out of the murk was one of the tall, Hawkwind music towers, leaning perilously on its foundations. At its base, a hole was blown in the park wall, and a pile of masonry partially blocked the road. Lord Rudolph swerved and jammed on his brakes. He brought the van to a halt.

The Sonic Prince climbed cautiously out, followed by Lemmy and Astral Al. Outside, the air was deathly still, and smelled faintly rotten. They clambered over the bricks to get a closer look at the tower.

The instrument box at the top, where the Delatron and amplifiers were housed, was completely shredded, as though hit by a small bomb – probably a hand grenade or a shell. The Sonic Prince winced. Hours of work lay in ruins. More importantly, vital equipment and spares were lost.

'Prince! Over here!' Lemmy whispered, urgently.

The Prince turned. The other two Hawklords had climbed round to the far side of the tower. From the ghostly glow of their bodies, he could tell they were looking upward at something on the scaffolding.

With a sinking heart, he went over to them and peered up into the gloom. Several small, black shapes seemed to be caught in the metal supports. They were the bodies of the tower operators.

'Must have been changing shift when they were killed.' Astral Al spoke with rancour. 'They've been strung up and had their throats slit.' He looked down at his feet and moved them along the ground. The gravelly surface was tacky.

The three Hawklords felt sick, and stared nervously about them in the dark. There was still no sound on the air.

'If only this bloody cloud would shift!' Lemmy shivered in the heat. 'Come on, we've got to get back to the commune and find out what's happened to Dougy and the equipment.'

They were turning to leave, when a slight sound came from behind the corrugated sheets at the base of the tower. They froze. It sounded like a squeak. They turned towards the noise, and waited.

'Probably a rat,' the Prince hissed. 'Now the music's off, and with all these corpses about . . .'

'Better to make sure. You never know . . .' said Lemmy. He lifted up his hand and displayed a huge steel spanner. The other two gaped. 'Got it from under the seat,' he said grimly. 'I agree with the Baron, and I ain't taking no chances.'

He smacked the heavy head of the deadly implement against his palm and held it there. Then he advanced menacingly towards the tower.

The squeak came again, louder. It changed into a positive shriek, and a figure burst out from behind the sheet metal. It took off at top speed. Lemmy hesitated, and then ran after it.

Seconds later, he re-emerged out of the cloud, clutching the spanner in his teeth. In one arm he carried the struggling figure. He held his other hand across the captive's mouth.

'Couldn't let him go . . . he might have raised the alarm,' he said. His breathing level had scarcely altered.

'Who is he?' the Prince asked. 'Friend or foe?'

'I don't know. Let's get him back to the van and find out.'

They clambered back over the bricks. By the van's lighting, they could see it was one of the Children. He had his eyes closed, and he was still silently screaming into Lemmy's hand.

'Give him a shake,' said Thunder Rider.

Lemmy shook him violently, not daring to take his hand away. Eventually, the man opened his eyes. They were wide and shining with fear. When he saw where he was, and who he was with, though, he stopped struggling. Lemmy let his grip go and the man broke free.

He took several more moments to regain himself. Then he spoke.

'Thank God it's you, Hawkwind. I thought you . . . you . . . I . . .' He broke off. Shuddering took hold of him and he collapsed sobbing on to Lemmy. Lemmy raised his arms, shocked. Thunder Rider scowled at the other Hawklord and took hold of the man's arm to provide comfort. After a while, the stricken man raised himself again.

'Now, listen carefully. You're among friends,' Thunder Rider said to him, firmly but kindly. 'Who did we remind you of? It is very important.'

The man swallowed. 'Him!' he shouted, unable to control himself once more. 'Him . . . out there . . .' he pointed a thin, rigid arm out of the door into the blackness. Lemmy slid the door to, partly to prevent further sound escaping, but also because he felt safer.

'Cool down, will you?' he asked, more disdainfully than he intended. 'We're not exactly looking for trouble ourselves. Just tell us who "he" is, will ya?'

The hard words seemed to work, for the man suddenly grew more collected and quiet.

'The Major, or whatever he is . . . he glows, like you . . . spooks,' he replied. 'This crazy world . . . I don't want to live any more . . . I'm out of my head . . . I can't stand it . . .' He sunk his head in his hands.

'We don't know this Major – tell us about him?' Thunder Rider asked, patiently.

'He's the main one . . . the others don't glow,' the man went on. Whether or not he had heard the question, they couldn't tell. 'Him . . . like an army . . . they came and killed us . . . so quick . . .' He shook his head vacantly. 'So quick . . .'

'Sounds like the dreams we had,' the Moorlock commented. He turned to the man. 'Try and think,' he said, 'how many soldiers are there, and how many of us have they killed?'

'Hundreds . . . they killed hundreds of us, out there . . .' he indicated the park. 'You'll see the bodies . . . just lying on the grass . . . they left us to die . . . They've got guns, and . . .' He gasped again. 'This pain in my head . . . ever since the music stopped . . . the Horrors, they've been bad, real bad, worse than before, Thunder Rider . . . the death music too . . . its unbearable . . .' He rocked backward and forward, clutching at his head, as though trying to tear away the bone.

'He's obviously in a much worse state than we thought,' the Prince said. 'Better let him rest.'

'Not yet!' said Hound Master, unexpectedly. 'I feel for this guy as much as you do, but he looks like he's going to peg out – we've got to find out what's been happening before he does. It may be our only chance to get this crate back safely. Ask him where this army is camped now? The action's obviously over, and my bet is that they're congratulating themselves somewhere.'

The man dropped his hands, and stared levelly at Hound Master for a brief haunting moment. 'That's right . . .' he panted, 'I'm dying . . .' A gleam came into his eyes, and he started to loll drunkenly. 'But I don't mind what you say, friend . . .' He held out his hand to Hound Master, and laughed manically. 'Go on, take it . . .' Hound Master drew back, uncertain. Then, impulsively, he took hold of the other's hand, and squeezed hard. 'You're right,' the man gasped deeply '. . . too, about that ghoul . . . he took over the Palace . . . with all his men . . .'

'Did anyone escape?' Lemmy asked the man, who was now lying in Hound Master's arms, his final burst of energy spent.

'Yes . . . into the ruins . . .' he whispered. His head fell to one side. Hound Master straightened it, and slapped his cheek, urgently.

'What about the Gate? Did the soldiers go there?'

The man opened his eyes, and nodded. 'Bad . . . bad . . .' Then his head fell to the side once again, and stayed still.

The Hawklords were silent. The stygian darkness outside seemed to intensify. It filled them with dread . . . They had little time for grief.

'We've got to get to the commune!' Thunder Rider shouted.

He helped lift the body from his lap, and then grasped at the controls. The engine leapt to life. Soon they were bumping and jerking off again on the agonisingly slow journey through the endless shadows.

THE INTENSIFYING DARK

They inched cautiously forward through the gloom, headlights blazing. Eventually, they reached Portobello Road. In the dark, it was impossible to tell exactly how much destruction and slaughter had been wrought. The shop fronts were still caved in, and most of the buildings gutted, as they had been for months. But there was slightly more rubble and other debris in the road, and some of the houses that had been occupied were now derelict.

As they passed the ruins of the Convent, they saw more bodies, lying like grey dolls among the wreckage. The corpses stared lifelessly up into the muddy cloud. Some were flung face down, their limbs impossibly bent.

With lowered spirits, the Hawklords began to realize that the deranged Child had painted a terrifyingly accurate picture.

'They can't all be dead,' Thunder Rider whined through his teeth, gripping the steering wheel tightly. 'Doug and the others must be alive. They must be around somewhere . . .'

No-one could answer him. They were filled with a mixture of rage and fear. Rage, that Earth City should have ended so quickly without a chance to prove itself, that all their friends had been murdered. Fear, that Earth was now surely doomed.

What now was the point of carrying on? What reasons had the Hawkwind Gods given them their powers, except to cruelly mock?

They turned the corner and began to roll silently, jerkily, downhill towards the flyover where, not so long ago, they had first tested the Delatron's powers. Now, there was not a sign of life in the blackness.

Then, above the noise of the coasting van came the sound of shouting. It seemed to be coming from directly ahead of them, on the far side of the viaduct. Thunder Rider braked suddenly and flicked off the headlamps. He flung open his door and jumped out, crouching by the flank of the van.

The others climbed down after him with their music guns, and waited. The shouting grew louder, and more excited, though they still couldn't see who it was. The voices were gruff and aggressive.

'I think we've been spotted,' Thunder Rider said. 'They're moving towards us. Better get away from the van.'

As quietly as they could, they begun to move towards the shop fronts, down the street.

'What about Higgy?' Stacia suddenly whispered loudly. 'He's still in the back!'

They stopped, abruptly.

'Christ! I'll get him,' the Baron said. His large, dark shape detached itself from the group and disappeared into the murkiness. As soon as he had gone, a burst of machine-gun fire exploded in the silence. A rain of bullets smashed into the ground up the centre of the street.

'Halt! Or we fire again!' A loud, harsh command pierced the darkness, and in the dimness they began to make out the advancing shapes. The figures walked confidently forward, with the aid of powerful torches which nevertheless were scarcely visible. Their boots scraped noisily over the ground.

'There can't be more than a dozen of them,' the Light Lord whispered. 'Let them have it with the guns!'

They pressed themselves flat against the wall, and waited until the invaders were almost upon them. Then, arms outstretched they turned on the small battery of music guns in their hands. A sharp, jarring crash of music rent through the air as the miniature Hawkwind tapes began to play. The tunes were indistinguishably mixed, but shoved through the tiny Delatrons they had an instant, hideous effect on the men in front of them.

'Here we are!' Thunder Rider roared as the figures began to scream and clutch at their heads. 'Now get a load of Hawkwind music. Remember! You'll never vanquish the Hawklords!'

The men let their weapons fall to the ground. They staggered about and eventually they fell themselves.

'Don't turn your guns off!!' Lemmy yelled above the noise. 'Kill them! Kill them! Let them see what it's like, the bastards!'

He ran forward and picked up the sub-machine gun. Then he sprayed the writhing figures lying in the road with sound, and they shuddered and fell still. He turned off his gun and pocketed it. He stooped down to retrieve one of the fallen torches with his free hand. Its beam still stabbed frozenly into the dark, lighting the swirling vapours with a ghastly glow. He picked it up and played it on the inert bodies lying on the ground.

'So they are soldiers,' he confirmed in the silence that had returned once again. The Hawklords came over and crowded round the scene. The light picked out the dead men's uniform.

'. . . British soldiers at that. Where the bloody hell have they come from?'

They heard the sound of approaching footsteps and spun round. But it was only the Baron. He emerged from the darkness, supporting the Scotsman under his shoulders. Higgy was on his feet, groggily staggering along.

'Thanks,' the Baron said to them through gritted teeth, as he drew close. He propped his heavy burden up against the wall. 'The bullets missed me by a sliver!' He slapped Higgy lightly round the face. 'Come on me beauty, you'll have to walk a bit better than that.' He turned round to look at the bodies lying in the centre of the street, illuminated by the fallen torch lights.

'That's a few less we'll have to deal with,' he said, coldly. 'What now?'

'We'd better see what's left of 271,' Thunder Rider said grimly. They looked at one another hesitantly through the dark. Then they gathered the torches on the floor and returned to the van. Higgy was still dazed; now he was suffering from the Horrors again. They had escalated unbearably and he was moaning and swearing, continually wiping his hands down his face and the sides of his head.

'Don't worry, we'll soon get something permanent set up,' Hound Master said to him once they were inside again. He pressed a fresh cartridge into the player, and instantly the Chief Roadie began to feel better.

Hound Master started the van up, and soon they were outside the Yellow Van Commune, peering out at the lightless building. They could see by the headlights that vicious fighting had taken place. Bodies were strewn about on the road; some slight attempt had been made to heap them along the sides, presumably to make way for the military vehicles the soldiers must be using.

The door leading upstairs to the Commune had been broken off its hinges, and there was no sign of life at all in the building.

'I'd like to meet that Major or whatever he is!' Astral Al growled. They were reminded of the description of the ghost-like figure that glowed in the dark, like themselves.

'Come on, let's get out and have a look,' the Baron said, sliding back his door and climbing out. They took the torches, and held the music guns at the ready. By the light of the torches they could see that the entrance was badly damaged, and most of the plaster had been stripped off the inside wall.

'Must have been a grenade!' Lemmy said. With sinking hearts they climbed up the old stairs, and shone their torches in every room, half expecting to see a massacre of their old friends. But each room they came to was empty. Tables and chairs had been overturned, and most of the other furniture had been splintered.

They gathered in the room they once used as a lounge. The mattresses and cushions had been ripped and slashed. The room was full of feathers and foam pieces. This was the room where they had left their standby equipment.

It was gone.

'We've got nothing to play with!' Stacia cried out, aghast.

'They must have taken the lot with them . . .' the Moorlock said. 'What've they done with it all? You'd think that if all

110

they wanted to do was to prevent us using the instruments, they'd have just smashed them.'

'Whatever they've done – we're sunk, unless we can get them back,' Thunder Rider said. 'We've got to try and find Dougy and find out what's happened . . . if he's still alive,' he added grimly.

THE FORMATIONS OF THE ENEMY

As the War Lord finished speaking, a loud explosion came from outside in the street, accompanied by a blinding flash of light. The Hawklords froze. Then Stacia ran to the window and looked down. Debris from the explosion was still clattering, and the music that had been coming from the Mercedes had stopped. She made out the dim outline of their van – or rather, what remained of it. The body seemed split open from the roof, and its front seemed to cave in. Here and there, a few embers from smouldering combustible material were still glowing redly, struggling to burst into flame in the claustrophobic stillness.

From further up the street came more sounds of shouting, but she could not yet see the figures which she knew were advancing.

'Get away from the window!' Liquid Len shouted at her, after she'd told them what had happened. 'That's another patrol party come to relieve the other lot. They saw our van . . . heard the music, took no chances.'

'They must have blown it up at a distance to avoid the effects of the tape,' Lemmy said. 'We should never have played those tapes – it's bloody obvious now that they'd attract attention.'

'We can't hang around, that's for sure,' Thunder Rider said. 'We better get out of here before they arrive and lob a few grenades inside.'

Hurriedly, they moved out of the room. Their magical bodies left faint traces of phosphorescence behind them in the grave-like darkness. Astral Al took the lead downstairs, lighting the way with one of the torches. At the bottom he killed the light in case it were visible in the street; then he edged himself cautiously round the doorframe and peered out through the dense cloud.

The advancing soldiers were now quite close, and he realised that there was going to be no way they could evade them without being seen.

'It looks like another little battle!' Thunder Rider whispered sardonically behind him. 'Get your guns at the ready, and lie in wait!'

The fuzzy silhouettes of the soldiers came into view, checking the ground with their torches as they moved. They were not so confident as their other colleagues had been. The Hawkwind music had given them a bad time, and made them wary. They approached with caution, rifle nozzles pointing threateningly at the darkness in front of them. They had stopped shouting now, and only the sound of their heavy boots crunching unevenly on the ground could be heard.

They reached the wrecked vehicle and began probing about in the debris looking for clues to its identity. Close to, Astral Al could see they were a small detachment of about twelve men, not unlike the other group they had encountered. They wore the same hard, tight-lipped expressions, and moved stiffly and mechanically about. They were armed with self-loading rifles, except for a sergeant who held a sub-machine gun at his hip. He was looking warily about the buildings. One of the soldiers found something in the roadway and picked it out with his torch. It was the panel from the van bearing the HAWKWIND emblem.

'Looks like it is them, sir,' he said to the sergeant.

'Pity they weren't inside,' their superior replied, coldly.

He turned his attention briefly to the panel. 'They can't have got far away and they probably aren't armed. I want all these doorways checked. They must all die . . . Let one of them go, and Mephis will have us shot.'

The Hawklords in the open hallway tensed. They would be discovered and their advantage destroyed.

Astral Al screamed out. He leapt into the street. Simultaneously he pressed the button that activated the music gun in his hand. A beam of pure, concentrated Hawkwind music blasted into the midst of the surprised soldiers. The Sergeant spun round, straight into the music's path, and got thrown to the ground before his practiced fingers could operate the deadly weapon in his hands.

The other Hawklords came out behind the drummer, and soon the air was charged again with the jarring clash of notes and rhythms. The soldiers crumpled to the ground, their agonised faces staring uncomprehendingly at the Hawklords' fearful armoury. Their bodies twisted in pain. Then, they lay still.

Astral Al ran forward, the snub nose of his gun containing the speaker cone, still blaring. He played it at close range over the bodies, then turned it off. He knelt down in the sudden silence and felt around for the sergeant. Almost too late, he saw a dark shape move against the wall. Before he could move to defend himself, it sprang out and threw itself on him. Strong, thin fingers clamped around his throat, and a shrill, demonic voice rent in his ears. For a second, he was taken off guard. Then, instinctively, he knew that he need not worry. The instant his brain had received the alert, a feeling of supreme physical power far stronger than any that he had felt before, flooded into his being. Effortlessly, he reached up and ripped the struggling man from his back. With super, Hawklord strength he flung his assailant back against the wall.

From behind came a beam of light as Lemmy turned his torch on to the fallen soldier. Now they could see it was in fact the sergeant. He was sliding down the wall, a thin trickle of blood running from the corner of his mouth. But he was still fully conscious. An evil sneer crossed over his face.

'You think you've won,' he gasped. 'But you're losers . . . all your friends and kind are dead. You'll never defeat us . . . you Hippies have gone . . . you have lost . . .' His face twisted with pain and mocking laughter burst out of his throat. 'You're

113

all doomed! Look . . .'

His head lolled, and his death gaze fell for an instant on an object on the floor. Then he collapsed and lay still. The stunned Hawklords stood paralysed for an instant. Then Astral Al reached across for the small, rectangular object. It crackled as he drew it closer to him.

'Some sort of walkie-talkie device,' he said despairingly to the others. 'That can only mean that we're going to have more visitors – if we hang around here too long.'

'What does it matter . . . we might as well be dead if what that soldier said is true,' the Light Lord spoke morosely.

'Don't say that!' Astral Al said, his new super body still trembling with energy. 'We can't give up. So long as we still live . . .'

Their ears pricked. The unnatural dark pressed in on them. From somewhere behind its dense wall came the sound of vehicles. Their engines were screaming and whining as they approached, obviously in an attempt to cut the Hawklords off.

'Sounds like heavy company, Al,' Thunder Rider said grimly. 'I don't think we can chance tackling them.'

'They don't seem to know about our guns yet,' Stacia observed. 'Hot Plate only managed to make these eight.'

'They do now,' the Prince said, indicating the dead sergeant. 'It'd be safer to leave while we still can. We're probably heavily outnumbered and we'd be able to overthrow them better if they didn't know our location.'

'Then what are we waiting for?' the Baron asked. 'Let's go.'

They started to run away from the approaching army, picking a path with their torches through the scattered obstacles in the road .Since the van and the cartridge had been blown up, Higgy had fallen prey again. He was half pulled and half shoved along by the Baron.

They reached the flyover and then stopped abruptly. More vehicles were advancing from in front of them.

'We'll have to keep going. It's our only chance. If we can reach the cross-roads in time we'll be able to escape them,' the Baron said.

They ran on, stumbling through all the impediments. Then

114

the sound of the vehicles ahead of them grew suddenly louder. Bright, powerful light burst out of the cloud, cutting them off.

'Back!' Thunder Rider yelled. 'Tavistock Road.'

The Hawklords turned and started back along their tracks. But out of the dark ahead of them more light stabbed. A sound of squealing brakes announced that vehicles on both sides of them pulled up.

'Make a circle!' Thunder Rider yelled again, desperately. They formed a tight group around Higgy, facing outwards. They turned on their music guns to full volume, and filled the street with lethal sound.

But now they faced their match.

Over the discordant melée produced by their own equipment, came a rising tide of opposing sound. They listened appalled as fleeting snatches of the songs that were playing rose and died away. Sinatra's *My Way*; Ray Charles' *I Can't Stop Loving You*; Tony Blackburn's *Chop Chop*; The Carpenters, Yes and 10cc . . .

In the brilliant glare of opposing headlights they made out the shapes of the loudspeakers mounted on the roofs of the parked trucks. For a brief moment, the two sounds clashed and vied for supremacy. Then the more powerful speakers of their opponents gradually transcended their battery-operated hand guns, and the Hawklords felt the horrifying effects of the Death Music start to take over their minds.

THE ROTTING DEBRIS AND INSECTS OF NIGHT

The cell smashing sound continued to mount in effect, until it reached an almost unbearable intensity. Then it levelled off as the two opposing sides threw everything they'd got at each other. Once again, the barriers between nightmare and reality started to break down as they came into the grip of the Horrors. The mighty Hawklords struggled to fight off the demonic

115

psychic visions that assailed their senses, that tried to take over their being and destroy them utterly.

The soldiers stood outside their trucks in front of the blazing ring of headlights, sensing victory. They fired endless rounds of ammunition at the group. From behind, they were backed by a constant rain of fire from jimpies mounted on scout cars. But the bullets slowed down as they entered the field of Hawkwind force, and dropped harmlessly in piles at the Hawklords' feet.

But their less powerful equipment was gradually fading, and the area of protective energy around them was beginning to contract rapidly.

The sudden unleashing of magical energies charged the malign air. Electric colours began to pulse and flash at the juncture of the two fronts. The door of one of the Land-Rovers opened and a tall, thin figure stepped down. He was dressed impeccably in officer's uniform, and was obviously of a high rank for the privates on either side of him stopped firing briefly, and saluted. He surveyed the scene for a few moments, then, as though not a part of it, he began to walk stiffly towards the trapped Hawklords. As he drew closer, they could see a cruel smile playing on his features. He stopped, and gave a signal to his men. Immediately, the lights from the vehicles were extinguished, and the battle continued in the dark. Now, the Hawklords could see that the figure in front of them glowed, like themselves, and they knew that at last they had met with Mephis.

The phosphorescent shape in front of them began to ripple behind the flashing colours, as though performing a macabre dance. Its arms stabbed at them accusingly, and its face stretched and shrank. Its whole body convulsed and shook with insane, soundless laughter.

Another mental explosion burst inside the Hawklords' heads as the power in their batteries began to dwindle. The Forces of Darkness reared ever higher around them. They felt the corrupt tentacles of the Death Lord's evil mind squirm inside their heads. Its poison sapped their will and tried to break down their last holds on reality. All but one were succumbing.

116

Astral Al recoiled from the touch. Inside him he fought blindly, instinctively, to bring the pieces of his mind together, and from somewhere in his being came the directive to move. He didn't know where to, or how, but he knew from his guts that move they must. Instinctively, his body strained to the left, towards an area of deeper black in the nearly invisible shop fronts. Resolutely, he mustered all his available energy, and brought his leaden frame into motion. Pushing weakly at the others, he managed to communicate his intention.

Still keeping his music gun trained on the soldiers he shifted the other Hawklords slowly towards the open doorway. They responded to his touch like sleep-walkers. Soon they were inside the shop and moving along a passageway. Behind them, as the boundary of the force field shifted, the bullets started tearing into masonry, and the building began to tremble dangerously under the impact.

Gradually, they moved through the house. Slowly, they reached the back entry. Then, out of the direct path of the Death Music, they began to revive, and their super minds were able to start thinking again. Shaking himself free of the painful, stroboscope-like trance, Lemmy flicked on his torch.

They were close to the old Hammersmith to City underground train line that crossed alongside the flyover, but here the bridge had ended and a steep embankment took its place. They clambered up it, music guns still playing.

They started to run down the old line in the direction of Westbourne Park Grove. Only then did they turn their guns off to save power. From behind them, as they did so, they heard the besieged building collapsing in a roar of masonry. Then the Death Music fell silent.

'They daren't follow us out here!' the Prince said, fully recovered. The effects of the Death Music had cleared remarkably quickly – no doubt due to the power of their new Hawklord Personna.

'They can't drive their lorries on a rail line, and they don't seem to possess any portable sound equipment to come after us with.'

'That's all very well, and also very agreeable,' the Moorlock grunted, as they continued to increase the distance between them and the soldiers. 'But where exactly are we going?'

'At the moment, anywhere where we can completely lose Mephis and his band of ghouls!' Lemmy replied from up front.

'Then we better leave the tube line,' Stacia said. 'It runs very close to the main roads a little further up.'

'Good thinking!' Thunder Rider told her. 'We can turn off down one of the side streets and lose ourselves in the ruins.'

The embankment had become considerably less steep now and in parts it more or less levelled off into adjoining land. Cautiously, they made their way through a mass of tangled fencing and eventually came out on to a street lined with what seemed to be large, abandoned warehouses rotting in the dark.

'Where to now?' Thunder Rider asked, slightly put out.

'We better stick in one place, until this cloud clears away,' Baron Brock suggested. 'I think we ought to find a way into the building and make a base. Mephis and his men won't bother searching for us in the dark.'

'That's what you think,' Lemmy called back softly. 'Get ready for another assault.'

They froze. More figures were coming silently towards them, shuffling unnaturally slowly out of the blackness.

The Hawklords started up their music guns once again, and pointed them directly at the advancing shapes. But this new set of assailants continued to bear down on them, unaffected.

THE STRATIFIED LAYERS OF TIME

The figures continued to approach out of the murk until they came within reach of the torches.

The rays fell on pale, emaciated faces with feverish eyes that seemed to hunger for the light and the discordant music. Then, Stacia let out a cry of delight. She ran forward and hugged the leading member of the ragged band.

'Dougy! It's Dougy!' she screamed, above the blare of the music guns.

The other Hawklords stopped playing, and stared in startled disbelief, trying to discern the features of their ex-manager, who stood wretched and shaking before them. Warm heartedly, they clustered round, and the two groups embraced one another.

'We knew you'd make it!' the Light Lord exclaimed, relieved to see friendly faces again. 'They tried to tell us that we were the last . . . that you were all dead . . .'

'We almost are, mate,' Actonium Doug managed to grin. 'It's been bloody murder here since you left. But we reckon we've worked out a way of keeping underground undetected.'

'How many of us are left?' the Baron asked. He always had a warm spot for Actonium Doug – he was glad to see him again still with his mind intact.

'No more than a hundred, Baron,' the other replied. A downcast look came over his features. He looked at them calculatingly. 'Now, we're a hundred and eight . . .'

'Good on you, Dougy!' Thunder Rider said, slapping him on the back. 'You always had a shrewd head for figures . . . and knew how to take advantage of them! Show us where you've been hiding out and tell us exactly what's been happening while we've been away.'

Actonium Doug turned, and together the re-united party stumbled down the street. They followed the warehouse wall for a short distance, until they came to a part where a hole had been blown in it.

'They've been combing London systematically,' Actonium Doug explained as he ducked inside, 'destroying or acquisitioning all the electronic equipment they can find in order to defeat us. This area's already been searched.'

They entered into the building. Inside, the torches picked out a jumble of criss-crossed beams, and smashed boxes with their clothing contents pulled out and scattered about at random. As they walked through, numerous insects scuttled out of their way into the heaps. The Moorlock shuddered.

They were led into a pitch black area at the end of the building, hidden by stacks of old boxes apparently placed at random. Hawkwind music was playing faintly from somewhere in the dark in front of them.

'This is where we're living at the moment,' Actonium Doug told them.

At first, they could make nothing out, except a large, cleared space in the darkness. Then Lemmy's torch found a collection of huddled people lying and sitting on the stone floor. They were all in pretty bad shape, and could scarcely move to greet them. In the centre of the huddle was a single Delatron, and a battered looking record player which was churning out the *Space Ritual*.

The Hawklords were sickened by the sight. But they were heartened too, for they had been mentally prepared to find no-one but themselves alive.

'Most of them are too far gone to respond to you,' Actonium Doug said. 'The only fit ones left I picked to come out and meet you.'

'Meet us?' queried the Prince, puzzled.

'Yes, we knew you'd arrived by the music you were playing. This thing . . .' he indicated the player, 'it's on its last legs, and often as not doesn't work. Well, we've all been suffering badly from the Horrors, and then when they started to clear up at intervals, we guessed you were around somewhere. Then we heard the guns firing. There's not been much activity tonight from the other side and sound seems to carry like electricity through the cloud. We were just setting out to see if you needed help, not that we could have given you much in our condition – when we bumped into you outside. At first we thought you were Mephis because you glowed. Then I heard Lemmy's voice . . .'

'You gave us a nasty shock,' the Moorlock accused, good naturedly.

'Sorry about that, mate – but what do you think you did to us? I thought you must be bloody spooks! So what's with all this shine, anyway?'

The Prince described the transforming incident at Rotting-dean. As he spoke, they found somewhere to sit in the dark.

120

Then Actonium Doug related what had happened to Earth City in their absence.

'As soon as you'd bloody gone, a load of carrier planes came over – must have been a few dozen of them, and we expected trouble right away. They must have been unloading and organising themselves for quite a while, because nothing happened until the next day. Then suddenly everywhere was swarming with troops. They attacked the stage area first, completely demolishing it and slaughtering anything and anyone who moved. Then, systematically, they spread out, wiping out everyone and destroying the towers. They were moving quickly because our music really screwed up their minds and they wanted to get it stopped before they cracked up. The taped music isn't as powerful as live music, for some reason, but by this time we couldn't get a band together. All the equipment had been wrecked . . . except for the standby lot,' he added, to ease the alarm he sensed on the listening Hawklord's faces. 'We rescued that. Next they started on the Gate, and they met with more resistance there, I can tell you. But, unprepared as we were, we were no match for their weapons. Mephis and his lot drove the few of us that remained into the ruins, and here we've remained ever since. They sent out parties to look for us to begin with, but we kept evading them. Then, this cloud suddenly came down . . . queer like, almost as though we were being aided . . .'

'You probably were,' said Lord Rudolph, thinking of the magical transition stage at the Inn.

'They've not been bothering us since,' Actonium Doug continued, 'except with this search and destroy mission they've embarked on as regards equipment. Somehow, they've got advance knowledge of your return, and they've been making London as inhospitable as they can for you.'

'They're probably frightened you'd make a come back, too,' Thunder Rider observed. 'Well, now we're all together again we're going to. I've been feeling a lot better since I've known definitely that there are survivors, and now I can feel my Hawklord blood starting to boil. What say you, men?' He looked round at them sightlessly through the dark. They

121

chorused their agreement.

'I'm ready!' the Baron said, menacingly. 'I've been saving up a lot of hard feelings for this moment . . .'

'Here, here!' Lemmy concurred. 'Let's blow the bastards off the face of the earth!'

For almost the first time since they had been given their new powers, they were able to begin exercising them. Most of it, as Astral Al had discovered wrestling with the sergeant, was latent. It developed as situations arose which demanded it.

'First we must get our gear back,' Astral Al said. 'We can't do anything without that . . .'

'And a place to play, to blast them all out of existence!' Stacia exclaimed. She remembered dancing on the first day of the Hawkwind concert – how the music had warned her of the impending disaster, and the manifestation of the Powers of Darkness. It had been a vague, unspecific warning then, and she hadn't known what to do to combat the force except to continue dancing. But now the dreadful happenings of the past few days were clearly etched upon her mind, and she felt the same feelings of concern, only a thousand times more strongly.

'Here's to Earth City!' Hound Master shouted.

'Aye, aye!' Higgy agreed, stimulated.

A happier, optimistic feeling crept into the stale air inside the warehouse, and the Hawklords reached for their music guns. They blasted a few bars off into its rank, humid oppression.

THE AUTOMATIC EYE

Moorlock, Actonium Doug and the Baron set blindly off from the warehouse, glad to be away from the dank, infested building of doom.

They picked their way through the almost tangible darkness, unable to use their torches much for fear of alerting the numerous patrols that now combed the streets. They passed the once teeming Mountain Grill food store, smelling of death and decay again.

Then they reached Blenheim Crescent, where the Acid Sorcerer's stronghold lay. It was impregnable and unscathed in the cloak of dark. According to Actonium Doug, it had been shot, bull-dozed, attacked by battering ram and in desperation, bombed – but all to no avail. A magic more powerful than Mephis kept it locked and barred to all but Hawklords and Children.

The group edged carefully along the pavement, keeping close to the remains of the ornate railings and walls that once protected the derelict terrace of Victorian houses. As they approached, a ghostly, pulsating glow of colours emanated from the gloom ahead of them. The magical, cybernetic house loomed into view. The Moorlock winced.

'Look what they've done to Victoria!' he blurted out in alarm. 'What's she done to deserve that?'

The building was surrounded by an electrical force field of flashing, crackling colours. The jagged sparks jumped along the eaves and brickwork. 'We must get in quick and calm her down,' he said, desperately.

The Baron laid a restraining arm on his shoulder.

'Don't do anything rash. Look!' He pointed to a scout car in front of the house. A kerosene lamp stood on its bonnet, casting a dim, yellow light through the swirling vapours. A group of soldiers was talking quietly by the open door. Every so often one of them looked towards the building, then fingered his rifle nervously.

'A pushover!' Actonium Doug murmured. 'Transport too. What are we waiting for?' He brought out the music gun he had been cradling inside his jacket. It was playing at an almost inaudible volume to help reduce the effects of the Horrors he was still susceptible to.

Together, they switched on their guns and stepped out into view. The startled soldiers spun round. One of them tried to reach for a cassette player that was strapped against his chest. But he and his comrades stood no chance in the path of the

123

Hawkwind music. Their bodies started shaking in the deadly sound. Screaming and clutching at their faces, they fell to the ground, where they twitched and convulsed until, mercifully for them, they lay still.

The Hawklords and Hawkmen stepped over their bodies and raced up the steps to the house. They had no time or inclination for respect.

'Victoria! Victoria!' the Moorlock crooned in a disconcerted voice, stroking the porch walls and the entrance doors.

The doors responded immediately to their presence, and opened to admit them. Once they were inside they closed, sealing them off, protecting them from the dangers outside.

'Mike! Mike!' A sensual, feminine voice replied, echoing round the stark hallway. It seemed to come from everywhere and nowhere. 'So you've returned. I wondered where you'd been. I've been so upset and lonely since you left . . . but I've been a good girl,' the voice added, pleased with itself. 'I didn't let anyone in, like you said not to.'

'Oh my love, my Victoria!' the Moorlock moaned, deeply wounded. 'Don't you worry yourself another instant! I'll be right in there with you to give you your favourite treatment . . .' He bounded down the passageway, away from his startled companions who watched him leave with their mouths agape. He disappeared through a door that seemed to lead down into the basement.

'Oh well,' the Baron scratched his head in disbelief. 'I suppose it takes all kinds. I had no idea though that . . .' He trailed off, amazed.

They stood for a few moments, uncertain what to do next. The emergency equipment that Actonium Doug had managed to salvage from Yellow Van before the commune had been invaded, was stacked next to them, but they needed to collect other equipment and they had no idea where to look. Then the Moorlock returned sooner than they thought, his face beaming.

'That's sorted her out!' he exclaimed. 'Now we can get down to business. Come with me and I'll show you where the gear we used for DEEP FIX is.'

124

They followed him through the door, down a short flight of varnished, wood steps into the basement.

Down here, lay Victoria's heart – bank upon bank of computer consules, together with some of the strangest looking instruments that they had seen.

'A mixture of magic and electronics . . .' The Sorcerer said, sheepishly. 'You're the first people I've let look at her insides. She's a bit shy, actually. That's why she's not speaking much. But come on . . . we don't have time for pleasant diversions,' he finished with a mysterious chuckle.

He led the way to a store room where the equipment was stored.

The Baron darted forward and picked up a guitar. He cradled it lovingly, and brought it out into the light. It was the Moorlock's Stormbringer II. There was one thing to be said for the Sorcerer, he thought – he didn't skimp. He was blatantly lavish.

Soon, they had brought out all the equipment – including a set of drums and several powerful amplifiers and speakers. Well pleased with the haul, they carried them upstairs and deposited them in the hallway. Then the Moorlock disappeared again. He returned a few moments later with his stereo system and tape recorder.

'We'll need all the electronic stuff we can get, I suppose,' he said, adding them to the heap. 'Now I'll show you where the generator is.'

They followed him into a sound-proofed room at the end of the hallway. A brand new, unused engine had been installed.

'An emergency measure, in case the house power failed,' he explained. He found a spanner and began to unlock the motor from its foundation. When it was free, they lifted it up and staggered under its weight to the front door.

'There! That should give them a kick in the arse!' the Moorlock exclaimed triumphantly, after they had laid it down. 'Now let's get them into the Land-Rover while we still can.'

The Baron walked to the door. It swung open and he peered warily out into the blackness. The faint glow of the lantern on

125

the scout car bonnet still glimmered feebly, no more than six yards away.

'Seems clear,' he reported.

Working rapidly, they hefted the gear into the back of the vehicle. When they were nearly done, the Moorlock made one last journey into the basement. He returned almost immediately, visibly saddened. Together, they left the house, and the doors closed behind them, keeping at bay the evil forces.

'Bye, bye, ever watchful eye,' the Moorlock said to it, as they drove slowly away, down the pitted street. 'Be good.'

TRACERIES OF GREEN LIGHT

The dingy, sunless cloud grew denser as the Sonic Prince and Astral Al approached Hyde Park Corner. Somewhere in its dark, enveloping fold was Hot Plate.

They could scarcely see more than an inch in front of themselves.

'Good job your sense of direction is OK,' Astral Al called out in a loud whisper, clutching at the other's coat tail as they moved across the road.

'Reckon I could get here in my sleep,' the Sonic Prince replied immodestly. 'This cloud's good for guerillas like us. We wouldn't stand a chance in the daylight. Pass me the rope will you? I think we've hit the wall.'

They had arrived at the west wall of the Palace. It stood before them, a solid high barrier in the dark. The Prince threw over the rope with a grappling iron attached. It clanged mutely, but held. Without hesitating he pulled himself up, feeling for the lethal spikes which he knew were mounted at the top of the wall. With superhuman strength he managed to lever himself out and manoeuvre himself into a standing position. He jumped down into the flower gardens on the far side.

A few seconds later, he heard a mutual thud next to him.

'You OK?' he called out to Astral Al.

'Couldn't be better.'

'Stick with me and you won't get lost.' They set off across the parkland, the Prince keeping a mental picture of the palace and its grounds in his head as they went. They skirted the private lake, and eventually reached more gardens close to the Palace. The historic old building was floodlit with powerful lights. From somewhere came a fearful, discordant noise which made them both feel sick. The Prince realized dimly that it was Bob Dylan's *Blowing in the Wind*. He shivered.

Across from them they could see the door which the Prince had used to visit the scientist. He hoped that, on this occasion, they would still be able to find him there. There was no saying what they would find now that Mephis had taken over the Palace as his headquarters.

Two guards patrolled the perimeter of the Palace, and at first there seemed no way the two Hawklords could gain entry. Their music guns would raise the alarm if they were sounded.

'We'll have to wait until one of them's on his own and somehow overpower him,' Astral Al said. 'I'll tackle him while you try the door. If it's locked, you'll have to break it open.'

Grimly, they waited on the edge of the light. Then, after a short while, their chance came. The two soldiers crossed one another's path, walking in opposite directions. The one moving towards the door bent down to tie up his boot laces, allowing his partner to move out of earshot. Astral Al tensed himself, then moved with considerable speed across the gravel to the crouching figure. Before the surprised man could react he keeled over from the blow. His head lolled slackly as he fell.

With equal speed, the Sonic Prince bounded over to the door and turned the handle. It was locked. With inhuman strength he smashed his shoulder against the heavy wood. It burst open under the impact – just as Astral Al arrived carrying the limp body in his arms.

'Get in quick! That other geezer will turn round any minute.'

They piled inside the small doorway into the dark interior. Astral Al threw the body to the floor, and then turned round to face the door again. He peered out. The other guard was returning warily. He had sensed that something was wrong.

'Come on, come on,' Astral Al muttered impatiently under his breath. 'Let's be having you.'

The frightened soldier drew parallel with the open door, and poked his rifle inside.

'You in there, Olly?' he asked, nervously.

By way of answer, the strong hand of the impatient Hawklord grasped the muzzle of his weapon, and yanked him bodily into the blackness. Before he could cry out, his neck too was hanging by a sliver of cartilege. Floppily, he joined his companion on the floor.

'Just a few tricks I learnt at karate school,' Astral Al informed the staggered Prince modestly. He closed the door and together they made their way to the secret stairway.

With the Prince in the lead, they mounted the ancient staircase, pushing their way through the cobwebs and dust up into the Palace attics.

'Here we are,' said the Prince at last, as they arrived at the laboratory entrance. 'Now let's hope Hot Plate has managed to talk Mephis into keeping him alive.'

THE BLANK EFFIGIES OF MANKIND

A tingle of warning shot down one side of the Light Lord's head. He stared into the intense blackness of the road from which the danger had emanated. In order to keep on course for Parliament Hill where the pitiful remnants of Earth City intended making a fresh stand they would need to turn down its path. But his psychic instincts told him that if they did so they would run into a patrol. They would have to go straight on instead, and take the next turning.

He touched the person behind him, and whispered the instructions. Then he continued moving forward, feeling his way with his feet across the road.

The wrecks of humanity that he and the other Hawklords had managed to revive at the warehouse followed behind him. They shuffled and coughed. Some were unable to stifle the occasional groans of pain and weariness. But the party kept going.

Liquid Len kept going. His growing psychic awareness enabled him to sense parts of his surroundings that were normally hidden from view. He knew roughly where they were and providing they could evade the patrols, he knew it was just a question of time before they would arrive at their destination.

At last they reached Chalk Farm. As anticipated, there seemed to be less troop activity out here and they were able to move more freely. Mephis appeared to have a limited number of men and was concentrating them around the area he was most familiar with.

Now all they had to do was follow a straight route up Haverstock Hill all the way into Hampstead. From there it would be easy to find their way to the Heath. By setting up a fresh base there they hoped to take the attackers by surprise.

They groped their way through the deathly blanket of darkness for several more hours. Eventually, they reached the small knoll of Parliament Hill that lay at the edge of the open land. It was not an obvious hiding place for a band of tired fighters, and it had the advantage of altitude.

They climbed up to its rounded, wooded summit and fell exhausted among the skeleton remains of invisible trees that they could only detect by touch. Motionlessly, they waited for the arrival of the equipment.

Stacia and the Light Lord waited on the road below while Hound Master and others who were fit enough did what they could to raise the desperately low spirits of the Children.

They waited for what seemed like hours in the pitch dark for the Baron and the Moorlock to arrive.

A slight breeze blew, laden with the faint smell of human carrion – there still seemed to be no escaping the horror of the carnage. It would continue to take its toll until the new stage was erected, and live Hawkwind music was once more blasting out. Now that they were Hawklords and immune to the Horrors they would be able to play for longer periods without tiring. Taking turns, they would be able to keep the music going non-stop until more automatic equipment had been built to help protect Earth City. And of one thing they were quite sure – they would never leave their posts again until Mephis and the Death Generator were completely smashed.

The growl of an approaching vehicle crawling in low gear broke their thoughts. They dropped to the ground, out of sight. The Land-Rover's headlights appeared faintly in the cloud, then more brightly. It pulled up alongside them, at the gates to the park. The door squeaked open, and a familiar figure climbed out. The Light Lord had no difficulty in recognizing who it was.

'Baron!' He stood up and ran forward to greet him. Soon, they were all out on the pitted road, hugging and kissing.

'We thought we'd never make it,' Actonium Doug explained their lateness. 'We've had a hell of a job avoiding patrols and clearing roads in the dark – no-one's ever had cause to come out here, so it's just been one long endless traffic jam, most the way.'

'We've only just arrived ourselves. Try hiding a hundred. sick people in a street when a patrol passes!' Stacia exclaimed. 'Have you got the gear though? That's the important thing.'

'All present and correct, madam!' the Moorlock replied. 'I think you'll find it all safely on the back.'

'Good, then let's get this crate to the top of the hill and get it unloaded,' the Light Lord hurried them up, moving agilely about in the small area of light.

He and Stacia began leading the way, while the others climbed back into the army jeep. Soon, they reached the encamped survivors and began humping out the equipment. It was not long before the instruments were wired up to the remaining Delatron, and the generator topped up with diesel ready to be kicked into life.

D-RIDERS

Eagerly, the Hawklords took up their positions. They had played on a thousand different occasions, for many different reasons. But this time the stakes were higher than they'd played for anywhere. The life or death of humanity was in their hands. If any part of the complicated circuitry which Higgy and the Baron had improvised failed, Mephis would triumph over all. For the first time in its history Earth would pass solely into the clutches of the Devil.

The stage was weakly illuminated by torches hung from the rotting branches. Around it, in a circle, lay the prone figures of the Children, most of them too far gone to realize the significance of the moment.

Through the blanket of cloud came a muffled roar as Higgy started up the generator. Tremulously, Hawkwind tested their instruments. The riffs and chords stabbed bluntly, disappointingly, into the black murk. But though the sound itself would not carry far, the emanations from the Delatron did.

Almost immediately, a mighty wave of pleasure swept through the dying Children. Those who had managed to stay conscious sent up a ragged cheer. The others stirred restlessly in their death sleep.

A surge of power ran through the Hawklords. Their electric steeds leapt and bucked beneath their touch. Intuitively, they began jamming. Hound Master loosed a volley of drum rolls. His wild eyes flashed menacingly in the torchlight. His gold mane flew from side to side as his body became the eternal thudding of his drum, as he fought the longest, hardest battle of his life so far . . .

The Baron played a series of low, fuzzed guitar chords, drawing on the limitless energy that seemed to lie in the air all around them. His sure, purposeful playing picked out the notes of *Time We Left This World Today*.

Thunder Rider stood at the ready, straining all over with pent-up energy. He held an old, dented sax to his lips, waiting for the right moment to join in. Eventually, it came, and the haunting, wailing sound began.

They felt the invisible wall of Dark Force that had choked the city depart, billowing and writhing away into the wastelands outside. Phantom shapes flashed, departing, across their minds. Pictures of the soldiers running and stumbling to their vehicles, jamming the roads in an effort to flee the destruction of the Hawkwind vibrations. Pictures of Mephis, grimacing with rage, skulked in their wake . . .

They played for all they were worth, caught up in the need to win the battle of Earth. The salving music doused the frustration of the agonizing separation from their instruments. They played simply and powerfully, without their usual batteries of synths and melatrons. Thunder Rider quivered with fulfilment.

As the wave of deathly oppression lifted, they were reminded once again of their mission – to build a new world. Once more, they had been given the footing they needed. Now they were determined to start afresh.

The claustrophobic cloud that had cast London into impenetrable night for so long began to unfurl. Their music hammered at its sickly, grey belly, battering it back. Gradually, the weak and watery daylight of a new dawn began to filter through. A large, pale sun emerged, riding high behind the vanishing, swirling shreds.

A second, louder cheer rose from the stiff and starving assembly on the hill top. The constant dark had done much to prevent them from recovering. They hugged and embraced one another in delight as the volume of sound increased, speeding unimpeded across the silent, newly emerged ruins.

From the early days of being a small, rough and ready rock band able to jam anywhere at a moment's notice and bring impromptu gratification to the audience, Hawkwind had gone full circle. They had passed through the electronic sophisticated phase and put on full scale tours. Now they were a simple, but vital group again.

Now was the Spacecraft's greatest moment – called from beyond the edges of time to free Earth from the Dark Web of

Evil. It remembered a hundred other missions, all victories over the Straights. Isle of Wight in 1970 where the ship made its first real impact, outside the gate, playing for free . . . the Charity concert at the Roundhouse for The Greasy Truckers in 1972 . . . Liverpool Stadium . . . Chicago, Detroit, New York and Los Angeles . . . called from the depths of space to fight for the new society of Children of The Sun.

Now its mighty engines thudded and strummed like they'd never done before. The complex of writhing, stabbing sounds spun off the wooded magical summit of Parliament Hill. The days of the black, mindless, visionless, selfish shape that for so long had dug its grey, parasitic roots into the minds of men, which had strangled their originality and freedom, and sapped the strength of their youth in order to perpetuate its colossal, satanic empires – the days of this blight on humanity were numbered.

CHEMICAL ALICE

Raptly, the Sonic Prince listened. He raised his head in the dark staircase of the Palace as the warming vibrations of the music melted into his being.

'Good for them! They must have made it after all!' he exclaimed.

Astral Al smiled through the dark.

'Sounds like the troops are leaving,' he commented with a tone of mock hurt in his voice.

From other parts of the building came the muffled, calamitous sounds of movement, punctuated by shouts and screams.

'All the better for us!' the Prince replied.

He put his ear to the panelling once again, and listened for Hot Plate. No sound came from the laboratory. The faint worry that something was wrong with his friend began to nag.

133

Fearfully, he swung open the panel. It swung open on well-oiled hinges. A sudden, sharp smell of chemicals wafted out.

The room was lit weakly by the dawn.

Coughing and spluttering, the two Hawklords glanced at one another worriedly. They walked through. The Prince picked his way through the dimness until he reached the light switch.

'Here's hoping the generators are still on,' he said.

Brilliant strip lighting burst out of the darkness, painfully bright after the lightless conditions they had been used to.

The Prince blinked. He took in the chaotic state of the room, the bottles on the shelves had been raked off and smashed. Their liquids and powders allowed to mix and react on the horribly scarred bench-tops. Sensitive equipment which the scientist used to detect the Death Ray, was lying smashed and broken on the floor amid the drying, crystalline puddles.

Hot Plate himself was nowhere to be seen.

Frantically, the Prince began searching the laboratory. Then, Astral Al called to him in a shocked voice.

'Over here.'

Dreading what he would see, the Prince walked over to where Astral Al was standing. He was pointing at a large, tacky pool on the floor, unmistakably blood. A violent struggle had taken place, and the drying liquid had been splattered over the walls and cupboards.

The Prince looked stricken. 'So Mephis got him after all – just as he's most probably killed off all the life he had found at the Palace. The poor fellow. Poor us too. We've lost more than a loyal friend. Without him, it's doubtful whether we'll learn the secret of the Death Generator – or be able to combat it . . .'
He turned away, sick at heart.

Then his eyes rested unwittingly on the bloody wall above the sad puddle. In the mass of random splotches and streaks, lettering of some sort seemed to have been written. His heart jumped.

The dying scientist may have left them a message.

He scrutinized the crimson streaks closely.

There was no doubt about it. In huge, ill-formed handwriting the words 'Towering Minds . . .' had been written. Obviously it had not been intended to be intelligible to the soldiers who had shot him, and it had been left intact.

And it didn't mean much to the Hawklords either.

They stared blankly at the cryptic words, until Astral Al tugged at the distraught Prince's sleeve. 'Come on,' he said softly. 'We'd better go . . .'

THE BLIND CONQUEROR WORM

When Astral Al and the Prince returned, Parliament Hill was alive with sound and movement.

Someone had managed to find a few remnants of food and a weak and watery gruel had been concocted. Those of the Children that could make it on two feet were crowded round the blazing fire hungrily sipping at the hot liquid. Others were helping their less fortunate members by taking the food out to them where they lay. From the stage area – a piece of flattened ground well clear of the rotting trees – came the vibrant, welcome sound of the Hawkwind music. The players were still going strong, and so far there had been no trouble with the equipment.

'We just hope it lasts out long enough to clear the city of creeps,' Actonium Doug said sarcastically to Astral Al and the Sonic Prince, as they joined the throng round the fire. 'Want some of this?' He held out a rusty can of soup. The Hawklords shook their heads, gloomily.

'Sorry, I forgot,' he added hastily. 'You don't eat.'

'It's not so much that . . .' the Prince began. He shuffled uncomfortably, slowly shaking his head from side to side. He told them about the fate of the scientist. 'It's not so much the fact of losing a good friend and ally,' he concluded miserably, 'but his going kind of makes a mockery of all this . . .' He swept his arm around indicating the stage and the hill-top city.

'We might as well say good-bye to it . . . to life.'

Silence fell around the fire. Desperate minds tried to rationalize away the painful facts.

'Ye can't be serious, man!' Higgy shouted from the back of the group. He was holding a ladle in his hands, about to sip some of the hot gruel. He had made a remarkable recovery after the music had started playing.

'Never more so in my life,' the Prince replied. 'Work it out. Hot Plate was the only one who conceivably knew about the location of the Death Generator. He was working on that before he died. The rays are mounting in intensity all the time. We can't possibly hold out for ever, endlessly gigging. Sooner or later we're going to slip up, or something's going to happen to prevent us playing. Then, we're going to be exposed to a very high powered dose of rays. With Hot Plate, we had a chance of destroying the generator. Without him, we don't stand a chance. We don't have the equipment any more – it's all been wrecked – we don't know anyone who knows enough to suss it all out even if we had . . .' He broke off, emotionally. By now, the large circle round the fire had swollen as more curious Children had arrived.

'Maybe Hot Plate hadn't been able to find anything out, anyway,' someone suggested.

'He might have, on the other hand,' the Prince replied, lifting his head. 'And it's a chance we can't afford to miss . . . but it's true that we're OK for the time being,' he added, to avoid panic. 'We have time to try to do something . . .'

'There's no hope . . .' a hysterical voice interjected.

'Actually, there's a very slim hope,' Astral Al came to the Prince's rescue. 'We saw a message Hot Plate gave out before he died.'

'What did it say?' Stacia asked levelly from the front of the circle. She was hunched over her knees, staring fixedly into the flames.

The drummer recited the two mysterious words. The company fell silent racking their brains for the meaning.

'Towering minds . . .' Actonium Doug repeated. 'I feel I ought to know what that means, but you know what it's like . . .'

'Rings a bell,' the Prince admitted. 'What could it mean? Minds? Tower? Tower of minds . . .?'

Rudolph the Black flicked his fingers. 'Of course, it's that bloody Control contraption at Euston. You know, that thing that lay empty for years. Harry Hyams or someone built it. It eventually got taken over by the Government and used as a computer storage bank for the minds of the snotty nosed coddlers who couldn't take living outside any more. They're all still in there living it up so far as I know . . . Mephis must have left them alone, or sided with them, because the place is armed like a bloody warship. It's got God knows how many million minds on tape. Too spooky for me. Sends the shits . . .' He shivered, shaking his head, as the Prince interrupted.

'If Hot Plate was taken there . . . why?'

As he asked the question, the answer flashed back in his head. In the days when the Government's dwindling forces had tried vainly to contain the rioting, it had been common practice for insurgents to be shot and their still functionable minds transferred on to tape, for interrogation purposes.

It dawned on him what had probably happened. Mephis had grown impatient with the scientist's refusal to reveal information about the Hawklords and his research, and had had his body shot and his mind retained.

A feeling of overpowering revulsion for the perpetrator of the outrage boiled up inside him as he thought of the suffering their friend had undergone and was perhaps even now undergoing in his prison of electronic hardware.

Through clenched teeth, he enlightened the still puzzled assembly. 'Somehow – I don't care how – if he's in there, we've got to get him out.'

He turned abruptly and stalked over to the stage.

LUNGS OF PAIN

Thunder Rider let the sax fall round his grimy, sweating neck. He and Hound Master wearily left their positions as Astral Al took over the drums. Lemmy and the Baron let drop the instruments they had been making do with, and the Moorlock stepped in to carry on the wailing, sliding notes of steel.

The freed Hawklords walked with the Prince and the others who had followed him over from the fire. They found a place to rest, away from the volume of sound. They listened with increased dejection to the bad news. When he had finished, their faces were set firmly once more in their usual grim cast.

'We were just getting it nicely together,' the Baron complained tilting his brown hat back with his hand and wiping the sweat off his forehead. 'Now we've got to start all over a bloody gain. We should never have left Earth City in the first place. We'd have been better off fighting the way we were . . . with cool heads, and scientific knowhow. I'm beginning to think you were right, Light Lord.' He looked towards Liquid Len in acknowledgement.

'Like it or not, we're lumbered with being Hawklords now,' said Thunder Rider. 'What we've got to discuss is how to get access to poor Hot Plate's mind . . . if we can. Anyone know anything about that?' He glanced from face to face.

'Can't help you there, I'm afraid,' Actonium Doug said. 'I got to know about the interrogating through a reporter I met at a Press Release party. I don't know anything about the technical side.'

'Then we'll have to find out from someone who *does* know,' the Prince said agitatedly. 'What about the Reporters who work there? They must know the set-up.'

'Sure – they know all about it,' Actonium Doug replied. 'They have a funny kind of set-up running. The dudes who live inside the computer – they actually live in a sort of mental state – so far as I can make out, they're controlled by the Press. The Press are into a power trip, and Reporters can actually go inside the computer themselves to check out the scene and then come back out into their bodies again. Pretty weird if you ask me.'

'That's our answer, then!' Thunder Rider exclaimed. 'Somehow, we've got to get acquainted with a member of the Press.' A flicker of a smile crossed his weathered face.

'How do we do that?' the Prince asked.

'They're pretty down on sex,' Lord Rudolph said. 'In fact, nearly all the Straights are. I heard something ludicrous, that sex is punishable by death in Control. We could blackmail one of the Reporters and get what we want that way.'

Despite the extreme gravity of the situation, the seated Hawklords laughed in amazement at the disclosure.

'Well, the poor buggers!' the Baron chortled, unable to hold his sulky composure. 'I bet they're all as randy as hell! Getting one of them to comply should be a cinch.'

'The next question, then, is how do we go about trapping one of them?' Thunder Rider looked around once more. This time he didn't have to look far. All eyes had fallen on Stacia. She sat upright, angrily shaking her hair as she realized their intentions.

'Oh no you don't!' she retorted hotly. 'You aren't laying that on me!'

'Easy, easy,' Lord Rudolph, who sat beside her, reached for her gesturing hands and brought them down on to her lap again. 'You don't need to do anything improper, baby. All we need is a little bit of feminine charm . . .' He flashed his best smile.

Stacia pursed her lips.

'You don't need to do anything except get the guy in a compromising position,' he continued. 'Leave the rest up to us. I'll personally do the guy over if he tries anything.'

Their eyes gazed expectantly at the Hawklady. She wriggled uncomfortably. There was no way out. She was the only woman in the group, and unless the fellow they picked on happened to be gay – extremely unlikely, she told herself – they would be stuck. The future of humanity had been dumped into her lap. She couldn't honestly refuse.

139

'You bastard!' she declared.

'Good, then we can take it that you'll help,' Thunder Rider stated. 'Good on you. Now all we need to do is work out the details.'

'Like *who* are we going to choose, and where?' asked Lemmy, ominously, cleaning his nails with a huge matchete-like knife he had taken to carrying around with him. 'It's about time we had a bit of action. I'm getting bored.'

'It shouldn't be too hard to pick one of them up,' Actonium Doug said. 'While we combed London for spares to build the towers we got quite close to Control. Just a few blocks away there's this amazing little club on its own they've kept going, a hangover from the old days – what's left of the Straights, the Press, a few down and outs and, would you believe, a few seedy looking girls. One way or another, the landlord's managed to stay open mainly by keeping in well with the lot at Control. Must be about the only bloody surviving establishment of its kind in London. But if it's still there, it'd make the perfect pick-up place.'

'Sounds like a good old whore house to me!' the Baron chortled. 'Their kind of society must be pretty desperately in need of something like that. Well, that's it all sewn up! We've got 'em by the balls.' He rose to his feet. 'Might as well get it over with if it's got to be done.'

'You've forgotten one tiny little detail,' Stacia said, determined to get on an equal footing again. Everyone turned to face her. 'When we've trapped this guy, and I suppose photographed him . . . when we've got him to help us, which one of you super heroes is going to be the one who goes inside the computer to contact Hot Plate?'

'Uh? What do you mean?' the Baron looked blank.

'Well, you know, Dougy said,' she continued confidently, 'those Press guys go *inside* the computer when they want to communicate, and become one of the minds. Which one of you is going to do that?' She rested her hands on her hips and looked around at them with an amused expression.

'Me,' said Thunder Rider unexpectedly. It was his turn to take the stares. 'I'd already thought of that. I'm going to be the one who goes inside.' He looked at Stacia wryly. 'I kind of like the idea. Ready, Baron?' He stood up and joined the other Hawklord. 'I suggest we take a small party with us, no more than about five, including Stacia. That means we need two more people.' He looked around.

Hound Master and the Prince rose to join them. 'Count us in,' the Prince said. 'I'm not missing out on this for anything.'

The group of Hawklords was about to break up and attend to urgent matters, when the sound of a plane droning took their attention. They looked up. In the clear blue, afternoon sky, an Indian Airways 747 was limping over, its jets misfiring.

'Looks like we're still as popular as ever,' commented Actonium Doug happily. 'Now we've given Mephis the boot they're all starting to come in again. Like old times.'

'Mephis can't have got far away,' Thunder Rider warned. 'He'll be back on us the first chance we give him.'

ENCOUNTER OF MINDS

Seksass lay back in the chair inside the entrance booth. He fixed on the rubber skull cap and set the timing mechanism for his awakening. Then he examined the tiny blue pill in his hand. He held it up between forefinger and thumb.

'Here we go again,' he said, frustratedly, opening his mouth. He popped the pill inside and closed his eyes to wait, feeling the havoc its powerful chemical action played on his stomach ulcers.

The Twinny Triad Case still wasn't solved. That filthy Hippy music had started up again. A potential ally in Mephis to help fight off the overpowering forces, had fallen – the Colonel and all his men had vacated the city just as some kind of law and order was on the point of being returned.

He decided that today he would have to bring the case to an end, come what may. He would try a direct, surprise approach on the two known deviants, and hope to glean information on the whereabouts of the third – the arch villain, instigator of the whole horrible affair.

His mind dissolved in black streaks and whorls as he sank deep into the mini-death caused by the drug. Then the electronic appendages of the computer began to take over. Out of nothing came jumbled pictures and fleeting, mixed-up sensations as his mind began to re-orientate. He passed through the fragile biologic barrier that had contained him all his life. His mind 'awoke' abruptly in the vaporous, ghostly world of the computer.

He had materialized inside an unfamiliar room. Unconcerned, he stood up and faded through the door. He stepped out into a street. Instantly, he recognized the landmarks and the styling of the buildings. He knew whose world he was in. It was the creation of one of the ex-Mayors of London – Reginald Throssle, who had lived some fifteen years ago.

Perpetual twilight fogged the cobbled street, lined with Dickensian shop fronts and quaint gaslamps. There was a damp, clingy feeling in the air. Seksass was glad to get out of the morbid old man's fancy.

He accelerated and glided into a modern area, where the first contact lived. Most of the occupants in this mental zone thought alike, and the creation was a product of their collective minds. An ideal place to find saboteurs and other unsavoury characters.

He entered a skyscraper block and drifted up twenty-seven flights of stairs to a penthouse suite. Through the walls he saw John, one of the known Twinny Triads. He had been kept under observation for some time, without being made aware of the fact. From time to time he changed his reality by moving to other surroundings, but the Press now had an identity fix on him to make sure he didn't slip through the net again.

The suite was nicely imagined. It overlooked a faded, colourful version of the long gone Piccadilly Gardens in Manchester, the city John had originated from.

Seksass phased in through the walls. He stood in front of him.

A brief flicker of shock crossed the subject's face as he looked up from his writing desk, where he had been working. Immediately, he composed himself again, evasive and resentful of the intrusion.

'Invasion by Thought Police,' he stated mockingly. He had a snobbish, Queen's voice, and wore a monacle on a gold chain and a velvet smoking jacket. His finger-nails were well manicured. On the polished table top by his elbow stood a half-full bottle of Glen Grant, together with two empty glasses.

'Company?' queried the ghostly Seksass. He flashed his Press Card. Before John could stop him he had sprung across the room to an ornate French bureau where he had seen the subject's eyes inadvertantly stray. The wood felt spongy, smoky to the touch. He opened the mother-of-pearl doors. Inside, he discovered a silver-framed photograph among piles of papers. It showed an attractive, smartly dressed woman with long, golden hair and hazel eyes. On the reverse side it read: 'Jacqueline, love and kisses, January 1980.'

Seksass grinned wryly. John's face suffused with angry red blotches as he rose from his desk. 'My con-fid-en-tial property . . .' he spluttered.

'Private lives affect the rest of the community!' countered Seksass smugly. At long last, he had the lead he needed.

'I keep myself to myself!' John replied, hotly.

'You know that's impossible in here. You must conform to the standard morality. No sex. Where does Jacqueline live?' Once again, he caught the other off-guard. He spun round and crossed the plush, maroon carpet. He leafed the top sheet from the subject's writing pad.

'Hey! You can't do that!' John screamed, clutching at the Sex Reporter's arm. Seksass retaliated with a smart kick in his crutch. His subject collapsed on to a couch, gasping and moaning in pain. Rapidly, Seksass moved to the door, and smiled.

'Thanks,' he said. 'You've been a great help.'

He floated down the empty passageway outside and left the draughty building. He was still grinning with pleasure at the speed with which, after all the months of fruitless search, he had succeeded in acquiring the elusive information. The tactic of inflicting psychological pain never failed when the conditions were right. One could always count on an habitual reaction to stimuli when the occupants of the computer were challenged offguard, like that kick. Really, there was no need for John to have felt pain – after all, he was no more than a collection of memory particles. But, instinctively, he had.

He walked nonchalantly out through the quiet gardens of John's overpowering memory – a sunset below the roof-tops, with dusk just falling; a few pigeons exploding out of emaculately kept flower beds; the noise of sparrows drifting across from all corners of the square; spittle on the tarmac walks; a few tramps wrapped in the last edition of the Manchester Evening News already stretching out on the benches; the imagined noise of late, Saturday shoppers coming across from old Market Street.

Then the colours began to grey together, and he left the area, en route for a surprise interview with the girl.

Eventually, it was time to return. He could feel the clarity of the sensations that reached him beginning to blur and fade. Engulfing blackness took hold of him. Once again he became the mindless void of emptiness as the computer de-coded his mental engrams and re-stimulated the synapsal gaps inside his brain.

Images of the booth began to swirl around him. He was free of the effects. He lay still for a moment to regain his balance before unlocking his harness. When he felt better, he stood up and vacated the booth. He could never feel entirely well, he reminded himself as he staggered weakly across the hall, while the Hippy music was playing.

Groggily, he made his way up to the Editor's office to file his report. But the combined effects of his ulcer, the journey into the computer and the musical emanations told on him.

He opened the Great Man's door and almost fell inside. He managed to steady himself. Distantly, he realized that the Editor was in the throes of delivering a lecture to a roomful of Pupil Press Investigators. A film was playing. His boss was commenting on the images that were flickering on the screen.

With distant pleasure, Seksass realized that the film had been processed from the computer record of the assignment he had completed. Through the haze of approaching delirium he heard the Editor's authoritative voice barking on in its loud, clipped tones. He was explaining how the Press worked and why it was necessary to the computer occupants.

'. . . sensational raw material of this nature,' he said, referring to the picture of sexual acts on the screen, 'is carefully edited and with other news items, continuous news bulletins broadcast to the occupants. When slanted right, local internal news serves to define the permissible boundaries of amoral behaviour, strengthening the social structure of the community – a necessity in our case where virtually the entire population of the planet is living inside a computer, and all "individuals" are part and parcel of the same basic mind of man. Only minor indulgences in idiosyncratic behaviour by the individual is permitted. The nostalgic attempt by John, for instance, to reinstate his lost bodily self through seemingly overt sexual relationships with the deviant girl occupants, is strictly dangerous magic. It could never come off, but can never be allowed. One of the functions of our agency is to make sure by the process of feed-back already mentioned – a process incidentally, very similar to the methods of control used by the old newspapers of the pre-Dawn era, only a thousand times more effective – that this never happens.'

The Investigator pulled himself back through the door and closed it. He couldn't possibly see the Editor in the condition he was in. Instead, he decided to return to his office to rest. Later on he could go out to the club to see if a change of scenery helped any, and then if it did, he could approach The Editor again after the Government tea break.

HEADS OF COLD FLAME

A dull, regular thudding sounded in Seksass's ears as he started off, away from the heavily fortified entrance of Control. It was some time before he realized that it was his own heart beat, amplified with the recent strain and the excitement of the journey – he always got like this when he decided to find a woman, mainly because of the fearful penalties involved. Somehow, sex became more of an attraction when there was a punishment. The greater the punishment, the greater the attraction. When the sentence was death, as it was for a man in his trusted position, the urge became irresistable. Many of his colleagues had woken up one day to discover themselves to be in this unfortunate predicament.

One relieving factor was that most of the people who worked for the Government at Control had become hooked to vice, except for the very top echelons who gave out they were immune. It was these people one had to be careful of, and many a luckless Press Cadet had found his chances of promotion blackmailed from him by a game-playing rival.

He set his course for the Blue Lagoon club, situated in the heart of the ruins. The landscape had altered drastically since Mephis had arrived. Most of the ruins in the central area had been bulldozed totally flat for security reasons. Heaps of masonry had tumbled on to the road. Stilled demolition machinery lay about abandoned wherever the soldiers had left it.

At last he reached the club, a single, scarred rectangular building standing on its own on a razed plane of splintered wood, twisted metal and tumbled bricks.

He parked with difficulty. Pop music – *Country Roads* by John Denver – was playing from batteries of speaker cones mounted outside the house as he got out. He began to feel much better already as the cheery music soothed him.

Inside, the rickety, decorative building was almost empty, except for a few Reactionaries who lounged at the makeshift bar. They sneered at him as he entered the neutral territory, friends of no-one except themselves. Their one, single-minded objective seemed to be to smash Control and all its millions of minds.

He glanced round the silent room, heavy with thick, fading carpets and rich, musty upholstery. Some corner tables were occupied by enlightened colleagues with their girl friends, and he nodded to them.

Then he noticed the young, very attractive woman sitting at a table on her own. His heart started thumping again, as he made his way across to the bar. He ordered a drink – the landlord special, brewed from moulds and sugars; it had taken a lot of getting used to at first. Gradually everyone had grown to like the acrid, warming taste.

Outwardly composed, he walked over to her table.

'Mind if I sit here?' he asked her.

'Sit yourself where you like,' Stacia replied coldly.

Taken aback, he realized that there was something appealingly different about this woman. She was not a prostitute. For one thing, she had no client come on; for another she was too attractive. She had a strong, finely boned face, shining raven black hair and an unusually healthy, natural complexion. Her presence in a place like this mystified him. One part of him wondered dimly what she could possibly be up to. The other, stronger part fell in love with her.

At first he was cautious, not wanting to get involved intimately. But the literally fatal dangers of that soon washed away as they drank more and she became less cold. They chatted about each other's lives. The object of his love, though, still had a peculiar stiffness about her character that he couldn't fathom. They drank more. He ceased to think about her flaw – as he saw it – and indulged himself in his feelings.

Forgetful of the respectable assessment he had made of her, he asked to accompany her home. When she complied, he staggered to his feet and reeled across the room – much to the amusement of the Reactionaries.

They stepped outside in the painful brightness that glared off the heaps of shattered concrete and mortar. They got into

147

the car. He drove across several miles of the waist-high rubble until they arrived at a terrace of broken, rotting houses on the edges of the plateau. She asked him to stop outside the end terrace.

'You're a Hippy?' he asked, in sudden alarm.

'No,' she shook her head, pushing the door open. 'This was my father's place.'

He found himself in a dark hallway. Deep down inside him he started to panic. But she caught his arm and led him upstairs to a room on the first floor.

'Come on, this is what you wanted, isn't it?'

Confused, he followed her inside. His head was swimming. The room was drably and sparsely furnished with a bed, an arm chair and an antique screen.

He faced the woman, about to say something. Then he stopped as he realized that she was already partly undressed. She had half undone the buttons of her lace blouse, and was standing submissively before him.

His blood pounded.

There was still an air of detachedness about her that he didn't like. But all thoughts of protecting his life and his career had vanished. He would love her, whatever she was like, whatever she did to him . . . Desperately, he fell towards her and clasped her rigid figure in his embrace.

An explosion of bright flashes lit the room. With horror he realized that he had been tricked. He broke weakly away, clawing at the air for support.

Merciful darkness rushed up to him, as he fell unconscious to the floor.

'Ugh!' Stacia shivered with revulsion in the front seat, as the Sonic Prince started away in the reporter's car. The owner's reviving body lay across the knees of the other Hawklords, who were squashed uncomfortably in the back, dressed in straight clothes, and with attaché cases. 'Ugh! I couldn't stand him! Now that it's over, you're not getting me to do anything like it again.'

'Don't worry, we don't need to!' the Baron said. 'You did a good job. It won't be long now before we've got Flabby Features here showing us how to get at Hot Plate.'

'Then we can locate the Death Generator and . . . wooph!' the Sonic Prince let go of the steering wheel and threw his hands in the air. 'Earth City will be free to flourish like never before!' He was feeling pleased with the operation.

'We don't have much time to lose,' Thunder Rider said. 'We've got to get in this afternoon, otherwise his disappearance will be noticed.'

'Stage Two of the Plan!' Hound Master agreed. 'Forward to the stated place, Prince!'

They arrived at an intact block of buildings close to Control, and got out. Warily, they carried the complaining, struggling figure of the reporter through a doorway and into a back room. Stacia remained thankfully outside. She kept watch.

The man's face was white and taut. He obviously thought they were going to hit him.

'Don't worry,' the Baron said gruffly. 'Nothing's going to happen to you if you keep your cool. We're not murdering bastards like you lot.'

They helped him up, and gave him some water. The reporter drank it thirstily.

'What do you want then?' he gasped. 'I'll do anything you like, but don't let those pics get into the wrong hands,' he blabbered.

Thunder Rider patted the Moorlock's camera which hung

inside the smooth suit jacket he was wearing. 'Like we said, don't worry. If you do what we say, you can do what you want with them.'

Hurriedly, he explained what they wanted.

There was a pause as their prisoner digested the plans.

'You can't do that!' he started, excitedly. 'It'd never come off! We'd all be shot as soon as we reached the guards. They aren't fools . . .'

Lord Rudolph approached the drooling man and took him by the collar. He put on his fiercest expression. 'Listen, it will come off, and you're going to make sure that it does, or . . .' He indicated the bulge of the camera.

'OK, OK,' the other spoke breathlessly. 'We'll do it. But I'll still run a risk, whatever I do.'

'*We're* running the risks, mate,' the Baron retorted angrily. '*You've* already *run* yours.'

Seksass gulped as the Hawklord's meaning became crystal clear.

'Right,' Thunder Rider said, looking around. 'Everyone ready?'

They smoothed themselves over. They tucked the stray wisps of hair down inside their collars and brushed particles of dirt off their suits.

Hound Master and the Baron tidied up Seksass. Then they filed outside.

'All clear?' Thunder Rider asked Stacia.

'Quiet,' she replied, recovered somewhat. 'They've not got the manpower to patrol anywhere except around the base of the tower. I walked to the end of the row and had a peep.'

'Good. Let's get going, then,' Thunder Rider turned to the Baron and the Sonic Prince. He unstrapped his camera and handed it to Hound Master. Stacia and Hound Master would keep watch on them as they tackled the guards. If necessary, they would run for help.

They got into the car and drove cautiously to the corner of the street. From here, they could see the base of Control a few blocks away. Perfectly symmetrical, it towered glassily out of the jagged disarray of the ruins. A platoon of guards patrolled its base, each armed with sub-machine guns and belts of grenades. Armoured, manned personnel carriers were stationed at the corners, covering all possible routes of access.

'Right!' Thunder Rider hissed at Seksass. 'Change places with me and drive us up.'

Unwillingly, the Press Reporter did as he was told.

'You better act natural!' the Baron growled from the back seat. They started off again, bumpily. 'Remember. If anything goes wrong and we don't return, that camera back there gets shown around.'

The driver flinched. Then he became perfectly composed under the threat of certain death.

The car drew smoothly to a halt beside the steps that led up to the entrance. So far, the soldiers hadn't interrupted their routine. Now four of them came forward. They opened the car doors, guns at the ready.

'Their usual procedure,' Seksass whispered through the corner of his mouth.

The hard, featureless faces of the soldiers came briefly into view as the doors were politely but firmly opened. The disguised Hawklords held on to their attaché cases and climbed out. Wordlessly, Seksass produced his identity card and showed it to the guard by his door. The man grunted. He waved him away.

Likewise, the three Hawklords produced their faked cards. The Sonic Prince switched on a modified low power version of his music gun. It was hidden in his pocket. With its focussing nozzle taken off and its volume down, it immediately began to send out soundless rays in all directions.

The effect on the guards, already suffering from the effects of the live music, was instant. They visibly gulped and shook under their poker straight faces.

'All right,' one of them grunted miserably, after the cards had been only cursorily examined. 'You're OK.'

Relieved, the Hawklords began to climb the steps, chatting casually. Then, they overheard the voice of one of the soldiers talking to his companions.

'I'm not satisfied . . .'

They tensed again. Seksass sagged under the strain.

'Halt!'

They halted. Heavy boots clattered up the steps.

'Show your cards again,' a rock faced guard demanded.

'Of course,' Thunder Rider smiled politely, drawing his card out of his pocket. He held it for them to examine, wondering how they were going to escape.

Then from across the street, came a clatter of machine-gun fire followed by a loud explosion. Part of the wide flight of steps errupted in smoke and flame. The air suddenly filled with flying chips of concrete.

Aghast, the Hawklords and guards turned towards the commotion. A mob of raggedly clothed people had appeared in the street, shouting and firing at the tower. The Baron realized what was happening. His face cracked into a broad grin, and he began to push them up the steps, away from the line of fire.

'It's the bloody Reactionaries!' he cried. 'They've staged a siege. What a time to do it!'

Without further prompting, they ran up the steps and through the swing doors. Seksass raced to the lift. They followed him inside. At the second floor the doors opened and they walked calmly out across the marble floor.

No-one payed them any attention as they made their way over to the booths. The few Straights who were there were at the windows, watching what was happening outside.

Seksass went to the hatches, while they waited for him at a vacant booth. He returned a moment later with two pills and two access cards.

'What have you got two for?' Thunder Rider asked, suspiciously.

'One for you, and one for him . . . whoever it's to be.'

'There's no other. I'm the only one who's going in,' Thunder Rider stated.

'How do you propose to get your friend's mind out, then?' asked the Reporter, genuinely amazed.

'What do you mean?' the Baron asked aggressively. 'Don't you try any funny business mate, or you know what'll happen . . .'

'I'm not being funny!' Seksass hissed in a loud whisper. He glanced nervously over his shoulder. 'If you want to get him out, you need someone to act as a receiver.'

There was an ominous silence.

'What? To take his mind in . . . inside . . .'

'To put two minds in one body. It's the only way. Your friend's body will have been destroyed.'

The Hawklords thought rapidly.

'Someone will have to volunteer,' Thunder Rider said. 'We've got no time to waste.'

'It'll have to be you, Baron,' said the Prince. 'Lord Rudolph and I are the only ones with the right technical knowledge. We'll have to stay behind to make sure we don't get tricked by our friend here.'

A cold shudder ran down the Baron's spine. He knew there was no way he could refuse. It seemed that before long, everyone would have to make their fair share of sacrifices, until the malign Death Generator was overthrown.

'What will happen to me?' he asked Seksass gruffly.

'You'll be OK,' the other assured him. 'As a person you won't disappear, if that's what you're bothered about. Come on, quickly, make up your mind . . . they'll be on to us any minute.'

The Baron hesitated, disliking the way the tables had been reversed. Finally, he consented.

'Right,' the Reporter said. 'Quickly, get in there.' He indicated a vacant booth. 'Wait for me – I'll be back in a minute. We go in this one,' he said to Thunder Rider.

Watched by Lord Rudolph and the Prince, Seksass strapped the tall Hawklord into position. He put on the skull cap. Then he pressed the token into the slot among the dials and set the timing mechanism. He handed Thunder Rider the blue pill.

'Here. Take this. Once you cross the barrier, you'll have just three minutes in which to find your friend. I daren't give you any longer.'

Thunder Rider took the tiny pill and placed it on his tongue. Then he lay back tensely and waited.

The booth was cool and fresh. A faint rubbery smell came from the skull cap. Gradually, his surroundings began to fade and panic gripped him. But fighting was no use. The heavy blackness took hold of him. It sucked him down, away from the twisting, bending face of the Reporter – the last impression he had of his existence.

FRAGMENTS OF THE WIND

Out of the lifeless, timeless limbo came a sickening vortex of lines and shapes. They spun crazily in front of the Hawklord, flickering and flashing like an old movie. He fought his way up to the top of the tunnel, struggling for breath. Then, the spinning stopped. The coloured patterns came together.

Hazily, he made out where he was. It was a factory of some kind. Work benches with machinery on them covered the floors. A massively exaggerated clock was fixed on the far wall, sternly surveying the motionless scene. The factory was deserted. It was immaculately clean, as though no-one had ever worked there.

Something was wrong with the reality. The colours seemed jaded. The solid objects, like the furniture, didn't seem solid. They reminded him of holograms – three-dimensional pictures he had seen projected by laser beams. He looked down at his body. It looked the same. He touched it. It felt cold and cheesy. Cautiously, he reached out an arm and touched one of the wooden benches. It felt spongy. He pressed harder. To his horror, his arm began to go through the wood. Instinctively, he drew it away – still intact.

He remembered his mission. If the Reactionaries managed to break in, they would probably bomb the computer. If they were overpowered by the guards, then the guards would remember they had four intruders to find. Either way, he didn't fancy the consequences.

He started to walk down the gangway leading to the door, his feet sinking into the soft wooden floorboards. The further he walked, the further he sank, until he was up to his knees.

Nervously, he wished he were not so heavy. He put effort into trying to walk more lightly. Thereafter the wood became shallower. He managed to walk on its polished surface.

The trick of movement, he suddenly realized, was to use his thought power.

His confidence gathering, he reached the door. Gently, he pushed it open. He was about to step through. A voice came from behind him.

'You've come in reply to the employment advert, have you?'

He spun round. At the end of the gangway stood the ghostly shape of a man. He was dressed in a black suit, and had a pink carnation in his buttonhole.

'You needn't slink away like that, girl!' the figure said. 'I won't bite you! Come over here and let me have a closer look at you.' The man was squinting at him.

Thunder Rider decided to comply . . . in the hope of gaining knowledge of Hot Plate's whereabouts – though he approached with caution, disliking the way he had been referred to as a girl.

'That's a good girl. Come on now, let me see you . . . why, you're *not* a girl!' the man exclaimed, shocked. His manner changed to indignation. 'You're another of those long haired hippies! Listen here!' he exclaimed, backing away slightly. 'We came here to get rid of the likes of you . . . how the dickens did you get in, anyway? Has the system broken down out there? God in tarnation! I hope not, or we're all doomed!' He crossed his chest.

Confused, Thunder Rider looked down at his body. He expected to see the suit he had been wearing when he entered. In its place were his usual clothes. He touched his long, straggly hair. Another fact dawned on him. In here, there was no hiding from one's true identity. Whatever his appearance, though, he had had enough of Mr Dickens.

'Listen to me!' he demanded in annoyance, causing the man to jump back. 'It's true – your system's breaking down. Right

155

this minute the Reactionaries are trying to break in. But of that, I'm no part . . .' He broke off, wondering what he could say to this man to get him to listen to him.

'I'm an agent . . .' he said the first thing that came into his head. '. . . and I'm looking for a very dangerous man who has been put in here. He has with him an unstable psi-device which could wreck the entire computer. You've got to tell me where I can find him.'

The effect of these words on the man was instant. He paled.

'Wreck the entire computer? We've paid a lot of money to be here, you know! What sort of man is this?'

'A scientist.' Thunder Rider described Hot Plate briefly.

'A snooping boffin! I thought as much . . . Once you've started something good, you never leave it alone!' the man cried out. 'I don't know where he is. Why should I know that, out of all the millions of people in here?' He calmed down. Then he said thoughtfully, 'He was *put* in here, you say? Done something wrong?'

Thunder Rider nodded. 'For interrogation.'

'Ah well, that casts a different light on things! Those sort of people usually end up in the Work House.'

'The Work House?' Thunder Rider asked, astonished.

'Well you don't think we want them living with us, do you? We had to invent a place for them. It was an insult to us to put them here in the first place. The Army think they can use our computer like a private toy. Well it's just not on, and when I get out of here I shall write to my . . .'

'Yes, yes,' Thunder Rider said impatiently. 'Where's the Work House? The sooner I get to the scientist, the sooner I can get that device off him.'

The man fiddled with his flower. 'Of course, the device. Uh!' he looked up. 'What do you mean? Tell you where? I can't tell you that! There aren't any directions here!'

'Then how do I get there?'

'You can't, unless you think your way around . . . you have to use your head here, you know!' he added reproachfully.

'We don't have much time to spare,' Thunder Rider reminded him. 'Can you show me the way?'

The man looked horrified.

'What? Leave my shop? Never! I've spent years building up this business – I've thought it up from scratch, right down to the . . .'

'Bugger your shop!' Thunder Rider exploded. 'We have precisely two minutes – external time – to get that man out of here. Otherwise . . .'

He advanced menacingly.

'Under the circumstances, I quite see your point,' the other said hastily. 'You'll have to hang on though . . .' He held out his hand, distastefully. The Hawklord took hold of it, and almost dropped it again. It felt like the cold flesh of a corpse.

'I've never had to leave my postulate the whole time I've been in here,' the man complained as they set off. The Hawklord held on grimly. They began falling through the floors. Then they stopped.

'You'll have to try to *come* with me, otherwise it's no use!' he said in exasperation. 'Think!'

Thunder Rider tried to get into the feel of being an airborne passenger.

Abruptly, they were on a busy main road outside the factory. Cars and lorries hissed past on the superhighway. There were no drivers inside the cabins. Before Thunder Rider could comment, the scenery dissolved into grey. A second later, a new landscape zoomed out at them. It was a desert. Close by, stood a long, low building. It was featureless, and for some reason reminded Thunder Rider of a slaughterhouse.

'*That's* the Work House!' Mr Dickens said to him proudly. 'We built it in the most inhospitable place we could dream up. Now you're on your own.'

'You certainly did that, all right,' Thunder Rider murmured, staggered by the constant surprises this world held. He turned, but the factory boss had gone. He faced the slaughterhouse. He began walking as lightly as he could over the sand towards it. He began running.

Soon, he stood outside the large, sliding doors. He was about to hammer on them. Then he thought better of the idea.

Moving forward as heavily as he could, he phased his body through the metal.

Inside, a horrifying, breath-catching sight met his eyes. In his determination to move through the wall, he had apparently projected himself up on to scaffolding of some sort.

From the thin bar he perched on, he could see down into the rest of the structure. Standing, sitting, lying, floating among the bars were scores of human figures. Most of them wore miserably unhappy expressions. The remainder looked as though they had already cracked up.

Fearfully, Thunder Rider looked round for the way out. Terrified, he realized that the scaffolding, or whatever it was, together with its human flotsam, extended in all directions – above, below, all sides.

He forced himself to be calm. It was a dream, he told himself. When the three minutes were up, he would return to his body.

When the three minutes were up!

Anxiously, he looked around for Hot Plate. He was wondering how he was going to begin looking for him when a friendly, high-pitched voice came from behind.

'Looking for me, Thunder Rider?'

He turned frozenly. There, floating among the metal tubing, was the scientist.

'Hot Plate! Of all the coincidences!'

'Not really, old chap!' the scientist replied, grinning. 'All this is deceiving.' He waved his arms at the scaffolding. 'Took me a long time to work it out. In actual fact, only a handful of us are imprisoned in this mental nightmare society has schemed up for us. The structure you see extending beyond a certain point is a mirror image of us, endlessly reflected back and forth into for ever. You can move through it, too – it's three-dimensional. But all you do is move back into your own position again . . . like Einstein's bounded yet infinite universe. If you keep travelling long enough in any direction you eventually arrive back at your starting place.'

Thunder Rider's mind baulked in amazement. 'Why don't you escape?'

'That's the reason! This place is called the Work House

because you have to *work hard*, i.e. *think hard*, to get out. I stopped thinking when I realized the task was impossible. As we have no bodies to return to, we are here for all time – until the computer is turned off. Only the Press can get in and out.'

'Not any more!' Thunder Rider smiled. 'I fixed us both up some bodies.'

He slapped the other on his back. 'Good to see you, Hot Plate. We've all missed you.'

'Me too. I wondered how long it would be before you got the message I left – or even if you'd get it at all. I'll be glad to get . . .' He stopped. They both realized that he would never again be able to occupy his old bodily shape. He looked upset. 'What have you got rigged up for me, Thunder Rider?' he asked.

'You'll see,' Thunder Rider replied, unhappily. 'You'll be OK, don't worry.'

The darkness below the surface tugged at his mind.

'Quick! Time's up!' He thought desperately what he should do next. The scenery grew dimmer. It began to spin round and he felt sick. An idea came.

'Hold my hand!' he shouted to the scientist. He reached out and grabbed the flailing arm. He began falling into the dark well. Something heavy tugged after him. He let go his mind and fell into the blank nothingness . . .

BRAINSTORM

From the drawing room of Asgard House the man in white looked out through the large French windows at the sweeping bank of freshly mown lawns. It curved gently away down towards the flower gardens and the figures of the other guests taking the afternoon sun in deck chairs.

It had been the same view for weeks as the unusual heat-wave had continued. There seemed to be no let-up in the clear

159

blue skies and the hot sun, nor was any forecast.

The dreams had started soon after he had moved into Asgard House. At first they came sporadically with their omens of doom, and their content hadn't been all that heavy. But gradually they had increased in frequency until now he received them nightly. The most alarming and puzzling aspect to him personally was that his crew were always depicted as being in danger. They were shown to be lost and struggling in the terrifying scenes of destruction.

The cinematic dreams had commenced with shots of the wretched environment, then humanity in a constant state of war. As the months drifted by he had gradually been allowed to see more. The world lay devastated. Only a few survivors remained, battling against the unequal odds. His crew were out there somewhere in mortal danger, and he was never permitted to see where. The dreams never showed specific details.

When he called his crew up individually on the phone, they were always in. In fact they must be getting fed up with his nightly checks on them, he thought in exasperation.

For the thousandth time he resisted the urge to scream out with frustration. He tried to calm himself. Everything was normal, he told himself.

He reached for the bottle of pills on the polished veneer beside him. He unscrewed the cap and shook two tablets out into his mouth. Then he sat back and relaxed again, watching the guests sunning themselves. He had invited his friends to steady his nerves and help him take his mind off the subject of the dreams. But all they did was laze around all day, sunning themselves and drinking his booze.

He continued staring abjectly out of the open doors. Beyond the chairs and the blooming gardens, the green causeway swept down to meet the rhododendrons and cyprus trees. From behind the trees came occasional glimpses of the red double-decker buses making their journeys into town.

The scene in his new Hampstead home seemed normal.

If only he could get someone to listen to him. But the few whom he had told thought there was little significance in them.

They chose not to believe.

In desperation, he brought his arm up to the sides of his greying head and pressed his hands hard against the bone. His prematurely lined face contorted with the tension he tried to release. His fingers grew white.

He kept the accumulated, unbearable feelings of frustration inside him. It was the only way to avoid going completely out of his mind.

SCREAMS OF THE DYING

The sound of shouting and gun shots from outside seemed to be diminishing. Tensely the Sonic Prince leant over the inert body of Thunder Rider, trying to determine whether or not there was any life in the staring eyes. He had been watching Seksass closely, but the Reporter had done nothing to arouse his suspicions.

'Listen,' the Prince said to him anxiously. 'You said he would be coming round. He's not.'

'He will. Give him time,' the other replied. He was shaking from fear of being caught by the guards. Now he had been seen with the Hawklords, he would be branded as a traitor and shot.

The timer in the booth read three minutes fifteen seconds . . . Thunder Rider began to stir. A groan cracked from his lips. His eyes blinked slowly several times. Then he brought his freed arms together. He clasped his hands.

'Thunder Rider!' Lord Rudolph slapped his face. 'Hurry it up!'

Seksass disappeared. A moment later he re-emerged with the staggering Baron.

The Baron shook his arm free, angrily. 'Get your hands off me!' Shaking his head, he went to help revive Thunder Rider. Together, the three of them got him out of the booth and they walked him up and down outside. Eventually, a more alert look came back into his eyes.

'OK,' he said weakly. 'Let's get out.'

Together, they ran for the lift shaft, watched by a crowd of grey-uniformed employees. The Sonic Prince took the rear, warning them off with his music gun.

Seksass called a lift. Then he waved them towards the emergency stairs nearby. They clattered down the stairs, and emerged into the entrance hall on the ground floor.

Ahead of them, through the glass swing doors, the fighting was still going on. The soldiers had gained the upper hand and were finishing off the remaining pockets of resistance who were hiding in the buildings opposite. Some of the guards had retired into the building. They spun round when they approached. Before the Hawklords could fire their weapons, a spray of bullets was fired into them. The unhappy Reporter caught the brunt. He slid slowly to the floor clutching at his crimson chest. His eyes gazed uncomprehendingly at the Hawklords as he fell, and words formed on his lips, but he rolled away and lay still.

Then, Hawkwind music shrieked out jarringly in the echoing hallway. It was the guards' turn to roll. Their weapons clattered to the floor. They fell in agony, clutching at their heads and hearts.

The Hawklords ran to the doors and flung them open, music guns turned full up. They pointed them at random into the backs of the soldiers. They ran zig-zagging down the steps. Playing the guns continuously over their shoulders, they darted across the road.

Most of the soldiers were now incapacitated by the music, and in their wake they caught a glimpse of the victorious Reactionaries leaping out from their shelters and running towards the tower steps.

Stacia and Hound Master were waiting for them in the Reporter's car, as the three Hawklords sped round the corner of the block. They backed up when they saw them coming. Stacia flung open the doors. They clambered inside.

'Just get out of here as fast as you can!' Thunder Rider

yelled at Hound Master. The car engine whined and the gears crunched together. The car shot forward, throwing them back in their seats.

'That how you mean?' Hound Master grinned. 'Why the hurry?'

'You'll see . . .'

Behind them a brilliant light burst, followed by a loud, rumbling explosion that shook the roadway. Sheets of flame licked up the side of the tall Control tower. Then, a vast explosion erupted from inside the doomed building as its power supplies caught. The concrete materials it was made from began to de-stress. The floors bulged out, pushed by a fierce red glow. Then they began to collapse slowly downward on top of one another. An artichoke-like cloud appeared, spurting out dust and smoke.

Hound Master gave the car all it had got, before the debris started showering down. Swerving and skidding round corners and obstacles, he drove on for about five minutes in silence. Then, he slowed the car down.

'Looks like we're clear,' he said shakenly.

'I thought we'd had our lot there!' said the Baron, as they drove more sedately back towards Parliament Hill. 'That's another bloody ruin on the map . . . and another big drop in the population,' he added. 'The Reactionaries must have gone up with her. They obviously didn't expect to set off the whole bloody works.'

'All thanks to our music,' Thunder Rider added morosely.

'Don't take it that way,' the Baron responded with feeling. 'It couldn't be helped. It isn't such a bad thing anyway, you know. They would have got us, or others like them would have got us, in the end.'

'I know that,' Thunder Rider persisted. 'But there were a lot of innocent lives lost . . .'

'It couldn't be *helped*,' the Baron reasserted. 'What else could we have . . .'

His sentence was cut short by a further tremoring in the ground. The explosion behind them had finished. Only a drifting pall of black smoke now marked the spot where

Control had stood. The new tremors were much stronger. They seemed to come from all around.

They mounted in intensity, until the landscape outside became a blur of jogging, vibrating forms. Hound Master braked suddenly, stopping the car.

A blunt cold pain gnawed at their insides. Their skins felt clammy.

'Uh, Christ! Now what?' the Baron shouted out, his face contorted with pain. He held on to his seat as the shaking continued to grow worse. The feeling was similar to that produced by the Death Generator, only more accute.

Outside the car, the vibrating air was beginning to fill with clouds of choking, impenetrable dust. Over the low rumbling sound that was generated came the loud, harsh roar of crashing masonry as buildings started to collapse around them.

When the effects were approaching the threshold of bearability the trembling stopped. The obnoxious physical sensations subsided. Soon, apart from the occasional fall of bricks outside somewhere in the dust, the Hawklords were sitting in an intense silence.

'I thought we were supposed to be immune to the Horrors,' Thunder Rider managed at last.

'Maybe our immunity is wearing off,' Stacia remarked, sarcastically. She was nursing a bruised forehead where she had banged into the windscreen.

'Or maybe,' came a peculiar, high-pitched voice from the back seat, 'the intensity of the Death Generator was momentarily stepped up.'

Astonished, they turned. The Baron was sitting bolt upright. His eyes were staring blankly ahead of him. His mouth was moving.

'Hot . . . Plate!' Hound Master pronounced uncertainly, in recognition of the voice. An eerie, prickly sensation ran up and down his spine.

'That feeling could only be attributed to the Horrors. But the fact we haven't got the Horrors now and didn't have them before the attack, leads me to conclude that either the Generator was somehow stepped up, or momentarily, our protective powers decreased. Myself, I believe the former explanation to be more likely,' Hot Plate spoke.

The Hawklords fought to speak through the vocal paralysis that gripped them. In their hurry to escape, they had forgotten about the mind transfer. They had not even had the time to check if the operation had been successful – or if they had been tricked. But there was no denying now that the dead Reporter had done his work – good or bad it remained to be seen.

'Well . . . that's a possibility,' said Thunder Rider at last, struggling for words. Like the others, he was unable to grasp the idea of the Baron being anyone but the Baron.

They began to adjust to the new member – a mental hydra with two minds. As Hound Master got the car underway again, they began to ask it questions.

'What about the Baron . . . can he hear what's going on, and speak back . . .?' Stacia asked in a concerned voice.

In reply to her question, the glazed eyes on the Hydra's face flickered, and the facial muscles altered slightly. Then the deeper voice of the Baron croaked out.

'I can hear you all right!' he said, irritably. 'But it's hard getting it together. Still, it's got easier already, so I'll . . . we'll,' he corrected, 'We'll get along OK together, I suppose . . . This is the weirdest trip I've been on, I don't mind telling you,' he added. 'This beats everything. I wouldn't like to live like this for ever. I hope we can figure a way out of it . . . bloody Jesus!' he exploded. 'There's not a single private thought left in my head! Hot Plate's no saint either, I've discovered.' The Hydra gave a peculiar, comic grimace. Then its face altered again. A new expression appeared.

'Don't worry Baron!' the high voice of Hot Plate said

humorously. 'I'll not reveal any of your little secrets if you don't reveal any of mine!'

Hound Master stared unbelievingly ahead of him at the road. Events were happening faster than he could adjust to. Nothing seemed real any more. Anything could happen – and usually did. He felt uncomfortable because some other thing was trying to get at him, too. It was some disturbance he had inside him, but he couldn't think what it was.

Staggered by what had taken place, the Prince spoke next. 'What did you find out about the Death Generator?' he asked the part of the Hydra that was Hot Plate.

An expression of reluctance flashed across its face. At first, it didn't reply. Then the scientist spoke through its lips.

'Thought you'd ask me that sooner or later,' Hot Plate said, evasively. 'Before Mephis got his sadistic hands on me I managed to find out quite a lot. But my discovery isn't going to make life easier for us. It might make us feel like giving up . . .'

'Go on, go on,' Hound Master said impatiently from the driving seat. 'We've taken everything else. We can take one more thing.'

'Well, I'm afraid to have to tell you that the Death Generator is virtually unstoppable . . . short of taking the whole planet to bits. Remember I was trying to locate it by tracing the source of the Death Rays? Well, I succeeded. I'm almost one hundred per cent certain that it's buried at the centre of the Earth!'

'Then we'll never be able to stop the Death Ray . . .' Stacia gasped, an expression of horror on her face.

'Doesn't look like it,' replied the scientist grimly. 'I don't see how. I also discovered that it's still rising in intensity – that's partly why I think that little jolt we received before was a freak taste of stepped up Horrors. To make things worse, the intensity is rising more strongly and at a faster rate than our music. It'll only be a matter of time before the effects escalate to such a degree, our weapons will be powerless to . . .'

'You said our magic only protects us up to a certain level,' intoned Thunder Rider. 'That means we're all going to be gonners. First the Children will die, then us.'

No-one commented.

Hound Master squirmed uncomfortably in his seat as he listened. Something was trying to come over him, but he kept shaking it off. He shook himself and tried to concentrate on driving – but the strange feeling persisted. At first he wasn't sure whether it was his reaction to the terrifying news. But then he realized that it was to do with thoughts already inside his head. Since they had become Hawklords his ability to perceive supernormally had increased. Uncomfortably, he tried to allow whatever was tying to happen, to happen. But the feeling for some reason couldn't quite form.

Through a panic of confusing thoughts and impressions he looked out at the road ahead. They were only about half way to the Hill. Anxiously, he gripped the wheel. He tried to bring his head under control.

But everything was falling to bits.

THE COLD, DYING WINDS OF EARTH

'We can't let Earth die!' Hound Master suddenly screamed.

The strange, psychic attack now had him fully in its grip. It was not altogether unpleasant – in other circumstances it could have been ecstatic. But it exaggerated his feelings. He was unable to think properly. His body felt flexible and warm. Even the car and the crumbling streets outside seemed to waver and bend. He fought to keep control of the steering wheel. He couldn't allow himself to let go – though he wanted to with all his heart.

Then, on top of the fluid, melting landscape outside his head, he saw the ghostly outlines of a grassy plain superimpose itself. He watched with disbelief and horror. Instinctively, he realised that the scene was an ancient one, pre-cars, pre-rockets, pre-pollution.

In the distance he saw the towers of an unfamiliar city. On the yellowed grass in front of him were scattered human skulls and bones, and the freshly slaughtered bodies of strangely dressed warriors. The sky was a bloody red, pierced by the crescent of a younger Moon. Fearfully, he noticed that the pale, aquiline form was surrounded by great birds of prey, shrieking and flapping over the dead and dying.

Desperately, he fought to dispell the vision. But it persisted. The fated plain became more real and vivid. The smell of the blood wafted to him on an otherwise fresh and cool breeze. From somewhere behind came the rustle of living leaves. By his side, a horse whinnied.

Startled, he turned. Other, living warriors on horseback were assembled there. There were nine men altogether, naked except for loincloths and shiny, armoured girdles protecting their vitals; wide, shiny arm-bands, and sturdy boots decorated with mysterious designs. On their heads were fierce helmets, made of antlers, eagles' wings and horns. Each warrior carried a bladed lance of lethal length and keenness. At their sides, harnessed to the sleek and gleaming steeds upon which they rode, were sheathed mighty jewelled swords, each heavy enough for three ordinary men to wield, and solid, glinting shields bearing the proud and fearful emblem of the Hawk.

In awe, he realized that they must be the Hawklords of old – remote ancestor agents of the Hawk Gods, who like themselves were obliged to lead the ceaseless fight against the Forces of Darkness and Chaos for all time.

As suddenly as the scene came, it began to disappear. The mental force that had taken him there through time and space began to lift him through the blurring colours and into a grey, cold void.

The void disappeared and he found himself standing on a high, windy ridge, surveying a lush valley. At this distance, he could see that the plants and trees below him were like nothing he had seen before. Their huge leaves, tinted with reds and blues, grew thick and close on the ground. Many small clearings had been made among them. He noticed modern-looking

168

buildings with clean, simple lines, and minuscule people scarcely discernible moving about in their grounds.

His eyes took in the scene slowly. His mind tried to adjust to the boggling change. Gradually, he made out the dimensions of a massive, translucent bubble spread over the peaceful valley, almost indistinguishable from the air.

He became painfully aware of the barren, rocky mountain chain upon which he stood. As he watched the scene, a fleet of benign-looking saucer-shaped craft appeared in the sky. They cast deathly shadows on the paradisical civilization in the valley below. Out of their bellies stabbed burning rays which ate through the protective bubble and scorched the earth. In seconds, the valley had become an acrid patch of burning, smoking wasteland – an entire people, or so it seemed, wiped out before his eyes. A desperate, useless feeling welled up inside him.

Sickened, he turned away. A tall, robed figure stood beside him. Its eyes were burning red, like the rays. Its skin was a smooth, pewter colour. The being shimmered and flickered, as though projected from a great distance across time and space. As he watched, its mouth opened in a crack. No sound issued forth, though words formed inside his head.

'Do not be afraid,' the voice said. 'The form you see before you is a manifestation for you to focus on. Its looks were deemed appropriate for your tastes, but unfortunately the appreciation of beauty is subjective – even to Gods!' The creature laughed.

The Hawklord struggled to find words, but he felt drained of energy. He could only listen to the Hawk God in timid fascination.

'The beautiful race you have witnessed – the Baasark – were not so beautiful as you suppose. They took Earth from the Throdmyke centuries earlier, after their own home in a distant galaxy had been devastated. The Throdmyke – in the saucers – were merely repaying the Baasark a debt. The township you saw represents only a small fraction of the Baasark population, and the Throdmyke will not slip so easily through the defences of their other towns. But look . . .'

Hound Master looked to where the figure indicated. In the sky above the still smoking valley the Throdmyke had assembled their craft. Now a different ray emanated from their open hatches. Shafts of lurid, greenish light struck the ground. The rays tore effortlessly into the earth, gouging out a huge vertical passageway he could see no bottom to. From the underside of one of the craft, a cylindical object appeared, falling rapidly. It neared the open vent, and accelerated. It shot into the bottomless dark. Abruptly, the rays stopped. The abyss walls began to melt and slide together, sealing the strange machine inside the planet for ever.

'Ever since this time,' the Hawk God continued, 'the two races have been using Earth as a battleground. Drop-out elements from both societies, appalled by the magnitude of the atrocities, separated from their parents and went to live in caves. They were your descendents – Humanity.

'Unfortunately, your race was also affected by the Death Generator left behind, as you have just seen, by the Throdmyke.'

The sinister craft, their task performed, had fled to the edge of the horizon. Now, the valley was as barren and bleak as the windy ridge. He shivered. The figure of the God began to fade away, and then reasserted itself more strongly.

'The Throdmyke and the Baasark live no longer, but their war still goes on inside your heads – it is the eternal struggle between God (represented by the Baasark) and Evil (the Throdmyke). After centuries of oppression by the Throdmyke, Baasark forces in your own time are rising once again. *Their* weapon lies not in the centre of the Earth, but in your genes.

'Long ago, your cave-dwelling descendents were exposed to a controlling force which programmed you to fight the Evil, impulsive side of Mankind's character whenever it became dominant. It gave Baasark forces control over your Conscience. Twice in the history of Man, this programming has been triggered off by the Death Generator's fluctuations, and a magical battle has ensued between Men – some of whom have been influenced to the side of Evil, others to the side of Good. The legends of Merlin and King Arthur and the Hawklords, go back to the first Magical Era. Now, in your time, another era has dawned – the Throdmyke legacy of hatred and bitterness, governed by the Death Generator, which has grown steadily inside you and manifested itself as severe exploitation of the weak and the poor and as selfish raping of the planet for material wealth, has already destoyed the nations of Earth; the rising flood of Conscience and outrage implanted by the Baasark has once more countered the threat. Your invention of the Delatron has inadvertantly accelerated the process.

'You who were the Hawkwind Spacecraft, were five people who genetically evolved higher than the rest of humanity – if you like, you are the cornerstones of Baasark strategy. You have now become the feared Hawklords of old, the same who existed thousands of years ago, the ones whom you saw on the Plain of As preparing to take the legendary and evil City of Stones.

'Prepare yourselves likewise for battle – first, to defeat once again the arch agent of the Throdmyke; later, to destroy the Death Generator itself.

'But I say now,' the voice commanded, weaker and under great strain. The Hawk God's figure was scarcely visible. Hound Master listened intently for every word. ' . . . you will *not do this* to settle old Baasark feuds. The time has come to put a stop to this senseless battle. Humanity must be freed from the burden of a war that it never wished for in the first place.

'I now decree, that you and your kind have the right to live among Earth's bountiful riches. The Throdmyke and the Baasark are dead races – their war no longer matters. After you have destroyed the Death Generator, your task will be to restore Earth to her former glory, and fulfil the Hawklord prophesy begun but not fulfilled centuries ago. Your programming is weaker now, and you have the chance to break free of the chains that have held you for so long. Go . . . I can hold myself here no longer . . . remember Mankind must rise above the issues of Good and Evil . . . each man must become a god in his own right . . .'

The words had dropped to an urgent, echoing whisper that he confused with the wind. The shards before him disintegrated into nothing. The wind rose to a shrieking, howling pitch, as the ancient vista of rock around him crumbled away and he was sucked back into the grey void of nothing.

LINES OF BLACK CUT-OUTS

From his bed, the ailing figure in white watched the yellow and gold colours of the gaudy poster he had bought. It depicted eastern love couples entwined in ecstacy. He had watched in on many previous occasions, and grown bored with it. Now, in his semi-delirious condition its colours and lines writhed and twisted with new life.

The ugly dreams had become unbearable. Not only did they dominate his sleeping hours, but his waking hours too with their terrifying, realistic visions of planetary doom. His crew were dying in the dim chaos his burning mind was subjected to.

The figure of Odin appeared several times in the space of a few hours. It seemed to be trying to tell him something important. Its repeated presence could only mean that the dread catastrophe was about to take place.

He raised himself sluggishly.

He shouted out to be believed.

He kicked and twisted in his bed, throwing his covers to the floor.

The sane, faraway face of Rodney The Cook, one of the last few faithful friends, hovered above. 'Cap'n sir!' he cried out aghast. 'Don't worry – I'll get some more of that stuff the Doctor brought . . .'

'NO!' the man in white shrieked out, horrified. 'You don't understand! I DON'T WANT THE DREAMS TO GO AWAY NOW!'

His screams echoed back at him as though from a deep well.
'I DON'T WANT THEM TO GO AWAY!
'I DON'T WANT THEM TO GO AWAY!
'I DON'T WANT THEM TO GO AWAY!'
The neat, orderly world of Asgard House faded.
He fell away into darkness.

He was alone.

He was standing at the edge of a cold, dark tunnel. Odin stood at the other end in a circle of light. The God was beckoning to him.

Surprised, the man in white moved forward.

Soon he began laughing deliriously.

He felt happy.

He realized now that he was being taken away to fight, to save his crew.

DYING SEAS

When the Hawklord Drummer awoke, it was night. A vast, psychic transformation had taken place outside his head.

All of the Hawklords had been present on the ancient Plain of As, but had immediately been returned to the present time. Extra strength and fighting knowledge had been imparted to them by the ghostly warriors. Actonium Doug, absent from the Phantom Inn had been given lordly powers. The Children and the Road Hawks had been sent into a deep trance, where they had been shown visions of a future Earth – a utopia of green and fertile parks and blue skies and waters – the paradise promised in the Hawkwind Legend.

He was lying on the back seat of the car loosely covered with evil smelling sacking material. Groggily, he pushed it off him and sat up. Outside, he could see the darkened hill top pointed with camp fires and the dull glow of the stage.

Memories of the vision returned. He tried to push the car door, but found it already open.

Shaking his head, he climbed out.

As he got used to being on his feet, and the effects of the trance wore off, he began to feel a sharp chill inside his body.

'Ugh!' he shivered, hugging himself with his arms. 'The Horrors!'

He tramped across the rough grounds towards the stage. Dawn was breaking. Through the semi-darkness loomed the shapes of several stationary vehicles parked in a small compound away from the fires. Other small signs of growing affluence told him that the Children, aided by Actonium Doug had not been idle while he had been away.

But whatever fires had inspired their minds, they were now doused.

A gloomy, silent crowd was gathered round the stage, trying to absorb the healing Hawkwind music into their scarred minds. There were Eskimos, who must have arrived recently by plane, clad in the scantiest of clothing and shying away from the fires which they found too hot for their cold-adjusted skins. Among the drooping throng were Hindus, and a group of people who looked like South Americans. Unprotected mortals, they were all suffering severely from the Horrors.

He found the Moorlock sitting against the trunk of a tree close to the players. The Sorcerer had taken off his ceremonial robes at last, and now had on his more usual jeans held together by faded patches. An Upman burned in his hands. His once famous leather patchwork hat was tilted down so that he couldn't see the face.

He sat down next to him and listened to the half-hearted playing.

'Some pretty stylish stuff you took,' the Moorlock muttered under his hat. 'You almost crashed the car.'

'Don't be funny,' Hound Master replied. He told him about the Hawk God.

'He wants us to stop the Generator?' the other asked, looking up. 'That's a tall order.'

174

'Hawklords are supposed to do anything,' Hound Master commented wryly. He looked around him again at the Children. 'They're dying . . .'

The Moorlock nodded. 'Dougy got a load of medical stuff from the Palace. Stacia's trying to help the worst cases, but it's pretty hopeless. The drugs are only hiding the symptoms.'

'We've got to do something . . .'

'We are doing,' the Light Lord spoke up. He was sitting a few feet away from them, propped up by another tree stump. 'It's a question of time. Hot Plate thinks that the sudden escalation of Dark Power is out of character with the Death Generator's usual steady increase. He's gone off to investigate at some laboratories Higgy found near Baker Street . . . meanwhile we're supposed to be building new music towers, ready for a full-scale concert with all members playing to see what effect that has. The only trouble is we're waiting for Actonium Doug to turn up with the materials . . .'

As he spoke, Stacia burst through the trees. Her white face looked distraught and upset.

'I've tried everything, I really have!' She flung herself down in desperation. 'They won't seem to come round . . .'

Hound Master looked at her, alarmed. 'What do you mean? Who're "they"?'

'The Children in the shelters!' she shouted. 'The worst cases. They're unconscious. We must do something to help them before it's too late!'

Struggling to their feet, they set off to see what help they could give.

From the stage came the sounds of *Kings of Speed* – under more pleasant conditions, Hound Master thought, one of the best straight rock and roll numbers there was. Now the saving music seemed almost horrific.

The harsh, watery light of day washed coldly over them. The effects of the Death Ray gnawed hungrily at their insides once again, wrecking their minds.

CHILD OF NIGHT

From the scant cover of branches adorning his shelter, a Child called Cronan watched the distressed group.

'Only a short while now, and they will be yours, Master!' he whispered softly. His thoughts and words flashed across the dying landscapes of Earth towards Mephis. 'To think I once belonged to *them*,' he continued bitterly, eyeing the stage with loathing, 'laughed with them, ate with them . . . Now they've dwindled away almost to nothing. They're weak. We can strike them again any time we like. This time, I know you won't let them escape . . .'

A malign smile flickered across his scarred face.

ASSAULT AND BATTERY

The soundless, mocking thoughts of the imposter Child flew across the barren wastes towards the North.

Mephis received them.

In response, his mind expanded, sending out fingers of mental energy. Then the small monitor screen in front of him flashed on and began to translate the mental images into video.

Leisurely, he sat back in his maroon leather arm-chair. His scheme had worked perfectly. It had been an inspired flash of genius to fix up the agent, he told himself.

It was too bad, though, he hadn't been able to finish the Hawklords off. Timing had been against him. The power of the Death Generator was slow reaching its peak. From now on, they would have no such luck. He had the weapon which was already wiping them out.

Gloatingly, he arose from his chair and walked across the

carpet to a large bank of equipment. Lights flashed. A humming noise filled the air.

He ran his fingers rapturously over the controls of the Death Concentrator.

Soon, Earth *would* be his.

SONIC ATTACK

The warm, sunny bubble of light over London began to break up. The life giving sunlight began to flicker. It dimmed suddenly, and brightened again, as concentrated Dark Rays from the far North were increased in intensity.

Earth City shuddered.

Damaged minds twisted in pain and confusion.

Bravely, the Children fought back at the Web of Evil that had them in its grip. The Throdmyke curse from centuries ago seemed invincible. It drew effortlessly on the energy of the universe. The black, mindless, visionless, selfish Thing that had for so long dug its grey roots into the minds of men, strangling their originality and individuality and sapping their youth and their strength in order to perpetuate its colossal, satanic empires, was poised ready to achieve its logical fulfilment – the death of all life.

BOOK THREE

THE BATTLE FOR EARTH

SONIC ATTACK – PART II

Driving, thudding drum beats burst out into the flickering air.
Strident guitar notes howled and jerked across the empty ruins
surrounding the hill. Urgent sax wailed into the dying white
brain matter that stood about on the bleached, barren knoll,
blasting it with new life. The vibrating, machine-like voice of
Count Motorhead echoed explosively out of a hundred
speakers round the festival site.

> '*I got an orgone accumulator,*
> *And it makes me feel greater,*
> *I'll see you sometime later*
> *When I'm through with my accumulator . . .*'

Wildly, the invincible Hawkwind music, played by the last
fully crewed Hawkwind band, screamed out in a bold attempt
to fight off the mounting power of the Death Ray. The music
towers trembled and shook with the power of the sound. Extra
equipment had been installed on stage. The remaining Children
were packed tightly round the players, whistling and cheering
them on.

But after several hours of hard playing, scarcely a drop
occurred in the intensity of the Horrors. The barrage of
Hawkwind sound was unable to push back the Dark Force.
The Death Ray had reached the peak of Hawkwind's musical
power, and was starting to climb above it.

RIVER OF DEATH

Above the beleaguered death land, where the ancient battle of millennia ago between impartial, warring races long since dead was once again being enacted, an intensely bright star appeared in the starless sky.

It moved silently, effortlessly forward through the cold, dim light, its airy substance propelled by nothing more than mere emusement – as though chance impulse had led it astray from its true course on to a pleasant diversion.

It moved across a land torn with magical and psychic war, through a vast, blue cavern of perpetual night. Hellish fires burned in the ruins of the cities it crossed. On the horizon of gloom lay a single dome of natural light – now the sole outpost of life in a world of death and decay.

The sentient being on board sighed with relief at the sight. Hell was weakening him, as it weakened the bodies and souls of those he sought to protect. He gave his craft all the power he had left. Below him, the outermost ruins of the Dome City's vast satellite towns were starting to appear – the ghostly shells of what used to be called Luton and Watford.

The air ship lost height. The protective bubble of light hung in front of it like a massive, vaporous wall of gold.

The pilot reached out his hands to touch it as his craft burst through into the blinding sunlight. The City and its miles of peaceful ruins lay beneath him. A loud cheer of joy escaped his lips.

He skimmed across the still familiar Transport Depot at Hendon with its collapsed garages and workshops. Further on, he crossed the weird sculpture remains of the Brent Cross flyover complex on the North Circular Road.

Travelling at random he came to the parched vegetation of Hampstead Heath and Parliament Hill. The white tents and shelters dotted around the trees came into the view.

Anxiously, he reduced height, watching for signs of life, but apart from a few figures gathered around the edge of a stage, the summit of the hill looked ominously quiet.

'TECHNICIANS OF SPACESHIP EARTH . . .'

Recovering from the third hefty increase in the Death Ray in as many days, Actonium Doug looked up from his work at the blinding, silver object. Stupefied with amazement, he realized that the music it was playing was *Shouldn't Do That*, a very old Hawkwind number from their earliest days together. Although seemingly airy and light, the music was in fact powerfully and well amplified, as he could now hear.

At the centre of the glinting aura of sunlight was a strange, pod-shaped craft, about as deep and as long as a small car. Its prow and flanks were constructed entirely of a silver material that gleamed and flashed. At the helm stood a tall, erect figure, both hands placed in front of it, clasping the sides. He seemed to be guiding the silver machine towards them by thought.

Slowly the craft came in to land. Impulsively he waved at the figure inside. The figure stretched out his arms in a gesture of welcome, and shouted out:

'Welcome aboard brothers and sisters of the Galactic Patrol!'

Instantly, he recognized the drawling, bemused voice of Captain Robert Calvert – their long lost friend and one-time beloved pilot of the Hawkwind Spacecraft.

The craft settled on the bleached grass in front of him. Dropping the amplifier casing they had been replacing, he and Higgy bounded forward in awe to greet him.

'Captain Bob Calvert!' Higgy yelled out, slapping the wiry pilot on the back as he dismounted. 'Where th' hell did you spring fro'? We'd lost hope in ye . . .'

Incredulous Children ran over to the scene. The time

traveller seemed like a ghost. They could not comprehend his presence. Poet and vocalist extraordinaire, he had left Hawkwind many years earlier for new pastures. He had returned several times to do the job he loved most, but finally, he had vanished, leaving a legend behind him. They had never set eyes on him again. Like so much of their past, he had been assumed dead in the holocaust that wiped out Civilization.

Now, he stood in front of them, better in looks and health than they had ever seen him. His eyes were filled with a burning radiance. His face had a warmth on it that made them feel good to be alive again. And he was very much the old pilot they knew and loved and respected – the one who had invented crazy word machines, thrown instant poems like love into the crowds, whose spontaneous though erratic brilliance had for a while provided the driving power and inspiration for the group.

His thin, almost fragile figure was clad in jeans and jacket embroidered with rambling, psychedelic designs. He wore multicoloured, leather patchwork boots, a black hat and scarf and scruffy wool gloves with their fingers cut away. Badges, poems and messages sprang from his clothes, riveting their attention.

'Just the same old Captain!' Actonium Doug marvelled. He grinned affectionately, slapping him on the back. 'Howdya manage it?'

'That's a long story,' the Captain replied. Scenes and words clicked in his head. He lifted his hat and scratched his short, greying hair. Then he told them, in his off-hand way, about the years of agony and despair he had endured trying to establish his direction, of the faith he had retained in his old Hawkwind friends and in the group, of the way in which he had gradually become aware that his visions were the product of a mind sensitive to precognition.

' "The Wind of Time is blowing through me",' he quoted, raising his arms and unfurling them. ' "And it's all moving relative to me, it's all a figment of my mind in a world that I've designed. I'm charged with cosmic energy. Has the world gone mad, or is it me?" '

They clapped hands and cheered, the spectacle momentarily taking away the pains that tormented them.

'I ran on, from tree to tree, seeking sol-a-cis-i-tee, frightened all the while that I was going juvenile,' he ad libbed.

'I sussed it all out only after I was dematerialized and brought here,' he continued more coherently, as they walked towards the stage. The other Hawklords were still playing in the desperate attempt to fight off the deadening Dark Forces. 'I'd been getting these visions of for-bid-den doom that not all was right with you all. I didn't know why or how, because your albums were selling and you were always in the news. But I was still uneasy. I got these terrible feelings of foreboding. I'd been getting the same feelings, only not so strong when we used to play together. Then I realized that the feelings had their origin in the future. A lot of people thought I was crazy. But I knew you still needed me. I didn't know how. Then Odin, that's my mentor, finally brought me through. I "awoke" somewhere in your time. With his help I hunted around for components and with his guidance I built this,' he indicated the vessel behind him with a dramatic flick of his arm. 'At the pre-ordained moment I climbed in and flew off and came here!' He waved his arms about theatrically and smiled at them.

'On cue!' Stacia appeared, applauding his timing. 'Much later and the curtains would have dropped on us.' She put her arms round his neck and kissed him.

A look of consternation furrowed the Captain's brow.

'How much do you know about this world? I gather you're in some sort of war . . .'

They told him briefly about the series of catastrophic events that had occurred since the old world had collapsed, culminating with Mephis's attack and Hot Plate's rescue from the annihilated tower.

They reached the stage. The imprisoned performers waved grimly at them, unable to stop playing. They looked worn out, sloppily bashing their way through a number that vaguely resembled *Lord of Light*.

'Terrible noise!' Actonium Doug cringed. 'We've been

185

through our whole repertoire . . .' He put his hand to his forehead to steady himself from falling weakly.

Once more, a concerned, worried look came over the Captain's features. The people round about him looked drunk and vacant. Far fewer than could be accounted for by the number of shelters he had seen were present.

'What happened to them?' he asked agitatedly waving at the shelters. He could no longer bear the strain of the homecoming ceremony. The pretence at cheerfulness wasn't convincing. It didn't hide the obvious suffering his crew had all endured.

The ragged assembly fell silent, shuffling awkwardly and looking at the ground. Finally, Higgy, bearing the same drugged, disorientated look, spoke in a low, mournful voice.

'We had tae put the Children out . . .' He looked up at him imploringly. ''Twas the kindest thi' we could do! The Rays h' got so bad!'

The Captain looked alarmed.

'They're in their shelters,' Actonium Doug came to the Scot's aid. 'Higgy here and a few others are managing to stay awake on the top of the dope . . .'

The thin veneer of cheerfulness cracked. They were plunged back into the crippling despair.

As though their mood had sent out an invisible signal, the sunlight began to flicker unsteadily again, as though insufficient power were getting through to the solar orb's vital fires.

The air grew cooler. A gust of ice wind blew across the site. The Captain shuddered in recognition.

He had been in its frozen grip only moments before as he had hurtled across the land outside the bubble of light.

With an enraged gaze, he turned to face the Silver Machine lying on the grass. The Past, where it had taken him from, mattered nothing now. He belonged here, in the Future of Earth, where he was needed.

He turned to face his expectant crew. He smiled. Then he walked on to the stage.

LOST JOHNNY

Mechanically, mindlessly, Astral Al drummed on into day two of the final, mammoth rock session. If they stopped the music once, if a vital part broke down, they and the Children and everything they stood for would come to amend.

He played woodenly, numbed by the sheer monotony of going through the motions of drumming. He could no longer hear the sounds that clattered off the end of his drum sticks, no longer judge whether his beats kept time or not.

Instead of thinking, he stared ahead of him at the tiny white face that had taken his attention. It hovered somewhere in the small crowd in the trees. He seemed to have been looking at it for hours – and it at him, fixing him back with a strangely loaded gaze. On the one hand it seemed warm and benevolent, yet its very persistence made it appear sinister.

But he was past making objective sense of what was going on. They were doing all they could, and it still wasn't enough.

Savagely, he launched another assault on the drums in order to keep up. It didn't seem fair that Mephis should be able to have all the power he needed, while they had to rely increasingly on their wits . . . and that was the dubious way, being descended from Baasarkian stock, they had to fight. Their strength was supposed to come from within, from a sense of what was fair and honourable, from a feeling of love for their fellow brothers and sisters, and respect for their Space Ship Earth. 'And the meek shall inherit the Earth,' he muttered scornfully to himself.

The anaemic face hung in front of him, tantalizingly. Its vaguely familiar features niggled at him. He had seen it before, sometime during the last few days, but he couldn't think where or in what connection.

Nervously, he tried to ignore it. But his eyes had already been attracted too long. Now he felt it possessing him, controlling him. A solid, crushing force spun off it and entered his brain. It cut off his thoughts. In their place, terrifying pictures of Hell formed – expressionless faces of the ghouls amassed in their thousands; gaping, orange entrances of furnaces packed with corpses; convoys of creaking trucks moving tortuously across flat landscapes bathed in the clinical, bluish lighting . . .

Paralysed with fear, he tried fighting off the attack, but to no avail.

The face smiled triumphantly at him. It was warm and caring. It was cold and hating.

'Cronan!' he croaked out, horrified. He floundered in confusion. Too late, he had recognized the Child's shock of red hair and the evil looking scar down the cheek.

The demonic power possessed him.

INTO THE FUTURE

Over London, the sunlight flickered. The bubble of light protecting the City began to collapse, contracting inwards. Grim-faced, the Hydra and the Prince sat in their seats in the jeep, relieved to leave the stage whence they had been called from their researches. They watched the hollow shells of buildings and bleak, upright fingers of masonry skim forbiddingly past them. Whenever the micro-second blasts of darkness struck, their minds turned rigid with sudden pain.

'Can't you go any faster?' the Prince urged the Hydra, as they rounded a corner and skidded into Baker Street.

'We're going too bloody fast as it is!' the voice of the Baron rasped in irritation.

Gritting his teeth, the Prince fell silent.

Then at last, the jeep jerked to a halt throwing them forward. They jumped out.

A large, solid-looking building stood in front of them. Outside it, a faded letter board read: 'NEM Service to Industry – Electronics Laboratories' . . . though in its earlier days the imposing relic of Victorian England had obviously been used as a banking hall or a museum. Mephis had used it as his own research headquarters. Now, deserted but intact, it was an unexpected life-saving stronghold for the Hawklords and all at Earth City.

They raced up the steps and unlocked the doors. Inside, the building was dark and cool. The corridors were long and their walls lined with notice boards. The floors were layered with dust, scuffed and patterned by their own recent footprints. As they leapt up the wide staircase, the Hydra's facial expression and movement began to change. The Baron's scowling personna left. In its place appeared a more pleasing look. Its body began to take smaller, faster steps. By the time they had reached the head of the stairs, the character of Hot Plate had fully metamorphosed itself.

'There must be more properties of Hawkwind music still to uncover,' he said, anxiously clasping and rubbing his hands. 'There's probably a certain way of using it, or directing it. It's up to us to find out exactly what!' They arrived at the laboratories. 'You start the generator, Prince, while I readjust the detector. It shouldn't take us long to test the effects.'

He walked over to the bench where a new version of the Death Ray Detector had been built. It contained more refinements than the old model which had been smashed irrepairably at the Palace. As well as being able to analyse the Death Ray into its components, and measure their intensity, it also had its own mini Death Generator built into it. They were able to perform experiments they would otherwise have been unable to do.

The generator in the corridor spluttered into life, and the array of instruments hummed and clicked. He peered at the dials, and the madly swinging needles inside.

'Blast the fluctuations in current!' he yelled out in annoyance, as the Prince entered behind him and watched over his shoulder.

The Hydra sprinted along the side of the bench and tore off a sheet of graph paper from the print-out at the far end. He frowned as he read it.

'Just as bad as ever!' he said, showing it to the Prince. The

Hawklord stared blankly at the squiggly red line drawn by the graph pen, as the other's trembling finger pointed to it. 'That denotes what I call the Cyndaim wave frequency – the main ingredient of the Death Ray. If this reading's correct, then the actual Cyndaim level of the Ray uncountered by Delatron emissions has risen by twice . . .' He looked at his watch, ' . . . in only five hours! As the waves are in a fixed ratio with the other ingredient that means the Death Ray itself is now also twice as powerful as it was this morning! That means, as I suspected, the increase is linear, and the prediction I made still holds. Seven days of life at the most.' He crumpled the paper and threw it despairingly at the floor.

'Let's get started then,' the Prince said, his flesh creeping as he listened to the eerie words of doom.

He walked over to the Moorlock's quadrophonic equipment that they had set up on the opposite side of the bench. Wired to a Delatron, they had used it to determine the neutralizing effects of different types of Hawkwind music on the Death Ray. They had discovered that fast, heavy rock music was the best type to play, but the increase in power was marginal and not much help. While it had been playing, however, the Prince had accidentally knocked over a bottle of cleaning acid next to one of the large, teak speaker cabinets. As he had moved the vibrating cabinet out of the way further along the bench top, Hot Plate had recorded a slight momentary drop in the intensity of the Death Ray emanations coming from the Detector.

The observation, perhaps a fluke, seemed only slight. But it had sparked off the slender hope that their music could somehow be used to greater effect against the new, more powerful source of Cyndaim Waves they had detected in the North – providing the speaker cabinets were aligned correctly.

He turned on the set. The glinting needle lowered itself on to the disc with a slight hiss. Then, after a few seconds the awe-inspiring, death-defying opening bars of *Magnu* began to unfold from the twin speakers.

Hot Plate studied the dials, while the Prince, tape measure in hand, repositioned the thudding cabinets. Eventually, he had them precisely aligned in the formation that the scientist had specified, with the tiny comparator Death Generator.

The Hydra stood up, shaking his head.

'Nothing! Try moving the left hand one apart, keeping it exactly the same distance from the Generator.'

The Prince did as he was bid.

'Stop!' the Hydra cried out excitedly. 'That's it! Hold it there!'

The Prince ran to the Hydra's side. The needles were still swinging chaotically in their cases. They looked just as confusing as before.

'They've increased . . . that means . . .' the Hydra moved to the read out and checked the graph line '. . . look! According to this, the Death Ray appears to have *increased* by around 30 per cent . . . but that's because the comparator inside has been *depressed* by the music!'

They looked at one another, surprise breaking on their lined faces.

'That means we've increased our power by 30 per cent! Looks like we were right!' Hurriedly, he reached down to the cupboards below the bench top, and opened one of them. He rumaged around inside and then produced four extra speaker cones. Wires trailed from the back of them across the bench as he handed them to the Prince. 'Here. Mount them on a couple of retort stands and plug them in to the back of the deck. It won't strictly speaking produce an octaphonic effect, but it'll do just as well.'

Once again, the Prince set to work. Soon, the eight speakers were arranged according to the scientist's instructions. *Magnu* blasted out over the air.

Nothing happened.

The Prince moved each speaker in turn, in different combinations, carefully measuring the distances each time. But the emanations from the tiny home-made Death Generator remained normal.

'It's no use!' the Prince said in exasperation. 'We could spend all week trying to get them in the right positions.'

'We must keep trying!' Hot Plate urged. 'A thirty per cent

191

increase is good, but it just isn't enough. At the rate that the Northern source is increasing, we still won't gain much time. We need something decisive to . . .'

A loud explosion cut him off. Molten plastic splattered round the laboratory. Billowing black smoke coiled up from the Detector on the bench.

'You did it!' the Hydra jumped about. 'You blew up the Death Generator! That's better than we ever imagined! Hold those positions and let's take the co-ordinates . . .' He rushed around obliviously, smouldering where the blast had caught his garments. The Prince doused him with water.

Charred and dripping, he eventually finished his work, holding up a list of figures.

'Here it is! The formula for victory! . . . only . . .' he added gravely, 'now that we've got these, we've got the job of positioning eight batteries of speakers of sufficient power, round the source, at exactly the right distance and co-ordinates!'

'That's where the Captain comes in,' the Prince said.

'Eh?' the Hydra asked. A reprimanding tone entered his voice. 'I told you – we could never leave Earth City again. Our bodies wouldn't stand it – even inside Silver Machines.'

'We've got to take the chance,' the Prince pronounced with determination. 'There's no other way of doing it. We've just got to hope that in this instance, your theorizing will bend a little in practice!' He grinned at the scientist. 'Let's put Operation Silver Machine into practice.'

Together, they began to collect as much equipment and tools as they could salvage. Then they staggered downstairs with their load, and piled it all into the waiting jeep. They climbed into their seats, and set off back to Parliament Hill.

Above them, the sun began to flicker again.

Anxiously, they raced against time to save themselves and their home planet from being plunged into Darkness for ever.

NERVES OF NIGHT

Crouched in the awning of one of the shelters, Stacia paused in her work, struggling to listen to the words coming from the stage.

She was tending to the sick and dying, and had visited almost every home on the site. Most of the patients were still unconscious, but some were coming to again. She had found them desperately in need of her help and assurance. They needed someone to talk to, someone to tell them what was happening outside. Most of all, their agonised systems screamed out for the fast dwindling supply of sedatives.

Next door to her, Actonium Doug was busy fitting in the slabs of polystyrene they had decided to use for insulation. They provided meagre protection against the sonic radiation and the piercing cold wind that now swept across the hill top, but any improvement, no matter how small, was worthwhile if it helped the occupants to survive.

She frowned at the words coming from the stage. They were sinister. They were not Hawkwind words. Alarmed, she arose stiffly and looked out.

She noticed the frenzied figure of Astral Al shouting into the microphone. His voice was flat, and uneven. He gyrated about as though possessed. At his side, slightly behind him stood the Captain, his hands upturned in a gesture of helplessness. The other musicians wore puzzled expressions on their faces. They looked apprehensive about the incident, but they were unable to stop playing and intervene.

The malign words boomed coarsely out of the loud speakers round the festival site, filling her with terror. Intuitively, she realized that the Dark Forces had found a way through their defences, trying to erode away the precious time that remained to them.

The words grated harshly on the ears of the listeners, crudely persuading them to submit to their will:

> *'Children of the Light*
> *Don't try to understand . . .*
> *I'll see you all right*
> *If you'll take my hand . . .'*

Revulsion mounted inside her as she listened. She turned round to attract Actonium Doug's attention, but he was already standing at her side listening, open-mouthed.

> *'Your pale flesh is slain,*
> *It can't survive the Dark.*
> *Come and give me your pain –*
> *In return I'll give you LIFE.*
>
> *'I'll give you NIGHT!*
> *I promise you RELEASE!*
> *Just leave the Light*
> *And get eternal peace . . .'*

A subtle change began to take place in the air as the chanting continued. The feeling of tension lessened, and the cold wind was transformed into a mild breeze. Drug-like, the words made everyone feel peaceful and drowsy.

'Don't let it get you – try and stop him!' Actonium Doug yelled out to her. He flung down his cutting knife, and began sprinting towards the stage. Stacia followed behind him, her body and mind gradually melting in the seductive power, dissolving into warmth and sleep.

They ran in what seemed like slow motion, as in a dream. At last they reached the taut, spluttering figure of the drummer.

Close to they could see that only the shape of their friend remained. His face was contorted into a grotesque mask of uncharacteristic guile. The veins on his skin had lifted perilously out as his body was recklessly, impartially manipulated by the Dark Force inside.

They reached out to pull the figure down. As they did so, the zombie lifted its arms above its head to strike them. Actonium Doug got ready to ward off the blow. But instead a hideous look of pain crossed the zombie's contorted features. Its power drained away; its arms froze in mid air.

For a fleeting instant, Stacia saw behind the tortured eyes as the Hawklord within battled for life. The agonized eyes stared out at her for help. She gasped as the extreme emotions that were evoked brought her into sudden, blinding telepathic contact with him.

Momentarily, the mind of the invading ghoul lay open also. A horrifying, total picture of Mephis, his army of ghouls and their fortress retreat burnt in her mind. She saw the low, functional buildings of an army camp. Uniformed soldiers with deformed, blistered skins and grossly swollen bodies milled about on a shadowy parade ground, climbing into waiting cargo trucks. A large, stone tower, out of character with its surroundings rose from the site. At the summit of the tower, which she now realized was an Operations Headquarters, a ring of lights blazed from slit-like windows. Instantaneously, a picture of Mephis sat inside it, together with every detail of the Death Concentrator, came to her.

Aghast at the realization, she screamed. The brief, mental link severed. Once more she saw only the dummy face staring insanely at her.

Stiffly, the figure began to topple.

A stifled sound hung at its lips. It pitched forward limply into their arms, its face purple and blotched through lack of air.

CAVE OF TERROR

The ring of faces went black in front of him. Stacia's screaming went on and on inside him. Dimly, he could still hear the band playing. He lost consciousness.

When he came to, he was lying down inside a cramped, tent-like structure of some description. Its walls were lined with white bubbles. From outside, came the Hawkwind music like a stiff rod poking at him.

He shook himself and tried to rise, but his host body was

195

lead and wouldn't move. Memories came back to him, and he realized where he had been brought – inside one of the freak shelters.

A wave of nausea swept over him. The music rasped over his skin. He felt like screaming out, but that would draw attention.

Letting himself go limp, he remembered that he had to act as though he were still the drummer. He would be able to rise later.

His mind seemed enormous, like the inside of a giant cathedral. It was a composite of several peoples' minds. Somewhere behind him lay the Hawklord's mind, still barely conscious but lacking the power to assert itself. In front, he sensed two areas that were veiled by a grey anonymity. They were access parts to the minds of Cronan and Mephis, and he knew that they could be opened with a minimum of effort.

Mephis had not let him down, he thought happily. When he had been assigned the job of psychic spy he – Major Reginald Wessex Asquith – had been mortally afraid. 'Now Master, you have made me into a giant – bigger than I ever dreamed as a lad,' he whispered thankfully, hoping that his feelings were being received. 'I realize now that all I ever wanted was this kind of power. You have shown me the way to get it. Without you, I would have lived out my miserable life unfulfilled, unknown and unthanked. I am yours. I will do your wish on this mission and serve you to the death.' He saluted mentally in the customary manner.

A strong, forbidding power invaded him. One of the psychic portals opened in front of him. The vast internal thoughtscape of Mephis linked on to his.

'You have done well,' the wicked voice boomed into him. 'With you and Cronan, and the others that you will manage to occupy – gradually, as the Hawklords grow weaker under the power of my Death Concentrator, as the fool of a drummer had done, they will all succumb to you – we will be able to eradicate this last troublesome pocket of resistance to our rightful aims and ways. Then, the world will be ours! We will be free to conquer the other worlds that our ancestors set out to do so long ago – to claim back what is ours from the Baasark. When you discover the Hawklords' plans in more detail, I will instruct you further. Remember that the Baasark are clever to have outwitted us for so long . . . we must make sure this time that they are killed once and for all!'

The voice echoed away, and Mephis's thoughts departed.

The old soldier inside Astral Al's body waited, well rewarded by the praise and the value of the mission that had been entrusted to him.

WALL OF ZONES

The tall, jesterish figure of Captain Calvert, adorned with his strange costume and labels strode calmly about in the rising wind near the vehicle compound. He moved from person to person, supervising the construction of the Silver Machines.

Attempts to overcome the Dark Force by sheer music power had been abandoned. With full knowledge of the Death Concentrator they were now working urgently on the new plan.

The Hydra had returned to the laboratories to fashion the complicated printed circuits that were necessary for the thought-controlled engines. Steele Eye and the hardiest of the Children were at work on the basic structure of the platforms. The Prince was busily assembling the musical weaponry. Every part had to be accurately fitted if the machines were to be successfully used against the Death Concentrator. There was no room for mistakes. Their work had to be precise and thorough.

When the Captain had been transported through time and space, his mind had been imprinted with the advanced technical knowledge that he would need. He had set to work immediately, and had been surprised to find the craft's workings so simple. Few parts were needed to be found. The only difficulties lay with the circuitry and the amount of time taken by the physical building. He had been transported to a point several months ahead of the time he had been scheduled to appear at the tower. Most of the time he had spent hunting for materials.

On this occasion, they had to build four Silver Machines in less than a week.

As they worked, an unhealthy dusk began to fall. Already, at the end of the first of the seven days' life left to them, conditions had worsened drastically. The thin, energized plasma from the North now blew constantly, freezing the waning bodies of the Children. It howled and shrieked around the hill top. On the ruined skyline, where the dome of light was rapidly shrinking under the onslaught, the full effects of its negative energy were being felt. Dust and masonry were being hurled into the sky, forming a boiling, seething ring of cloud round the horizon.

Utterly determined this time to beat back the Dark Forces and preserve their way of life, they worked painstakingly at their task. They ignored the cold. They denied the paralysing insect fingers of the Horrors clawing up under their flesh. They worked on for the hour when their machines would be completed, ready to rise into the wind of lethal, destructive particles of Hell and sail impregnably to the final battleground.

SPIRAL GALAXY

The hours ticked by in the dimly lit laboratory where Hot Plate worked. Apart from the muffled chugging of the generator in the passageway, and the moaning of the wind outside the institute's thick walls, the large room was still and quiet. It had the same deathly silence about it that all the intact rooms that still survived had got.

Two of the circuits were complete. The third needed a few finishing touches adding to it.

Fatigued, he lay the soldering iron aside and stretched himself. Inside, he felt nervous and sick from the Ray. Then he resumed work again, forcing his concentration back on to the maze of wires and parts.

At last, they were finished. Now they would need testing. But to do so, they would have to be integrated into the other engine parts back at the construction site. Carefully packing the delicate circuitry into a box, he hoped that they would work first time. If they didn't, there would be no second chance.

He began walking towards the door, glad to be leaving the eerie work place. As he reached out to open the door in front of him, a tremoring began in the floor. Alarmed and puzzled, he stopped. He could hear nothing above the noise of the wind. But the vibrations underfoot grew stronger. Eventually the walls around him began to shake. Plaster dust puffed down at him from between the tiles in the ceiling.

He stood, frozenly. The memory of the car journey from Control after he had been retrieved from its computer memory, flashed across his mind. A similar Earth tremor had occurred. He had conjectured that it had been caused by the Ray. Now, with the knowledge he had of the effects of high intensity Death Rays, he was certain. Those earlier tremors had been caused by a test running of the Concentrator.

A lightening calculation took place inside his mind. Appalled by the answer, he again reached for the door. But the Hydra's body would not respond. It had become paralyzed with panic.

A voice rasped somewhere inside him.

'Get the hell out of here!' It was the Baron. His mind had been lying in the background, aware of everything that had taken place, and he didn't like what he saw. Gradually, he asserted his personality and the thoughts of the frightened scientist began to lose their paralyzing effect on their body.

His thoughts began to power the Hydra. Clutching at the box of circuitry, he flung open the door and stepped out into the pitch-black corridor. He fumbled in its pockets for the torch and snapped it on. Then, playing the beam of light over the dusty staircase, he began moving as fast as he could down the steps.

He ran out from the trembling building towards the waiting

jeep. Underfoot, the ground was shaking threateningly as he climbed into the vehicle.

Above the noise of the wind he heard the sound of falling masonry sliding and crashing about him in the dark before he flicked on the headlamps and roared off down the street.

HELL FIGHTERS

Obsessively, the Baron drove through the night, in all probability the last natural night of Earth. Dust from outside the protective dome had blown over, forming dark, tumultuous clouds that obscured the stars. His body glowed phosphorescently as he drove erratically from side to side along the road to avoid the bricks and other debris that were rolling out from the collapsing buildings. His headlamps splashed garishly against bleak, trembling walls. They picked out the hunched, scurrying forms of mutant rats and insects escaping the destruction.

The constant earth quaking seemed much worse than it was because it shook his whole body. His vision vibrated frighteningly and his already queasy guts felt like throwing up.

After about ten minutes, he reached Haverstock Hill, where most of the ruins had already been razed. The roads were clear.

Opening up the engine, he roared uphill, turning right at the top into the ruins of Hampstead Village. From there he could see the lights of the Festival on Parliament Hill and it was an easy drive up to the approach road.

He parked the jeep in the dark compound and jumped out. Fast, thudding Hawkwind music was blasting out from the stage. Liquid Len's lights were playing luminously on the trio who were playing. But the dark silhouettes of the Children whom he expected to see gathered round the fire, were not there. He walked closer towards the scene, and then he noticed that the rough framework erected by the Light Lord to carry his new lighting equipment, although in operation, was unattended.

Puzzled, he stopped in his tracks. He changed direction and walked towards the construction site, where a string of electric lights attached to posts were shining dimly.

Below the lights were the shells of the partly completed Silver Machines. They gleamed dully and trembled under his gaze. But the worksite was strangely deserted. Tools and wires were scattered about randomly on the earthen ground, as though they had been dropped in a great hurry.

A stab of fear and alarm flashed through him. Wildly, he looked about, and listened. Above the sound of the music he thought he could detect shouting. Stooping, he placed the vital box of circuitry inside one of the Silver Machines. Then, picking his way through the smooth, dead tree trunks with his torch, he advanced on the sounds.

The shouting grew louder as he approached the edge of the quaking hill near to the music tower. There in the dark, he made out the jumping, glowing figures of the Hawklords. They were moving frenziedly about, intermingling with other barely discernible shapes.

'Get your bloody cloven maulers off me!' an angry voice shouted out from somewhere in the mêlée. It was Thunder Rider.

Aghast, the Baron raised his torch and played it on the twisting figures. At first, he couldn't make out who they were fighting. Then his beam momentarily caught one of the assailants.

Involuntarily, he stepped backward. He drew in his breath at the sight of the vaguely human form he had glimpsed. Its blistered face and hunched form reminded him of his nightmare.

With a sinking heart he realized that the creature must be one of the enemy ghouls.

WALLS OF ENCLOSING SLIME

The feeling of despair that gripped the Baron was replaced by anger. It seemed to him that for each step forward towards victory that they took, they had to travel several steps backwards. There was always something or someone about, ready to chuck a spanner in the works.

An insensate rage took him over. Cursing and growling obscenities, he played his torch about on the debris-littered ground. With mad Hawklord strength, he lifted a huge bough and swung it high above his head. Letting out a savage cry of war, he ran forward through the dark to the assistance of his friends.

He pushed his way ferociously into the affray, flashing his torch over the mingling bodies. Hawklords, ghouls and Children were grappling blindly with one another, stumbling over the bodies of their dead. As they fought, their shouts and shrieks rent the cold, windy air.

Surprisingly, there were only a few ghouls. They battled viciously with an uncanny strength and speed that seemed to be wearing their opponents down. Their repulsive bodies were hacked and bleeding from knife cuts and blows, yet they fought on like machines, as though unable to feel pain.

The Hawklords and Children fought valiantly to prevent them reaching the stage. Choosing the one that was giving the most trouble, the Baron shoved his way through towards it. With an angry snarl he brought the heavy bough down on its head. Its hideous, weeping face turned on him. Ignoring its other attackers, it began to hobble towards him, wielding a piece of bright, jagged metal in its clubbed fist.

Taken aback by the ghoul's toughness, the Baron raised his bough and swung it down again on the loathesome face. For a moment, the creature continued to move forward. But then something inside its head broke. It began to fall, a terrified human shriek escaping from its swollen lips. Its glazed eyes brightened as the trapped human inside was momentarily given back its useless body. Then it toppled to the earth and lay still.

Unmoved by the shiver of stark terror which ran through him, the Baron turned and picked out the next assailant with his torchlight. He forged his way towards it, wielding his great club.

'You got here just in time, Baron!' a voice gasped from his side. 'We . . . weren't . . . very . . . organized . . . when . . . they . . . attacked . . .' the voice panted.

Flashing the light, the Baron made out the figure of the Light Lord. He was shoving at the crush of bodies to make fighting space. In his hand he carried a large wrench which he was using to strike out at the shapes of the ghouls whenever they became visible in the faint aurora of his phosphorescent body. 'Three of our best fighting men are trapped on stage – Astral Al's still out of his head! We've been completely out-numbered . . .' he yelled out.

'You've not done bad!' the Baron shouted back to him above the groans and thumps. 'Here's another one that'll wish it stayed in Hell!' For a third time his solid wooden club descended. It landed with a sharp crack against the neck of the ghoul that he had earmarked. The squat shape emitted a blood-curdling scream and fell to join its grisly companions.

With two more ghouls down, the battle gradually subsided. Exhausted, the Children staggered back to the fire, leaving the Hawklords to attend to the rest. Finally, the last ghoul was clubbed to its timely death.

Low in energy, the Hawklords followed the Children. Soon the small band of victors were lying around on the bleak knoll in front of the stage trying to draw in as much warmth as they could from the ailing fire. Actonium Doug piled on more wood, but the flames seemed reluctant to take hold in the thin wind and the vibrations from the ground.

'They fought like robots!' declared the Baron. He glowered. His blood still pounded in his veins with rage and would not settle. He looked around him, as though searching for other things to vent his wrath on.

'Flesh and blood zombies sent out by Mephis,' Lord

203

Rudolph told him, wincing as he attended to a gash under his eye.

'They were like the walking corpses I saw in my vision!' Stacia informed them. She nursed an injured foot with one hand while clasping one of the Children to her with the other, trying to share out some of her warmth.

The Hawklords' wounds were mostly superficial, and already partly healed by their magical powers. But the Children as usual were in a far worse condition. Much weakened to begin with, and propped up with pills, the Hawklords wondered if they would even last out the week.

'You better tell me how it happened,' the Baron demanded angrily. He glanced over his shoulder into the darkness. 'And how we're so sure there aren't any others out there . . .'

'There are loads more out there,' Thunder Rider answered him with irritation. 'I told you – Stacia saw them all heading towards London. But the fact they haven't got through in large numbers suggests to me that Mephis can't control more than a half dozen or so at a time by psi hypnosis . . . and while our music's playing, that's the only way he can get them in. Perhaps the zombies we fought were an assassin gang or some sort of scout party sent in to see what would happen. We'll just have to hope that no more are dispatched.'

'Maybe we don't have to hope about anything anymore,' the Light Lord called out morosely above the noise of the band. He put his hand on to the trunk of one of the shaking trees. 'This started up soon after the attack, Baron. At first I thought it must be something to do with the ghouls, but it's still happening. Maybe the whole bloody world's going to end sooner than we think . . .'

The Baron listened uncomfortably.

The memory of the laboratory flashed through his mind. He felt the horrible anxiety of Hot Plate's warning return. He wondered how best to relate the bad news.

'There's something you ought to know,' he began lamely. But before he could continue, he felt the scientist's mind forcing itself up to the surface inside him. 'Think I'd better let Hot Plate tell it. He can do it better than me,' he added.

The expression on his face changed, and the gathering round the fire, sensing another dose of bad news, looked desperately on as the scientist manifested himself.

PLANET OF DEATH

'It's hopeless to carry on!' Hot Plate's high-pitched voice pronounced mournfully from the Hydra's mouth. It was barely audible above the sound of the music and the noise of the wind. The survivors of Earth City had to draw in closer to hear him. 'I just don't see how we'll manage to get the Silver Machines off the ground in time . . .' His voice cracked with emotion. He looked at the Light Lord.

'What you say about this world coming to an end is true – literally!' He turned to the others. 'I'm afraid to tell you that the Rays concentrated by Mephis's machine have reached such an intensity that they're starting to vibrate the land . . . and I don't just mean the land around here. I mean the planet . . . the whole Earth is shaking! The Cyndaim waves reflecting back at us from outer space as sonic radiation are gradually vibrating the Earth to bits . . .' He paused again, shaking his head with grief. 'I guessed as much from the beginning. I knew if they kept mounting, this might happen. But the Death Ray on its own took so long to mount up that I thought we'd have plenty of time to stop it, so I kept my thoughts to myself. But now . . .' His voice trailed off despairingly.

No-one moved or spoke. They looked at him in horror and incomprehension. The scientist composed himself.

'By rights I should be dead. I'm not worried for myself. But I feel sorry for you . . . Unprotected by our music, none of us could survive for a split second. I didn't know the exact figure before, but now I know that at this level the planet starts to shake. I know the mass of our planet, and I know its composition, its strengths and weaknesses. I also know that the force that was needed to shatter the hypothetical planet now known as the Asteroid Belt is close to the present force exerted by the Death Concentrator. The old astronomers assumed that the planet was about three quarters the size of Earth and was made roughly of the same things. This means that Earth can probably tolerate a higher force . . . but it won't be long before that level is reached . . .'

One of the Children began laughing hysterically as the unspoken conclusion to Hot Plate's terrifying dispatch dawned on him. A strange calm had come over the others though. They looked transformed, as though the extreme conditions they were fighting under had given them extra rather than less determination.

Captain Calvert was the first to speak.

'You mean Earth herself will disintegrate under the strain . . . ?'

The Hydra nodded.

'How long have we got?' he inquired.

'I don't know . . . not more than a week. Maybe tomorrow, the next day . . .' The Hydra shook his head slowly as he spoke. 'I don't know exactly.'

'Then we may have *less* than a week to get the Silver Machines off the ground, to save Earth!' He rose to his feet. He raised his index finger to his greying temple. Then, after considering the information he had been given, he waved it admonishingly at Hot Plate.

'But you know your lack of faith in Mother won't help at all! If there is a discrepancy between the strength of Earth's core and that of your asteroid planet, then why not look on the bright side and assume we have one week?'

The Hydra fell silent. Inside, Hot Plate cringed uncomfortably ashamed of his paranoid outburst.

'Not to worry,' the Captain continued sympathetically. 'Nerves are running high.'

'All the same,' Stacia commented observantly, 'it'd be as well to assume both that we may have either one week or less than one week. Then someone could discover if Mephis himself knows what his rays are doing! For all we know we might not, and then we might be able to get him to stop the Death

Concentrator.'

'Our aim is to destroy Mephis, not to bargain with him!' the Baron's voice rasped out from the Hydra.

'Stacia's got a good point, Baron,' Rudolph the Black intervened. 'And it wouldn't be compromising. No-one wants the planet torn apart. The thing is, how do we contact him?'

'Easy,' Stacia replied. 'The Light Lord's best at psychic things. He could make contact with Mephis.'

Liquid Len looked up hastily. 'Not me. I'm no good at telepathy . . . I discovered that when I tried to psi you once . . .'

'All right,' Stacia persisted. 'Then what about the Moorlock? We've got a sorcerer right on our doorstep. So far we haven't used him much!' She pointed towards the stage where Lemmy, Hound Master and the Moorlock were playing. Of all the Hawklords, the Acid Sorcerer was the only one who still had any musical soul left. Their gloomy predicament for once seemed to be having a euphoric effect on him. He strummed forcefully across the strings of his guitar, while making involved chord changes. He sang the Deep Fix number *Rolling In The Ruins*, putting all he'd got into it. His unique, rich voice, with its slightly hysterical pitch was pouring vibrantly out of the speakers round the festival site.

Appreciatively, the Captain nodded to Stacia. 'Good idea,' he said. 'Well, let's put it to him. One of us will have to change places with him . . .'

'I reckon I could do that for a few rounds!' the Light Lord offered. 'Of course, there's no guaranteeing that my music wouldn't bring the whole bubble down . . .'

'We'll have to take that chance,' the Captain remarked, dryly.

BURNED OUT VISION

Those round the fire who were still able-bodied rose to their feet. They looked better rested and reassured than they had done. As they set out to work on the still incompleted Silver Machines, they glanced nervously about them into the unknown darkness.

Stacia sat behind with the Children to keep them company and to stoke the fire against the driving wind. She shivered, partly because of the cold and partly because of the intense blackness – but also because of the Horrors.

After her harrowing ordeal inside Astral Al's mind, her super mind and body had felt damaged, though she had not said as much. She had put on a brave front of normalcy. Her mind seemed to be impaired. She had difficulty fixing her attention on important matters. When the Horrors had increased, after the Concentrator had been turned up further, she had felt the terror symptoms many times worse than the other Hawklords – as though her nerve-wracked body had become especially easy prey to the Death Ray's probing fingers.

Several times she had felt the urge to give up the fight because of her inner state – to die, to be allowed to die. But she had fought on, as they all had to do.

After shedding some of its warmth, the camp-fire finally managed to eat through the brittle wood, and needed rebuilding. Painfully, she climbed to her feet and got more wood from the dwindling pile that Higgy had collected. If they were lucky, it might just last them through the night.

She threw on the pieces. The Children were mostly quiet, staring sightlessly at the fire or sleeping. They were still high on the effects of the sedatives, but their meagre protection wouldn't continue for long she thought, thinking of the last, half-filled bottle in her pocket. It certainly wouldn't go round all the Children – those who were housed in the insulated shelters would have to go without. Unhappily, she could only afford to give comfort to healthier members.

She checked over the prostrate forms in front of her to make sure they were still alive. They all were, but most of them would suffer horribly in the morning after their wounds started to be felt. A few were awake. She sat down again and talked to them. Although she felt ill and sick, it was the first time she had really been able to talk to them properly. Since the rock concert had started, it had demanded her constant attention.

They exchanged backgrounds, and listened sadly to one another's words. They were like weak and wounded soldiers fighting at the front line. Although they were confident that their side would win, they knew that in the end, they as individuals might not live. One of the Children with a bad leg injury had come from Paris. He and his girl-friend had set out with their children when they had felt the Hawkwind music. They were the only survivors of a squat that had been set up in the Boulevard St. Michel. In the early days of the political and social unrest, almost the whole of Paris had become a squat – the home of starving and desperate people – and when the reprisals started, reactionary mobs had roamed the streets of the City, purging it of the new Children of the Sun. Finally, when the end came for most men, the Child and his family had thought themselves the only survivors in the world.

Another person had come from Amsterdam – one of the few survivors of a more enlightened City. The people of Holland, like few other countries in the world, had made a concerted, last-minute attempt to help reverse the insidious effects of the environmental poisoning, but they had been swept under in the madness of the worldwide cataclysm that ensued.

They kept one another company throughout until a bleak, paltry light began to filter through from between the dust clouds in the East. Gradually, the light spread across the sky, but the wind still blew cold.

The Parisian and the Dutchman, together with a Hindu and a Mancunian who were still awake, groaned stiffly with pain. Compliently, Stacia took the last bottle from her pocket and shook out four powerful, tiny blue Narcolene tablets. She handed one to each of them. Then she rose wordlessly to begin her rounds of the shelters.

The wind whipped icily about the Hawklady as she stood before the first shelter awning, frightened to enter. Deep down, she knew that many of the sick Children might not have survived the chill night.

Instinctively she backed away. She went instead to the shelter where they had lain Astral Al. Now she was kicking herself that they had not foreseen the extreme cold that had been brought on by the lack of sun. Cautiously, she pulled aside the polystyrene block that sealed the Hawklord inside. She bent down.

The walls and floor of the shelter were lined with the white polystyrene slabs. They completely encased his body, leaving only a small amount of head and side room to manoeuvre in. The still, stale air inside seemed faintly warm, and she breathed a sigh of relief.

'Al?' she called, nervously, watching for a sign of movement in the masses of beard and hair on his pallid face.

At first, there was no response. Then his eyes opened and he raised his head woodenly. He smiled and made a stiff gesture with his arm.

'Hi . . .' he said flatly, 'I was just thinking of you . . .'

His face remained perfectly expressionless as he spoke.

Her first impulse was to show joy at hearing him speak, but her feelings were replaced with unease. She knew the Group well. Including herself, none of them ever woke up smiling.

She withdrew hastily. 'I-I'll be back,' she stammered. 'You're OK. I'll go and check the others.'

'No!' the voice rasped out. 'Stay here!' Its tone was authoritative, but there was a slight note of pleading in it, so she stooped down again.

Instantly, her wrist was grasped. She was yanked half inside the shelter. 'Let go!' she screamed.

But the Hawklord did not relax his grip. He brought her face to face with him. Horrified, she could see now that there had been no change in his condition. Behind the familiar mask of skin was the same cold presence she had experienced looking out at her when she and Doug had taken him frothing and foaming from the stage – only now the look was calmer and more calculating.

Her first thought was for the builders of the Silver Machines outside, and she struggled to escape to warn them of the threat. She brought the zombie's arm upward, and then slammed it down again. At the same time she pulled towards her to break his hold. Her wrist broke free and she staggered to her feet. Behind her she sensed a movement. She spun round expecting to see one of the Children from round the fire.

Instead she met Cronan. He had the same dead eyes in his skull.

Cronan.

In a terrifying flash of insight, she saw how the whole treacherous web of Dark Force had spread its evil influence insidiously into their midst. The recent events which had virtually brought Earth City to its knees had not just happened – they had been cunningly caused. And they would go on being caused: unless the web was exposed – Mephis would continue to receive advance information of their preparations for war. He would continue to know their weakest and strongest moments.

For a frozen moment they held each other in their stares. Then she launched herself forward to strike him.

The possessed Child lifted his arm and pointed a music gun at her. He pressed the play button. Immediately, *It's Amore*, the crippling Dean Martin number, began rumbling out of its miniature speakers.

A jagged, white slash of light leapt out towards her. Pain exploded from her head. She felt something break inside. Then she lost consciousness.

Gradually, she came to. She opened her eyes and stared up at the low, white roof of the shelter. But it wasn't her own eyes that were seeing. Her eyes were trapped behind an invisible barrier which imprisoned her. Her thoughts were powerless. They had no control over her body. She could not scream or speak.

In her place was a new power. Although its alien thoughts were clearly understood by her, she was helpless to fight them.

They were ruthless, sadistic thoughts – the mind of a Captain Roger Watson, who had striven for power throughout his army career, but had had to remain content with being a Captain. This person seemed to have total control over her rightful body.

By the side of her lay the body of Astral Al. Although he and she were not speaking, the controlling minds inside them were locked together in thought.

'. . . so we wreck the machines today,' the Captain's thoughts came unmistakenly at her. They were not words, but concepts and pictures which she found herself automatically translating into words.

'Stupid fool!' the Major, who occupied Astral Al's head, replied caustically. 'Of course not! We let them finish – *then* we sabotage. You must think of the psychological aspects, I am constantly having to tell you that . . .'

Aghast, she tried to fight the barrier, to force her presence back into control, but to no avail.

Then, a third consciousness entered her head. It was the most powerful and insane of all. It swept through the other minds and its voice echoed hollowly across her thoughts. It was Mephis.

'Ha! Ha!' the Dark Prince chuckled. 'So, my little Hawk-lady – you are mine after all!' His voice rose to its familiar hysterical pitch. '. . . to watch, to help in the downfall of the dangerous, misguided fools you call your friends. But stop – think how fortunate you will be! When their kind have gone for ever, you will still survive! You will not regret then what has happened! You will see after all that I am right!' The voice became hypnotic and crooning. 'Watch! – Queen of Darkness!'

The low, wicked tones melted away, leaving her with a feeling of helpless rage and anguish. Once more she felt her mind being moved.

PARANOIA

Through swirling, amorphous shapes on a screen in front of her, Stacia was barely able to make out the tiny figures of her friends. She stared with anguished eyes, trying to discern how many figures there were and who they were and what sort of predicament they were in.

The dark shadow of Mephis stood next to her. He was dressed in his ceremonial uniform adorned with numerous medals and stripes accumulated in war – but the being inside that facade was now far from human. It stood, loosely upright, hands pointed to its forehead, its evil mind concentrating thoughts into the screen.

The fog cleared. The picture suddenly clarified and she let out a gasp of concern as she recognized the room in the tower. The satanic creature clasped his hands behind his back.

'Now watch,' he said to her smugly. 'Those are your gallant Hawklords! Look again at the screen! I'll show you just how capable those weak, spineless cissies are of saving people . . .'

He put his fingertips back to his head. Abruptly, the screen changed, and a line of phantom horsemen came into view. She watched, horror-stricken, as the small figures of the Hawklords fired their guns, but in vain. She turned away, unable to watch.

'No! I would not let you miss this for all of Hell,' Mephis hissed. She smelt his foetid breath. Strong, clammy hands grasped her head. They forced her to face the unbearable pictures.

'Let go, you bastard!' she screamed, twisting and writhing in the steel bonds that held her. 'Those are my friends! You'll pay . . .' Her mouth went numb. She tasted salt as his fist struck her in the face.

'Now,' he said, smiling twistedly. 'You'll witness their death. And after they have gone, you'll witness the death of your precious City.'

'You're insane . . .' she began, an expression of disgust on her face. She fought hard to calm herself. Time was running out for the fighters. 'Even if you have no respect at all for our lifestyle,' she spoke quickly, 'can't you see we're not just Hippies, whatever you call us – we're Hawklords! The Hawklords who have already defeated you twice before . . . you'll not beat that power, Mephis! Why don't you stop your terrible acts now, while you still have the chance, and save yourself . . .'

'This time I *will* win . . .' the Lord of Darkness interrupted her, breathing heavily. She turned, startled by his sudden change of mood.

'I will win *this time*!' His voice mounted in pitch and strength. His eyes were glazed and bloodshot. He was staring straight ahead, arms outstretched, as though the merest suggestion of failure was sufficient to bring him to the brink of madness.

He sprang across the room towards the bank of controls. As he did so, the screen in front of Stacia began dissolving again into billows of cloud. A panic gripped her stomach. She reached out to where the Hawklords had been. The screen went dead.

'Thunder Rider! Lemmy!' she screamed out their names. Desperately, she closed her eyes tight around the last image of the Hawklords. Telepathically, she beamed as much energy as she could muster, hoping her vibrations would get through.

In the background, she could hear the Creature babbling. It shrieked insanely. She felt herself being moved from behind. She struggled violently in the psychic chains that held her. She stopped moving. She felt her face being hit again.

'Open your eyes,' Mephis screamed at her, enraged.

She obeyed. From the background, the notes of the terrible music came to torment her.

She saw the console in front of her. Mephis was standing by it, his hands moving over the controls. He was speaking frenziedly.

'*This* machine's your downfall. This is the reason why you will not succeed a *third* time! With its help, I process unlimited power. I am able to harness the energy of the Death Generator

214

and speed up the slow, steady increase in power which those fools designed into it so long ago! It concentrates its rays wherever I choose. London . . . your kind . . . will soon be wiped out! I shall be master over all! Earth will be mine! Nothing you can do now will stop me!'

A banging started up inside her head as she struggled to concentrate simultaneously on the Hawklords and the shrieking words. Her body craved submission in the face of hopeless odds, but her mind screamed out stubbornly that she must not submit.

From far away came the hideous laughter. Then the crippling music, worse than her chains, mounted in volume.

She felt her mind fading away back into the nightmare of her body.

WEBS OF DECEIT

From his position on stage, the Moorlock watched the tall thin figure of the Light Lord walk bouncily towards him through the early morning light. Wilfully, he brought the number they were playing to a close.

Lemmy and Hound Master continued playing as he unhooked the Stormbringer II from round his shoulders and handed it over in silence. Solemnly, the two Hawklords gazed at each other. Both knew the importance of the Sorcerer's task ahead. Then, wordlessly, the Moorlock turned on his heels and began walking away.

The austere morning light suffused dimly from beneath the bellies of the brown clouds. It was unable to warm air or land adequately. In the chill dryness in front of him, millions of dust motes blew, catching in his throat and eyes.

When he reached the northernmost side of the hill, he began walking down it across the quaking earth towards the flattened desert of rubble. He reached the desert's edge. He stopped and looked out.

The boiling skyline of cloud had advanced considerably as the power of the Death Concentrator had mounted. The quaking had increased, bringing down all but the sturdiest ruins, levelling out the old City. To his left stretched the drab, rolling hill-land of Hampstead Heath. The Rays from the Death Concentrator were not coming from true North – they came from the North West, across the ruins.

Resolutely, he drew his long coat around him and set out into the fierce headwind that was blowing. He clambered unsteadily across the jagged, vibrating bricks and projecting planks of wood, occasionally skirting fallen trees half buried in the rubble. For about twenty minutes he laboured. When he thought he had gone out far enough, he climbed to the highest point about him and sat down.

From his vantage point, he could look out over Hendon towards Mill Hill, where the wall of cloud began.

Linking with a mind that was unaware it was being sought, was always problematic. He needed to be far away from the interference of Earth City.

He stared into the cold stream of air and dust. The landscape grew black as he let his inner vision expand to infinity, feeling for contact with the Dark Lord. For a long while there was nothing.

'Master of Dark come out to me,' he invoked, to help his mental body advertise itself with sufficient strength. He hoped the Dark Prince would eventually realize that he was trying to make contact.

Soon, a subtle change took place inside him. Whereas before he had felt isolated, now the beginning of a conflicting force started to break its way in. Unable to feel satisfaction for fear of losing contact, he remained stonily entranced, allowing the Hellish communion to grow. He knew the opposing force was Mephis, for none other could reach him.

Suddenly, the two super lords were mentally locked together, each keeping the other at a respectful distance. For a moment, they grappled to gain dominance. Finally, the Moorlock called out:

'Halt this senseless battling, Dark Lord! It will get us

nowhere and lose us time!'

'You are right!' Mephis called back sneeringly. 'You will soon be vanquished! Why should I bother to engage myself in petty jousting?' He laughed hollowly. 'Why have you called me, Sorcerer?'

'To ask you to stop the Death Concentrator!' the Moorlock called back firmly. As he expected, his words were greeted with an outburst of derisive laughter.

'So? You have come to ask for my mercy! You have come to ask me to spare your wretched lives!' The Dark Lord's tone became harsh. 'In return for what, Sorcerer?' He spat the words out. The Moorlock stood his ground unflinchingly.

'No, Mephis! We don't ask for your *mercy* – we're fighters and we will fight to the end! We're not thinking of ourselves, but of Earth . . . you are aware surely that the Rays from the Death Generator, concentrated by your machine will soon rent the Earth herself. Our scientists predict that at the present rate of increase in the Rays this terrible event will occur within a few days at the outside. Is this what you intend? Are you so bent on our destruction that you will destroy everything?'

There was a short silence. Unexpectedly, a fleeting chink appeared in the Dark Lord's mental armour. The Moorlock was able to look inside and discover the truth. The chink opened and closed in a split second, but in that short moment of time the Moorlock saw that the words that followed were hasty fabrication.

Mephis laughed affectedly. 'You are more naive than I gave you credit for! Of course I am aware of the true power of my own machine!' He grew scornful. 'My scientists are not fools! Do you suppose that we will back down merely on the issue you propose? What happens to the planet after my existence is finished is of no consequence to me . . . and as any self-respecting fighter would do, I will continue to fight until I perish or all perish! No, Hawklord. You must grow up. There is no room on this planet for two of us. This time there will be no rabbit holes for you to disappear down!'

'Then there is nothing further to say,' the Moorlock replied, ignoring the other's prompting to bicker aimlessly. 'You may

217

rest assured though, that your days are numbered, that you will perish. It is you who are naive, Dark Lord. Down the centuries you have been beaten each time the Throdmyke power has risen. And each time you have not learnt from your lesson, but become the puppet of that mindless Death Generator.'

Again, the Dark Lord laughed. This time he laughed with confidence, as though able to predict with certainty the outcome of their bitter war and was genuinely not bothered one way or the other. 'Go your way then, Hawk Lord – carry that thinking with you to your death!'

The Dark Lord's presence departed and the trance ended abruptly. Uncomfortably, the Moorlock stared ahead at the wall of billowing cloud.

The lie still hung in his mind. It was not the fact that Mephis had said he had known of the Concentrator's lethal capacity that troubled him. It was the Dark Lord's words: 'My scientists are not fools!' with the implication that it was his scientists who had informed him of the full destructiveness of the Rays.

In the split second that his opponent's mental guard had been down, the Moorlock had seen otherwise. The information had been supplied from *outside* Mephis's domain. But precisely who had supplied it had been rapidly hidden from him.

The Sorcerer brooded. It didn't take much to put two and two together and come up with an inspired guess.

After a few moments' thought, he rose stiffly from where he had sat on the hard bricks and began to clamber back to the island hill. Whatever else transpired, its ailing inhabitants would have to be told that there could be no release from the Death Concentrator. Mephis was now quite insane, and he would need to be attacked by the resources of every man they could find.

Approaching completion, the four great Silver Machines rested at their earthen berth. Their silvery flanks quivered with the planet's vibrations, as though the powerful psycho-tronic engines that they had been fitted with were already impatiently coming to life.

Captain Calvert's eccentric figure moved intently about inside one of them, finishing off the engine and testing the wiring. A trail of cable followed him about, leading to a soldering iron in his hand. Of all the parts, in the end the engines had proved the most difficult to assemble even though an exact template existed for them to copy off. The delicate soldering work that had been required had been made nearly impossible on account of the incessant quaking.

Beside the glittering crafts stood the Hydra and the Prince, waiting tensely for the final flight tests to be made. They would soon know whether or not their desperate attempts to save the Earth had worked. Their arms hung limply at their side. Their tools were discarded on the ground. Nothing else remained to be done.

Behind them stood the other Hawklords, Higgy and a dozen Children who were still staggering about. Everyone who could, had attended to watch the tests. Mephis's macabre, lunatic intentions to destroy the world had aroused outrage, and they were all the more determined to see justice dealt him.

The Captain finished his work. He turned and stood at his helm, beckoning for the pilots to come aboard. Thunder Rider, Actonium Doug and the Sonic Prince stepped forward and walked towards their respective vessels. They climbed on to them.

As they positioned themselves, the Captain made a last minute check of his fleet. Then he returned to his post and gave the flying signals.

The small crowd, keyed with anxiety and anticipation moved

back to give them room to manoeuvre.

The faces of the pilots became tense with mental exertion. Gradually, three of the machines began to move. Colourful lights and sounds began pulsing powerfully out of their lethal transmitting equipment, and they rose slowly into the air. But they were unable to gain height. They began to rock violently, and went out of control. For a while they glided about unevenly at low level, almost crashing into one another as their pilots desperately tried to bring them under control. Finally, they sank down and came to a jarring rest.

On the ground, the Captain was still trying to raise his own craft. His face was rigid with concentration.

A groan of anguish escaped the lips of the waiting figures. The pilots clambered out with bitter expressions on their faces.

'What happened?' the voice of Hot Plate shouted worriedly as he ran forward towards them.

Thunder Rider threw up his hands in anger. 'Don't ask me!' he yelled. He stood still while his feelings subsided, though his agitation was emphasized by the earth tremors.

A white-faced Captain Calvert joined them.

'I don't understand it. My craft was working perfectly . . .'

'We must have wired them up wrong,' Actonium Doug moaned, his forehead crinkling in an agony of frustration. 'I thought it was all too good to be true.'

They stood around helplessly, buffetted by the scathing wind and the waves of sickness. Several more of the Children collapsed as they waited, and they were carried over to the warmth of the fire.

Five days had elapsed since Hot Plate had made a statement that mortal flesh had a week to survive. They had commenced their sixth day.

The Children were gradually dropping out of the race. Many in their shelters had perished in their drugged, immobile sleep from a combination of the cold, the Horrors and the physical shaking. They lay entombed and unattended because the manpower could not be spared to remove them. The only good news that Earth City had had was that the planet had so far remained stable. It had not yet begun to fragment under the strain of its harshest trial in history.

'We'll just have to strip them down and go over them again,' the Captain said in exasperation, after they had accepted the situation.

Grimly they bent to retrieve their screwdrivers and avometers. They climbed back up the sides of the Silver Machines, resigning themselves to yet another test of mental endurance.

Then a strangled shout came from Thunder Rider.

Instead of joining them he had gone to examine the Captain's inert machine. Now his tall, ragged figure was standing behind it, holding up a length of cable.

'No wonder your ship didn't sail, Captain!' he shouted out. 'It was scuppered!'

Electrified, they downeds tools and jumped from their craft. They ran towards him and crowded round as he showed them the cable. From its black insulating sheath protruded a mass of shining bare ends.

'Watch it!' he handed it to them. 'It's live. Someone connected it up to the generator and put a dose through the bloody machine!'

Disbelievingly, they stared at him. They were stunned and bewildered. It didn't seem conceivable that anyone from their own community could have done the damage.

Then, Actonium Doug broke the silence. 'The scab!' he shouted out in sudden rage. 'The bloody scab! Who's done this?' He turned and faced everyone in turn. No-one answered him. 'Well, who is it here who wants us dead?' he screamed.

Again they were silent.

Thunder Rider spoke.

'It's no use asking us, Dougy,' he said. 'Whoever it is isn't likely to say . . .' He paused, heavy in thought. 'But there isn't time for a witch hunt. We'll have to forget it until afterwards and concentrate on getting the damage repaired.'

'If it *can* be repaired,' the Prince commented mournfully. 'When you shove that much voltage through semi-conductor circuits it usually knackers them for good.'

As he spoke, several more of the Children collapsed and they

221

were carried away to the fire.

Desperately, the Hawklords fought off the sinking feeling of despair as the wall of cloud on the imprisoning skyline visibly sagged inward.

HORIZON OF GLOOM

Reeling from the sudden deterioration in their condition and the hefty punches dealt out by the Rays, the Prince struggled to stabilize his mind. His thought processes were gradually speeding up to an unmanageable rate inside his head and the dark paranoic fingers of chaos were pushing up from below, taking him over. But he knew that his Hawklord body could take more, if only he could manage to adjust it to the new level of Cyndaim emanations.

Slowly, he got on top. His body stang all over. His mind sang with the effort. More calmly, he again placed the screwdriver against the screw head.

Determinedly, he held it in place and turned.

Gradually the screw came undone. Carefully, he pulled the cover off the metal box that they had used as the housing unit, exposing the delicate circuitry of the Captain's Silver Machine.

The tiny parts were almost a blur in front of him, but he began painstakingly checking each one in turn. First he checked the components he knew were most susceptible to mains' damage. After he had tested one complete board, he started on another. Then, rewardingly, the needle on his avometer registered low impedance. Triumphantly, he unplugged the part it had been connected to and held it aloft.

'I've found one of them!' he shouted out. The others looked up from their work. They dismounted from their crafts and began moving precariously across the vibrating ground towards him. 'It's one of the op amps.'

'No luck with the other machines yet,' Thunder Rider reported glumly. 'But at least you've found out what's gone wrong with one of them.'

'I'll check over the rest of the works,' the Prince said, 'then I'll try to find a replacement.'

He set back to work while the others watched him. They drifted back to their own tasks. At length, he finished checking. So far as he could determine, the rest of the components were sound.

Clutching the shorted operational amplifier in his palm he climbed down and stumbled across the thumping ground. The whole of Parliament Hill was now beginning to disintegrate. Cracks were appearing in its surface, forming a loose scree of hard clay lumps almost impossible to walk on.

He reached the stage where the prone figures of the Children were lying. The life-giving camp fire was just about catching beneath a fresh tangle of wood. Bravely, Higgy was trying to bring it to life, blowing and fanning it with his hands when all the pointers told the Prince that he ought to be lying down resting. But the faithful Scot was forcing himself upright, determined to continue playing his part looking after the welfare of his charges.

Sitting unconcerned while he struggled were the two slouched forms of Astral Al and Stacia. Their second drummer had ventured out of his shelter a day ago. At the same time Stacia had fallen prey to his illness. To begin with the other Hawklords had been pleased to see Astral Al again after his long coma. But the depressed pair had wandered about the site, watching and asking questions. They didn't seem to take the slightest interest in the fighting.

The Prince's first impulse was to reprimand them again, but time was short and he thought better of it. He walked past them towards the stage where the Light Lord was still gigging. Lemmy and Hound Master played by his side. The trio stared vacantly at the Prince as he passed, and he realized that they had probably not seen him. He felt sorry for them. They had had to play without rest for almost a week, day and night, longer than anyone before them. Ultimately their invincible Hawk bodies would be able to withstand the not too strenuous punishment, but their minds would already have turned into mere automata by the boredom and the sheer demand placed on them.

He moved jerkily round to the back of the stage where a large pile of spent and cannibalized equipment lay. The pile had accumulated gradually over the period of hostilities, and had been added to by the jeep load while the roads had been open. Actonium Doug had driven out and brought in anything he could find that looked vaguely electronic. Most of the pieces of any worth had been already used though, and the stripped cases junked separately.

He examined each appliance in turn, searching for a part similar to the one he held in his hand. He found several, but each time discovered they were of a different type number. Frustratedly, he threw the last case on to the rattling heap.

He climbed to his feet. The stability inside him began to break down again. Desperately he thought what to do.

He stared out at the bleak wilderness of ruins that lay around them. For a long time he gazed at the boiling brown skyline.

The wall seemed to hypnotically lure him into its swirling, tumultuous vapours, offering him solace from the horrors of reality. In the foreground immediately in front of it his eyes came to rest on the outlines of the few super buildings still standing.

He stared blankly at them.

Gradually, out of his extreme desperation was born an extreme idea.

He remembered the huge, sturdy laboratory building at Baker Street. If it were still by some miracle standing, it might prove to be their only hope of surviving.

THE MAELSTROM

The thin, bluish plasma from the North swept powerfully across the shuddering vista of masonry and girder as the Sonic Prince set out on his precipitate journey.

Behind him in the fading daylight, the other Hawklords worked tirelessly on building defences against the wind and making Earth City as secure as they could for its few inhabitants.

A few hours of gloom existed in which to reach the laboratory before the landscape was plunged into icy blackness. While he was there, he would have to search for the replacement part, then undertake the dangerous journey back, guiding himself to safety by the lights of stage and fire that would be kept burning extra brightly on the Hill.

It was virtually an impossible mission – but the alternative was certain death for all. He patted his bulky pockets to check that his torch and tools were still there.

In front of him lay the boundary of cloud that merged overhead with the brown sky. It was no longer possible to see a distinct horizon. The energies of destruction outside had mounted to such an extent that the cloud was raging and boiling as never before. It twisted above him, rushing at a phenomenal rate towards the wall. It was spewed back again with equal force.

Underfoot, the bricks rocked and shook alarmingly as he stumbled across them. The shaking constantly grew and several times he lost his balance and perspective. He crashed forward without realizing he had done so and found himself trying to climb the vertical jagged wall that hung fleetingly in front of him.

Gradually he got used to making the right body movements and made faster headway.

As he trekked further away from the stage, the Hawkwind music grew fainter, until eventually it died away altogether. Soon all he could hear was the moaning of the wind round him, and an ominous rumbling of masonry that came from ahead. He found himself cut off in an immense sea of broken artefacts and wreckage.

The sea had its own laws that he had to obey. It had its own tides that inextricably mixed its parts.

In one roaring, sliding movement the surface ahead of him began to move forward. It started slowly and smoothly at first. He was hypnotized by the majesty of the sight and the vast power at play. Then the rumbling sound grew louder, and the surface began accelerating. Before he realized the danger, it began to carry him with it.

He was thrown backward off his feet on to the back of a firm, hard object. Horrified, he felt beneath him. His hands clasped the rough trunk of a tree and he gripped the crevices in its bark tightly as the treacherous ground many yards in front began to open up.

The tons of rubble began to slide rapidly downhill towards the centre of the subsidence, where it seemed to feed itself endlessly into the black, hungry mouth. As the tree moved towards destruction, the giddying surface became a huge funnel. Its circular walls heaved claustrophobically upward, cutting out the light and the view of the surrounding land.

Entranced, he stared at the looming vortex below him. It rushed up at him. As he was about to be tipped down it, the roaring stream of bricks in front abruptly filled the hole to its brim. The movement stopped.

Paralysed with shock, he lay back along the tree trunk, mentally exhausted. He stared up at the brown cloud streaking silently by overhead. Then, in disbelief he arose to his feet and walked into the centre of the depression. The bricks were still vibrating, but they had ceased to flow. The hole had been filled.

Shaken, he began to climb uphill towards the lip of the now frozen whirlpool of bricks. His mind boggled at the enormity of the landslide, and he wondered what workings of Mankind had finally given way deep below ground.

He reached the funnel's rim and once more he was exposed to the sound and touch of the rasping wind. Disorientated, it took his several moments to work out where he was. The sky had grown darker and dust from the landslide still hung in the air. Eventually he made out the glimmer of lights at Parliament Hill. He turned and stood with his back to it. Gazing ahead of him, he was able to make out the dim forms of the buildings almost enveloped by the brown cloud.

Resolutely, he set on his way towards them. He clambered on, occasionally encountering more surface disturbances of a smaller order. At times the debris around him seemed to be moving and shifting, like waves, burying his boots.

Thankfully, he reached the relatively solid terrain of Primrose Hill. He began running to make up time. With one mighty bound, the Hawklord leaped across the ozzing black mud of the Grand Union Canal into Regents Park. He passed the dried-up boating lake and the ruins of the women's college. Then he veered right and soon found himself standing on the jumping, trembling wasteland of what used to be Baker Street.

He peered intently ahead of him into the gloom. He was now very close to the cloud and the boundary of the Hawkwind musical power. The loud thundering explosions taking place where its front met the Dark Force's front, was ripping up the land and hurling the debris and dust high into the sky. In the midst of the angry, churning cloud he caught glimpses of fire and huge silver sparks.

All around him he sensed the presence of the tall, upright buildings standing in the sea of rubble. They were scarcely discernible in the dimness. They shook and quivered alarmingly, threatening to topple at any moment.

Pensively, he squinted directly into the wall of cloud, in the direction he knew the industrial laboratory to be. At first, he could make nothing out. Then, right at the edge of the seething black/brown mass, almost swallowed by it, he made out the low, solid outline of a building.

Uncertainly, he set out once more across the agitated land surface. The protective front ahead of him was steadily being pushed backward, and he was not sure how much time the building, if indeed it proved to be the right building, had left before it too crashed to the ground.

He staggered on, feeling small and puny beneath the vast curtain of reaction that was taking place before him, the seething by-products rising up high above and curling over into the brown ceiling.

His body screamed to return whence it came, almost seizing up with fear. But he forced it on.

At last he reached the black, trembling shape. With horror rather than gladness he saw that it was the laboratory. He cursed and praised the long ago Victorian builders. They had built it to last, with blocks of stone a metre thick, with steel thicker and tougher than most of its successors.

Through dust-filled air he could see that the building shook violently on its foundations. Large black fingers were crawling up its stonework. He realized that the building was cracking up. If the wall of cloud didn't get him, the collapsing building might.

Cruelly crushing the thoughts inside him he moved forward and up the shaking steps. Amidst a rain of falling slates and stones that were breaking off the building, he pushed his way through the door and into the black interior.

Inside, the convulsive darkness absorbed him, about to devour his identity for ever. He struggled frantically with the torch. Moments before he flicked it on, his body reached a new understanding with his terminal surroundings. The mouth of death calmed him. Paradoxically he found he was able to think clearly. His feelings of terror abated. As the extreme conditions existing at Parliament Hill had forced them to behave rationally and coolly, now he found himself doing likewise.

Flicking on the torch, he flashed it about him. The stone floor was littered with debris and dust that had fallen from the ceiling. He shone the beam on to the stone staircase. The steps led up into the roof of darkness. He made his way towards it and began walking upward. The building shook. Through its walls he could hear the roar of the main turmoil about to consume him.

He reached the landing and walked along the passageway

and turned into the laboratory.

Inside, everything was in disarray. Cupboards had fallen from their places on the walls. Their contents had been tipped on to the floor and mixed in with plaster and light fittings from the ceiling. It was a jogging, jerking mass of confusion, and he wondered helplessly where to begin looking.

He remembered Hot Plate had stored a great deal of their equipment in the cupboards and drawers in the sides of the benches. Moving towards them, he pushed aside the rubble on the floor with his feet and opened one of the doors.

It was empty. Most of what had been in it had already been cleared out.

Methodically he searched each cupboard and drawer in turn. A few boxes and packets were left in some of them, but they mostly contained useless items.

The feelings of terror began to return again. Fighting them back he pulled out the last drawer. He closed his eyes, and then opened them again. Beneath the torchlight he could see that the drawer was packed to capacity with small white boxes. Hurriedly he pulled out a few of the boxes and looked at the black numbering on the side. They were integrated circuits of one kind or another. Feverishly he began pulling them out one by one, searching for the numbers and letters he was after. He took out the last box. Turning it over he read the identifying panel in the torchlight.

It was a type pin compatible with the one he sought. It would do.

To make sure, he flipped open the lid clumsily. The box was brimful of the tiny, metallic spider-like amplifiers. Sagging with relief he closed it again and put it into his pocket. He emptied one of the other boxes and filled it with a mixture of the other components.

A nagging pain which had lain in the background inside him burst out. Semi-deliriously, he realized that it was the Horrors which had built up to an acute level because of his close proximity to the Dark Front.

His energy began waning. With great effort he turned and stumbled out of the room. He battled his way down the corridor. He reeled down the steps and flung open the heavy doors.

Outside, there was no light.

The dark, unfolded, rottenly out of the doomed building. It was night.

The noise of the chaos screamed in his head. Flashing his torch to the right, he made his way blindly through the pitch darkness, away from the sound of the cloud. He kept going on, stumbling across the turbulent bricks through the numbing cold of the wind. He left the empty building to its fate. Gradually, his strength returned and he picked up speed. He stumbled on until the roaring sound dropped slightly in volume. Then he stopped.

He flicked off the torch beam and stared intently ahead of him into the blackness.

There was nothing. He could see nothing.

Frantically he looked about him for the lights on Parliament Hill. But they were either too far off to detect, or so small they were indistinguishable.

Irrational fear gripped him again. It filled his lungs. Ruthlessly he tried to shake off the wild impressions. The lights ought to be roughly ahead. He tried to calculate. If he had walked in a curve, as suddenly seemed plausible, the lights would have moved to his left or right.

He turned his head though not his body, for fear of losing his orientation completely. He scanned the blackness for sign of the lights. He twisted his trunk so that he could see right round him by slowly turning his head. He looked up and down in case his visualization of the horizon was faulty. Tremulously he noticed a vague glimmer.

A delusion, he thought. Nevertheless, he began to reach out for it. It was his one, blind hope.

He snapped on his torch. He moved forward. After a few minutes his feet trod firmer, smoother ground. By the torchlight he saw by the dried, beaten turf that he had reached Regents Park. Overjoyed, he noticed that the light ahead had grown brighter.

Shining his torch in front of him, he started out again, this time with greater confidence. But now he had to face the great, heaving sea of debris and junk that lay between him and the dubious sanctuary of the besieged hill.

INFINITE NIGHT

The pallid, wasted face of the Child rocked with pain.

It tried to lift itself up. Then it fell back heavily into Actonium Doug's lap.

The lines disappeared and its skin became smooth. A smile crossed its features. Its lips parted.

The Hawklord bent closer to the man's mouth.

'I've tried to hold on as long as I could . . .' his weak voice whispered. '. . . even though I wasn't much use. I wanted to see us win . . . I wanted . . . to . . . help . . . build . . . the . . . new . . . Mother . . . Earth . . .'

His head slipped sideways before Actonium Doug could reply and he died.

The incessant quaking jogged and shook the lifeless body indifferently.

For a long while the Hawklord stared respectfully downward at the flopping face. Life was sweet. Living was often hard. Despite the almost insurmountable odds that had tarnished this man's life, he had died at peace – an incredible feat.

Bitterly he climbed to his feet and began dragging the corpse away into the darkness. He felt his way to one of the shelters and put the man inside. Then he returned to the firelight to wait.

There was nothing more they could do.

The fire had been stacked high with logs cut from the trees. All the remaining wood had been gathered and lay in a pile at its side. Behind it, shielding it, they had built a wind break from the jeep and an old battered lorry.

The figures of the Hawklords and half a dozen Children sat round the fire, together with no more than a handful of the semi-corpses. In the failing daylight hours, a search had been made of the shelters for surviving casualties. Only a few had been found, and their bodies lay closest to the fire, sapping its life-giving warmth.

They took turns on stage to relieve the boredom of the endless playing. Lemmy tended to a large oil drum filled with a watery consommé. It contained the last of the food and water provisions for the Children, and had to be watched constantly to prevent it being tipped over by the quaking into the flames.

Higgy gazed at him with a child-like expression of helplessness and fear on his face. He had started cooking the gruel, and then collapsed. He could go on no further, and was rapidly sinking into unconsciousness.

In the shadows behind them the glinting hulks of the Silver Machines stood. They had been dragged over from the construction site, so that everything the survivors needed lay within the stage area. After the Sonic Prince had set out they had worked on the machines again in a vain attempt to get them air worthy. But the mystery of their malfunctioning engines remained absolute. There still appeared to be nothing out of place.

The feeling of Horrors burned out their insides as they waited. There was nothing to take their minds off the pain. The shaking grew more acute and the wind shrieked louder and harder.

Most of the night had gone, but the Prince still had not returned.

THE DEAD LANDSCAPES OF EARTH

The land shuddered.

It jumped and cracked. Its heaving seas rose and crashed, flooding it. Its mountains broke and toppled. Its continents shifted. Fire began pouring once more out of the fissures as the heat at the planet's heart began escaping. Dust and smoke filled the satanic, bluish skies, trapping the heat. In places, the waters boiled away into steam as the planet gradually, momentarily, reverted to its older, primeval state.

THE DRAINS OF SPACE

Mephis laughed. His mind encompassed the globe, witnessing the destruction. Over London the sun began to rise once more. Its single, thin pillar hit the only piece of ground his thoughts were still unable to penetrate. But that pillar had shrunk. He had watched it being slowly eaten away day by day. Its final demise was a planet's rotation away. Then, the Hawklords would be dead! He would be able to turn off his machine! He would be the absolute ruler of Earth!

He returned his mind to the jaded reality of the Tower Control Room. Its walls and furnishings shrank distantly away from him, and he laughed self-consciously.

'Ah ha! The very matter of the universe fears and respects my presence! You'll all be a part of me soon! I shall bend you to fit my will!'

He moved swiftly over to the shying consoles of switches and dials that operated the Death Concentrator. They bucked and wavered under his touch. He watched the unwilling needle on the main dial moving gradually to its limit.

'Ha! You have to behave for me even now!'

The tower shook. Its stones groaned and ground against one another protestingly.

The Dark Lord turned and seated himself in his leather arm chair. He closed his eyes and brought his finger tips to his head.

The matter quivered and dissolved. His mind swam above and behind and through it. It reached the psychic plane and began to send out mental feelers.

THE DRUG TRACT

The cold thoughts probed for Her. They reached across the barriers of Time for Her. Eventually, they locked with the mind that occupied Her body.

'Still not coming out?' the icy tentacles mocked Her.

'Then think again of your Queendom! It awaits your control. It needs your feminine touch!'

Her mind recoiled from his sudden repulsive contact into a tighter space.

'I will not! I will not!' it cried out. 'My heart is pure! I will never be yours! I will fight you until I die!'

'You and I are one!' the harsh voice insisted. 'Fate has always bound us, though still you will not admit it. Deep down your heart knows, and you will eventually have to listen to that.'

It departed abruptly. She sensed it communing with the other parasites that had control of her and Astral Al.

'They are dying, Colonel,' the mind of Major Reginald Wessex Asquith intimated. 'At 1600 hours the one known as the Prince set out from the base to look for a replacement, but he will not survive! Now it is only a matter of hours before their power breaks down and our mission is completed.'

'You have done well,' the thoughts of his Master and executioner congratulated him. 'You will be well rewarded,' they lied.

The thoughts detached themselves. They broke free and contracted back into his waiting body.

The Lord of Darkness brought his hands down from his temples, and sneered wickedly. He had glimpsed inside the bubble of light! His sharp senses had consumed details of knowledge from the minds of most of the unwitting Hawklords. They had built a vivid picture of activities.

As the Major had reported, *his* victory – not *their's* as the presupposing idiot had suggested – was imminent.

A feeling of consuming pleasure rose inside him. He hesitated, wondering whether to indulge himself in its glow. So many times before he had been let down.

There was one last check he had to make first.

He placed his hand on the psi screen in front of him and switched it on.

The screen glowed and pulsed into life. Swirling misty patterns appeared on it. As he concentrated, they clarified. The large army of ghouls that he had dispatched to wait outside the explosive, fiery front of clashing forces appeared. They were camped on the burnt, pitted land that had been left behind in the wake of the explosions, waiting to ride in and finish off the Hawklords once their music had been stopped.

The screen convinced him. He was quite certain of victory.

Slowly he let himself lie back in the armchair. He let the feeling of ecstacy rise up inside him. It filled his being and radiated everywhere. He laughed.

He WAS the Master of the Earth! He had climbed on top of its ridiculous peoples! He was invulnerable! He was safe from their hatred and scorn! He had gained the sacrosanct position he had grasped for all his life.

The feeling grew even more powerful. It exploded inside him, and he realized with sudden anguish that there was more to the condition than he had thought.

His laughter turned into convulsive sobbing.

'No! No! No!' he screamed.

His insides twisted and shook with emotion. It wasn't *his* voice that was crying out. It was the voice of the small child who had once been given a ride inside an army tank many, many years ago.

He had set out then to become his present self. To escape the blackness. To fight the blackness he couldn't see inside of.

'Mother! Oh Mother! Mother! Mother!' he screamed out, slamming the table top in front of him and shattering its glass surface into a thousand separate shards.

BAND OF OPPRESSION

The blackness brightened as the sun slowly rose above the thickening cloud. The rest of the small hill top became dimly visible to the Hawklords who were standing at its edge, watching out over the desecrated City.

During the night the texture of the ground had become soft and rotten. It was riddled with gradually widening cavities, as though the soil itself were melting away like snow, its atoms collapsing on each other. A chunk of the hill had shaken loose, and a sheer cliff edge had formed.

At its brink, the Hawklords waited for the figure of the Prince. The hypnotic wall of cloud hung in front of them, its seething, sparking mass no more than half a mile away. They were enclosed all round by a terrifying dome that contracted momentarily.

Hawkwind music poured from the loudspeakers, stalling off oblivion. In its auspices the few remaining Children curled in a death sleep, unaware they were alive, unaware that they faced almost certain death.

STANDING AT THE EDGE

Somewhere in the flickering, jerky picture of grey rubble in front of the Hawklords a shadow moved. It tottered about, heading painstakingly in their direction.

As the poor light gradually improved, they made out a thin dishevelled figure crawling out of the dimness.

'It's the Prince!' the Baron's voice yelled out hoarsely.

The others said nothing. A glimmer of hope crossed their grim, set features as they stared out over the wasteland. The odds of the figure having located anything in the infernal, stony sea were a million to one. They watched until it had almost reached the dark tide of soil that fell away from the hill. Then they began tottering weakly along the cliff edge to where the natural slope of the hill commenced again, and climbed down.

'Am I glad to see you lot!' the Prince gasped, throwing himself down. 'Reckon I've tested our super powers to the limit.' He lay still, trying to control the unbearable feelings of the Horrors that clutched at his insides, twisting them up. The others stood round him waiting for him to recover. They were barely managing to hold on to their senses. The intense strain put on their bodies by the Rays affected their vision. Their bulging eyeballs saw only a small area in front of them, and even that looked grey and distant, flashing with white.

Their skins had turned an unhealthy hue of blotched, mottled colours glowing and pulsing with a savage brilliance.

'Did you get the parts?' Thunder Rider asked him anxiously.

The Prince nodded. He pulled out the boxes. He handed them to the Hydra who opened them and examined them.

'These are the ones!' the Baron announced. A trace of enthusiasm cracked their taut masks.

'Well let's *hope* then,' Actonium Doug muttered tightly, holding back the pain that throbbed inside him. He peered into the boxes. 'They look new to me. Maybe there's enough in there to use on the other machines. We could swop them for the old ones . . .'

'That's what I've been thinking,' the Prince said, rising stiffly to his feet. 'These op amps have a better frequency response than the others. We might as well replace the old ones if we've got enough.'

'We've got nothing to lose,' Thunder Rider grunted sourly. He turned and began leading the way back towards the fire.

They reached the relative shelter of the stage, and went to work immediately on the Silver Machines.

They unplugged the old operational amplifiers, and inserted the new ones. Then, once again they took up their positions on board to test them out.

They stood at their helms, bringing to bear their waning powers of concentration to activate the silent, psychotronic engines, watched tensely by the other Hawklords.

'Give them all you've got!' Captain Calvert shouted out, his face a mass of black lines standing out against the sickly colours.

The lighting equipment on the Silver Machines came to life.

Gradually, all four crafts rose, their flanks flashing stroboscopically through the jumping, shuddering air.

ASTRAL KILLERS

The long, boat-shaped craft with their batteries of speakers and lights packed on to squat masts, rose unfaulteringly up towards the low ceiling of cloud.

Smiles of surprise and relief burst out on the faces of most of the watchers below. Despite their seriously weak condition they began clapping and cheering. From the stage came a sudden change in the music. It had degenerated into banal, repetitive rhythms and colourless tones that had scarcely served its protective function. Now it burst into new and inspired life.

The Silver Machines started their descent, and soon the crew were climbing from their parked vessels to the praises of the ground crew. They hugged one another and slapped each other on the back. But the effort involved in being happy was too much. Weakly, they released each other.

'We must hurry now and send the crafts on their mission!' Captain Calvert croaked out. He breathed heavily. He staggered about, unable to keep his balance on the collapsing, cheese-like earth.

He turned and headed resolutely back to his ship. Then he stopped and stared incredulously in front of him. Among the blurred, jerking forms of the equipment on board, a figure was stooping down. It lifted itself upright, bringing something away from his vessel in its grasp.

The figure looked at him. He made out the blank, deathless features of Astral Al. The Captain's eyes flicked about in disbelief, checking over the other craft. Stacia was with the Hawklord. She was standing at the side of his craft, facing the stage, pointing a long, flat object in their direction.

'Saboteurs!' he yelled out, running forward.

Startled, the other Hawklords turned.

'Stacia!' Thunder Rider gasped.

'Oh no you don't!' the Baron's voice screamed out. The large shape of the Hydra lurched forward. 'Get your bloody hands off!' he screamed out.

A blinding flash of light exploded in front of them, forcing them to a sudden halt. Momentarily, they blacked out from the effects, and reeled backward. When they came round, they saw the gaunt figures and drained faces of Astral Al and Stacia. They were standing together in front of them. Astral Al held a Delatron in his hand. Stacia still held the menacing object that had arrested them with such force. Through their narrowed vision the Hawklords could see that it was a pocket tape recorder, its spools revolving and emitting small bursts of jagged light. Faintly, above the sound of their own band still playing behind them, they could hear the cataleptic strains of Elton John's *Daniel*, a most nauseating and stultifying sound.

'Well, you lousy motherfuckers!' the Baron shouted out in disgust. 'You double dealing pair of shits! You were right, Doug,' he said with loathing in his voice to the Hawklord at his side. 'There *is* someone from our own kind trying to kill us off. There they are! Their true colours start to show when the going gets tough!'

The two, featureless figures stared at them wordlessly. Part Hawklord, and part Devil, they were able to withstand both the negative and positive forces in operation. Now that their own Dark Forces had gained strength, their weaponry was invested with treble its usual power.

The figure of Astral Al spoke. Its tone was none that they could recognize. Its utterly alien, half-strangled sound had a vaguely military style about it.

'Your run is over, Hawklords! I have been instructed to eliminate you at the first opportunity that presents itself, in any manner I chose. But you may feel at ease, for I am an honourable man!' The voice chuckled. 'Now that I have discovered the effect our music has on you – a surprise to all, I can assure you, so close to your own stage – I would rather see you all dead now. Prepare yourselves for death, Hawk-lords!'

Astral Al's figure reverted to its stiff, wooden look. It appeared even more puppet-like as it swayed and shambled about trying to remain upright.

The equally rigid torso at its side began to operate the cassette player. With difficulty, its frozen fingers turned up the volume control, and the numbing music began rising in intensity affecting the mental control the Hawklords had over themselves, and drawing the killing, negative forces towards them.

MAGNU

The blinding, crackling sparks leapt out at the trapped Hawk-lords. Their minds froze, unable to co-ordinate their bodies.

'We . . . must . . . fight . . . it . . .!' Thunder Rider choked. 'The . . . Death . . . Concentrator's . . . got . . . so . . . strong now . . . that we're at the mercy of a stupid song . . . we can't let them beat us on our own territory . . .!' he finished, gulping for air.

The band played on behind them, as yet not much affected by the tape recorder which did not point directly at them. But they were powerless to intervene and help.

'You will be the next to die!' the alien voice mocked the players. 'In the meantime – watch your friends!'

The two agents stood in their stolen bodies, faceless and unknown, watching the destruction they wrought.

The collapsing, struggling Hawklords slowly lost conscious-ness as the Dark Power evoked by the music grew more powerful. But then, a sudden loud explosion came. It took place at the edge of their awareness. It was followed by a second, and a third loud report.

The crippling force that enslaved them ceased. Their mental faculties returned to them. The sound of the Dark music had stopped.

Puzzled, they looked up at the two agents.

They were still there, shaking and jerking, but the recorder had gone from the Hawklady's hands. Their blank faces were turned slightly aside.

Following their stony gaze, the Hawklords noticed a large, dark figure standing by one of the Silver Machines. They gasped in surprise. In the confusion, no-one had noticed that the Moorlock had not been with them. Now he walked unsteadily out of the gloom towards the agents, his arm dangling at his side. Clutched in his hand was a Magnum pistol.

As he approached, the figure of Astral Al raised the arm holding the Delatron above its head, about to hurl it to the ground. But the Hydra, already half way to its feet at the Baron's insistence, summoned all of its remaining strength and sprang forward. It caught the slow-moving arm in mid throw and held it until the other Hawklords came to his aid. The two zombies put up no resistance as the vital piece of equipment was removed from their grasp. They stood shaking and jerking just as they had always done. They stared lifelessly about. It seemed their satanic controllers had fled.

The Moorlock took hold of them, while the others began fixing the Delatron back inside the Silver Machine.

'Keep them well guarded!' Thunder Rider warned. 'Don't let them trick you. We want to see someone here when we get back!' He turned and smiled weakly. 'How did you manage the gun, Moorlock?'

The Moorlock grinned painfully. 'An old indulgence of mine,' he wheezed. 'I collected weapons and learnt how to use them.'

Thunder Rider punched him on the chest in a gesture of affection.

'See ya then . . .'

He turned his back on them and began striding languidly

towards his craft. His body seemed to move in slow motion, as though its shaking form were wading through syrup.

What had happened to the two agents made no improvement in the level of Death Rays coming from the Death Concentrator. When the Hawkwind power had been briefly impaired by the cassette player, their power had strengthened. The lethal wall of brown cloud hung only a few hundred yards beyond the edge of the hill. Its thunderous roaring drowned out the sound of their music.

Thunder Rider hauled himself over the lip of the Silver Machine and took up his position at the prow. The Sonic Prince and the Baron finished repairing the damaged engine. Then the Prince dismounted, leaving the other Hawklord standing upright at his helm.

Actonium Doug and Captain Calvert climbed aboard their respective craft.

The moment had come – the moment that would decide the Life or Death issue for them, the Children, for Earth.

An extra reserve of psychic energy came unbidden from inside them.

They focussed their thoughts on the sensitive psychotronic engines that lay in their casements beside them.

Slowly, unstoppably, the Silver Machines began to rise.

FLIGHT OF THE SILVER MACHINES

Unrestrained, the four Silver Machines lifted vertically away from the grey hill top. Their lights flashed through the dusty air. Their powerful music systems were activated. Hovering momentarily below the agitated ceiling overhead they veered out of sight into the tumultuous, cancerous wall of cloud.

Captain Calvert gripped on to the sides of his craft tightly, willing it to keep on going. The fearful strength of the clashing zones of power was unknown. They had no idea whether they would come out alive or if they would be able to survive in the

Dark territory once through. He closed his eyes as the impact came.

The deafening roar of the constant explosions sounded in his ears. The small vessel shuddered. It bounced upward, and then was sucked downward again. Stones and other objects whipped up in the howling wind crashed against its underbelly.

A white pain burst in his head.

His skin burned with the heat.

Borne on a sudden blast of air, he felt the craft being swept away at a terrifying velocity.

It kept going and he felt sick from the sudden unimpeded acceleration. He waited for the erratic, abrupt changes in direction that would result in the splintering of his craft. But the Silver Machine hurtled trustily along its trajected path.

The roaring sound abated. An icy stillness clung around him. Through closed eyelids, he sensed that a bright light was burning somewhere outside.

Puzzled, he opened his eyes.

The vast, blue cavern of the Dark World met his gaze. His ship had been flung out of the maelstrom that still raged behind him into a deathly silent, almost serene landscape.

His craft had risen to a great altitude. Thousands of feet below him he could see the churned, pitted earth lying in the wake of the battling fronts. Ahead, the satanic landscape stretched as far as the eye could see, its trembling surface of razed ruins and devastated countryside clear in every detail.

The air was perfectly still. There was no trace of the wind from the Death Generator. Despite the immense velocity of the Silver Machine, no wind resistance was felt. It was as though the molecules that composed it had somehow widened and they were allowing the molecules of air to slip through their sieve-like structure.

Still alarmed by his speed, he glanced behind him to see if the rest of his small fleet had come safely through.

The wall of black cloud rose in a vertical angry column, completely obliterating the shaft of sunlight. There was no sign of the others on its sombre flank.

Apprehensively, he looked all about him in the still, cold

243

atmosphere. Then, high above he noticed the three large, silver stars. They increased in size, indicating that they might be travelling towards him.

He waited patiently. Gradually the familiar outlines of his fleet became visible. They swept in and positioned themselves alongside him.

'All OK?' the Captain called across, relieved. His voice sounded tinny and remote in the strange air.

'Aye, aye, Cap'n!' Actonium Doug called back. 'Leastways, I will be when we've frizzled that arch-ghoul back into his elemental components.'

'Now, every man knows what he has to do?' the Captain reminded them.

'Couldn't very well forget with a bloody scientist chattering away in the back of my head!' the Baron's voice retorted irritably. 'When we get in sight of the tower we get into formation and keep the speakers trained on it, then still in formation, keep varying our height in relation to the tower, while closing in very slowly . . . not forgetting to keep our lugholes open for your radio-dispatched orders, of course,' he finished.

'That's right,' the Captain agreed. 'Then there's no excuse for mistakes. Now we better test out the radio.' Part of his mind still concentrating on keeping his craft airborne, he walked across the small deck to the Central Instrument Control Panel and reached for his ear piece and microphone. He switched on the miniature short-wave transmitter and receiver that had been built into it. The others did likewise.

'Calling all members of the Hawkwind Space Craft,' the Captain began. 'Can you hear me Baron? Over.'

'Can hear. Over,' came the reply.

'Can you hear me, Thunder Rider? Over.'

'Loud and clear. Over.'

'Can you hear me, Dougy?'

'Aye, aye, Cap'n!'

'Thank you crew. Switch off. Over and out.' The Captain put down his microphone and turned to them. 'That's good! Now the Ranging Unit.'

244

He flicked a switch that activated the laser.

'Right, Thunder Rider. The beam is on now. Can you sail across its path?'

Thunder Rider obliged, manoeuvring his craft so that it blocked the perfectly straight, minuscule beam of light emitted from the apparatus on board the Captain's ship. The Automatic Laser Ranging Unit, as they called it, was the brain child of Hot Plate. Its function was to provide a way of ensuring that all four craft were positioned accurately in formation when they approached the tower. If they were a few feet of line, the full destructive effect on the Death Concentrator of their octophonic music would not be attained. The device worked by automatically measuring the distance from the Master ship of any craft in its path. When the correct distance was reached, a light on the Captain's console lit up. Four laser assemblies were needed. Two, mounted at right angles, on one craft, and two similarly mounted on another craft. Used in conjunction with the short wave radio, these would enable the Captain to put the Silver Machines in the correct formation – and to keep them there.

He glanced down at his instruments. The first laser was working. So was the ranging equipment. Systematically, he checked the other laser on board his craft, and the two installed on board Thunder Rider's.

'All appear to be working correctly,' he informed them after a while.

'Then let's try to work out where we're going now!' Thunder Rider suggested. 'We've been hurtling along at a helluva rate for about a quarter of an hour, and so far I've not seen any sign of where we're going. If it weren't so flat below, I'd say we were almost at John O'Groats!'

Startled by his words, the Captain looked down. A cracked, rucked landscape slid slowly past them far below. Thunder Rider was right. There was no way of telling where they were.

'Reduce speed and drop down!' he commanded after a moment's hesitation. 'We'll try to pick out landmarks we recognize.'

He looked behind him.

The cloud had become a long thin pencil of black, standing on end. At its top, high up in the Earth's atmosphere, the higher part of the column of sunlight was visible, shining like a brilliant star. It lay behind them to their right, when it should have lay to their left.

'Move over to the left!' he shouted out again, as they began to lose height. 'We're heading towards the North East!'

Gradually, they directed their crafts further westward, and the pencil of cloud slipped into place behind them.

They were now only a few hundred feet above the ground and could see the true extent of the damage caused by the quaking. The cracks in the Earth's crust they had seen from high up, now looked wide and sinister. From this height, they could hear a continuous, high rumbling sound. The chasm walls shook violently, and large slabs of earth and rocks were falling away from the edges into the depths. Elsewhere, the land seemed to have reverted to the same cheese-like substance they had seen at Parliament Hill. At short intervals, small islands of ruins passed by, all reduced, like their London counterpart to a shifting, heaving rubble.

They sped on wordlessly, looking for familiar signs they knew – but there were none. Beneath their attempt at cheerfulness, they were now very low in spirits. The nagging prospect that they were already too late to save Earth kept surfacing in their minds. The severe physical and mental irritation produced by the Rays had become almost unbearable.

'We can't be all that lost if we're heading in the right direction,' Actonium Doug called out. 'In fact I wouldn't mind betting that's Birmingham ahead of us now.'

The razed townscapes skimming past below them became more frequent. Now, they merged into a vast sea of ruins that took up the whole of the land ahead for as far as they could see.

'I think you're almost definitely right, Dougy,' the Captain replied. 'If my memory serves me well, the next largish town to look for after we've crossed this is Stoke-on-Trent.'

Behind them, the thin column of cloud had now completely vanished from sight. But the star of sunlight was still visible. Setting their course by it they crossed the remains of the great

Midlands' City. As they flew clear, the Baron suddenly noticed something on the ground. He leant over the side of his craft and pointed downward.

'The M6! It's still intact!'

They peered intently overboard.

Below them a twin, shadowy belt lay. It stretched onward in front of them, meandering slightly. Occasionally, it disappeared, broken up by land faults. Only the rough shape of the motorway remained, but it was all they needed.

THE DESTROYING ANGELS

The paradoxical calm of the Dark World reigned over their minds, crippling their true beings just as, in a lesser way it had stiffled all Humanity. It had enslaved men with its power to confuse and burden with fear and ignorance. It had spread negativity and hatred. No man had been able to live purely by his instincts and observations. Sooner or later he had been compromised, bought out, beaten, institutionalized or murdered. When many had tried, courageously, banding together, the system cracked. The environment poisoned, every man except a handful had to die.

Now, the whole Earth must perish as a result.

Whipping up as much speed as they could muster, the Hawklords sailed through the ghostly, cavernous realm, following the dim trail of the M6 further towards the North. They passed the scars of Stafford, Stoke-on-Trent and then saw the giant scar of Manchester appear far to their right. Abruptly, on the demolished, levelled country below, the single, ugly projection of the tower came into view. It stood at all only by the evil power that was holding it together.

Its sight caused a shiver of terror to run through them. Memories of Stacia's description flashed through their minds.

Inside its stones lay a force more powerful than the planets, wreaking out the terrible vengeance of one forgotten race on another.

At a signal from the Captain, the four Silver Machines fell away from one another. They took up their positions loosely, then more tightly as their crew listened to the Captain's directions over the ear pieces.

Eventually, the precise formation they needed was attained.

The last Silver Machine slipped fractionally into place. As it did so, the Hawkwind music achieved maximum power. It pounded out from all eight speakers, giving a double-quadrophonic effect. The intense glow of whiteness emitted from the musical equipment in the negative air suddenly leaped out into long, jagged lines of crackling light. The beams joined together in a blinding white-hot ball of light several hundred yards in front of them.

Holding itself steady, the trapezium-shaped configuration of lights moved gradually forward towards the tower, its lethal ball of energy moving when it moved, crackling and spitting ahead of it towards dawn in the long night of oppression.

THE EMPTY SOUP

The jagged, jarring force inside the Dark Lord's head came again, interfering with his pleasant dream of the future. Goaded into sudden rage, partly by the intruding power and partly by the awful, persistent doubt of victory, he rose angrily from his chair.

He glared around him, feeling the hatred pouring off the walls.

The psi screen was the worst of the objects in the room. It had always had the most loathing for him. Now, impulsively, he lunged out at it. Gladly, it seemed to him, it toppled off the table top and shattered on the floor.

After the one had been released, they all wanted releasing. The material universe around him craved destruction. He was giving it what it wanted. He stopped.

The anger blazed inside him, unable to be released.

He felt disaster drawing close. His dreams and aims dissolved.

Inside, the intruder clamoured, knocking away his cells. Now he knew why he would not let it in. It was the part of him that spoke the truth, that he had never admitted before. Now, it was battering its way in.

The part that he refused to believe in gnawed its way up to the surface of worms and lies.

'Colonel!' the voice inside cried, filling him with terror. 'I have failed. The Silver Machines are on their way! I have tried to warn you but I could not reach you . . .!'

The thoughtscape flashed expansively in his powerful mind. Its urgency vanished. It vanished.

He had blotted it from his mind. He had denied it. He had not even bothered to check . . .

Part of him, the side he wanted to win, had been confident.

Weakly, he staggered towards the tiny apperture in the wall next to the Death Concentrator. He stared through the plate glass.

The four points of lights moved towards him across the sky. They grew brighter.

They merged and became a dazzling globe that came at him, filling his mind with its brilliance.

Inside him, the hollow, empty void of terror grew.

The universe screamed for absolution.

'All right!' he shrieked. 'All right! YOU CAN HAVE IT! YOU CAN HAVE IT ALL!'

He ran to his mapping table. He wrenched open the drawer.

His fingers groped frenziedly for the Magnum inside, spilling the sheets of carefully stacked note paper on to the floor.

Then, grasping hold of the gun and pulling it out of the drawer, he placed its snub nozzle to his head, and pulled the trigger.

The searing, cleansing point of light touched the tower.

A massive explosion shattered its stone.

The explosion boiled outward, absorbing the whole of the ancient stonework, releasing it from its agonized tyranny.

Then the explosion died away.

Only the emptiness remained.

WELCOME TO THE FUTURE

The Hawklords let the music play on until they were quite sure that the tower had gone. Then, their minds pushed to the limit of their abilities, they finally let the formation of Silver Machines collapse.

They flew back alongside one another. Already they were able to feel the rewards of their victory. For the first time, they felt the effects of the Death Generator diminish. The unbearable level of power the Rays had been forced to climb to, dropped to their earlier level.

The Hawklords cheered as the load was lifted from their minds. Once more they were immune to the Horrors – like the Hawklords they had first been fashioned into.

They raced back to Earth City through the blue, Stygian cavern that still existed about them. They approached the bubble of light which had reverted back to its pre-Concentrator size. It shone before them like a huge, intense jewel. As they watched it with longing, its light, airy substance began swelling out. The pillar of light standing on its roof broadened.

The light exploded out towards them. Its dazzling outer surface swept past them, plunging their crafts into brilliant sunshine. Clear blue skies appeared overhead.

Filled with awe, they watched the Dark World peel away as the natural light of Earth returned. It became a small black pillar on the horizon behind them. Then, it disappeared out of existence.

'The Death Generator . . . it's stopping . . .!' Actonium Doug was the first one to realize what had happened. He gasped.

'But that's impossible . . . we didn't . . .!' Thunder Rider began. A smile of sheer joy was appearing on his lips.

'Whatever made it stop, it wasn't us . . .' the Captain remarked happily. 'It must have stopped on its own.'

'That's bloody incredible . . .!' the Baron muttered, staring disbelievingly around him. 'There's not a stick left . . .'

The earth lay perfectly flat and still and featureless in the strong light. There were no buildings of any sort. Its surface was strewn with debris. Here and there, the runner of a large crack appeared. It was impossible to tell whether city, farmland or open country had once lain beneath them.

'We've achieved what we were ordained to,' the Baron proclaimed in a reverent voice.

'Eh?' Thunder Rider looked at him, puzzled. 'What do you mean?'

'The Hawkwind Legend,' the Baron said. 'Don't you remember? It said: "And in the future of Time . . . blah blah blah . . . the Hawklords will return to smite the land . . blah blah blah . . . the Dark Forces will be scourged and the cities and towns razed . . ."'

A strange feeling crept over them as they listened. It shook their bodies. They felt fulfilment . . . yet something was missing.

'That's right!' Thunder Rider exclaimed. 'And it went on to say: "The razed Cities shall be made into parks. Peace shall come to everyone . . ."!' He looked at them optimistically. Inspired dreams blazed in his eyes. 'As soon as we return . . .!' He jumped up in the air. Then he ran up and down the deck of his Silver Machine whooping in ecstacy.

They sped towards the island base surrounded by the scarred and pitted earth. The ruins had gone. Except for Parliament Hill, nothing at all remained of the vast City that had been London. Mankind had been given the chance to start again.

At first the hill top seemed deserted. Then they noticed two figures standing among the tangle of wires and equipment next to the grey circle of ashes. Gradually, as the strains of Hawkwind music reached them on the still air, they made out the huddled forms of the other Hawklords and the handful of Children lying in the lee of the wind-break.

The air crew brought the Silver Machines down as close as possible to the stage and climbed out. They ran across to Lemmy and the Light Lord who were playing.

The Hydra picked up Stormbringer II and plugged in. The Baron struck up a few chords and then joined in.

'You can leave off now, if you want!' he yelled above the wattage to Lemmy and Rudolph the Black. He glanced down at the Light Lord who was struggling with the drums. 'When we're through we'll sign you up, mate!'

Thankfully, Lemmy swung the bass guitar off his shoulders. 'So you stopped the Death Concentrator?'

'Yeah. Did you notice anything?' the Baron asked.

'Only a bloody great injection of pure bliss. The cloud went away. The wind stopped . . .'

'What's happened to the others?' Thunder Rider asked with alarm. He looked towards the wind-break.

'They're OK . . . just about,' the Light Lord shouted out. 'They probably haven't heard you've arrived yet. Most of them are asleep.'

Thunder Rider and Actonium Doug walked over to where the population of Earth were lying. Captain Calvert motioned to the Light Lord.

'I'll take my turn,' he said. 'I might be able to do better.'

The Light Lord threw the drum sticks at him. 'Suits me fine,' he said.

The populace assembled round the stage. Most of them were happy and smiling, despite the injuries they had sustained to mind and body. But some were still in a bad way, and needed treatment.

Twelve Children only remained. Higgy had recovered and was already helping the less fortunate members. Stacia and Astral Al appeared normal again. Their old familiar features had been restored. The robot look was driven from their eyes. They were happily embracing the grounded crew, exchanging experiences.

In the midst of the happiness, the Baron called out gravely:

'Will someone take this guitar,' he said. 'I can't play it any more.'

Astonished, they fell silent. They stared at the figure of the Hydra. Its jaws were set. Its expression was typical of the Baron's. The Moorlock stepped forward and picked up the bass guitar. He plugged in and started playing as the Baron threw his guitar away.

The Hawklord looked miserable. 'I don't know how to say this,' he began. 'It's just struck me that Hot Plate isn't . . . he isn't here inside me anymore. He must have . . . just gone . . .!' He opened his arms in a gesture of exasperation.

The silence grew. 'I know I never really got to dig the guy,' the Baron continued. 'But I lived with him . . . I knew his inmost thoughts. 'Besides,' he added, looking up and staring around at the rivetted faces, 'we owe him everything. If it wasn't for him we'd have never got the Silver Machines off the ground. We'd have never even understood the Ray . . .' He broke off, choked with emotion.

They stood sadly listening to his words.

'I . . . I didn't know . . .' Thunder Rider began helplessly.

The Prince, who had always remained closest to Hot Plate, looked mortified.

'Are you sure he's gone?' he asked.

'I'm pretty sure he's gone . . .' the Baron replied. 'I can't feel him.'

'He more than anyone should have been around to see the outcome of our struggle,' the Prince wept. 'Good luck on you, Hot Plate . . . wherever you are.'

'Aye! Gide luck o' ye!' Higgy shouted up at the sky.

They fell silent as each paid a tribute to the brave scientist – a true Hawklord.

LIST OF CREDITS

Producer/Director	M. Moorcock
Writer	M. Butterworth
Music	Hawkwind and The Deep Fix
Lyrics	Calvert, Moorcock, Brock, Turner
Military Advice	Captain F. Hawkins
Dress and Electronics Advice	Geoff Cowie
Ethnic Habits and Characteristics	Altrincham Town Library
Acupuncture Idea	J. Jeff Jones
Hawkwind Legend	Bob Calvert, Barnie Bubbles, M. Moorcock
The Hawkwind Space Craft	Friendz, Melody Maker, Press Releases, Album Sleeves
Technical Advice (Music)	John Celario
Musical and Magical Names	
Precise Alignment of Silver Machines	David Britton
Indian Advice	Linda Pugh
Technical Advice (Scientific)	Michael Ginley
Geographical Information	Ordnance Survey, Geographia Ltd. The London A–Z
Ongoing Help	Catherine Butterworth, David Jarrett, Alan Johnson, Sherry Gold, Trevor Hoyle, Kari Larson, John (who lent the albums), Paddy, Steve Greenhalgh.

THE PROPHETS OF EVIL
W∴W∴

From his remote, paradisal kindgom of Pashman, nestling deep in the Himalayas, came QHE! Armed with strange, mystical powers, Qhe and his bondsman, Willard, vowed to challenge a tentacle of evil that stretched out to engulf the universe. The mysterious group calling itself the Prophets of the Prophet, wilfully attracting, then squashing, its converts like flies, was only the manifestation of a far greater evil that schemed to rock the world at its foundations. Somewhere in the heart of the Sahara Desert lay the core of the operations, the nucleus of a power which threatened the whole of mankind. Only Qhe possessed the energies to locate and combat the megalomaniac will of a being bent on fulfilling its terrifying nightmarish fantasy ...   *50p*

THE ULTIMATE WARRIOR
Bill S. Ballinger

This is the future. Earth, ravaged by man's greed and bloodlust, is on the edge of extinction. In mortified cities live tight, hostile clans of survivors scrounging food from a barren environment. In this chaos, only one attribute has value: strength.
Now a strong man stands in the city square, offering his allegiance to the highest bidder. This is protection that the ailing leader of the Barony must obtain — if his one hope for mankind is to survive.   *50p*

VENUS ON THE HALF-SHELL
Kilgore Trout

Snaggle-toothed, white-haired, long and tangled, a product of the imagination ... a man whose exploits have been the focal point of one of our greatest contemporary writers, Kurt Vonnegut.

Now for the first time without lurid covers, comes Kilgore Trout's epic science fiction saga of THE SPACE WANDERER. An earthman with an eye-patch, levis and a shabby grey sweater ... a man drunk with immortality gained during a sexual interlude with an alien queen in heat ... a good guy whose only fault is that he asks questions no one can answer, like ... WHY ARE WE CREATED TO SUFFER AND DIE? *50p*

WHO FEARS THE DEVIL?
Manley Wade Wellman

From the strange world of the North Carolina mountains, in the shadows of their tall rocks, beside their waters, among their trees, come some of the weirdest tales you may ever read. Wellman's work is not bound by space, or time, and least of all by science ... it is unique, unsettling and strangely habit-forming. *50p*